The Storyteller's Throne

A novel by

Jocelyn Bates

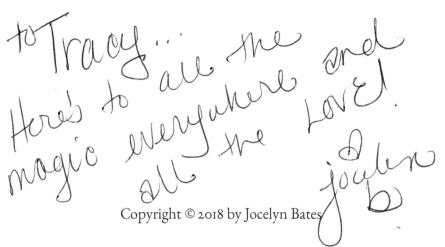

to Tracy...
Here's to all the
magic everywhere and
all the Love.
jocelyn

This book is a work of fiction. Any references to historical events, real people, or real places are used fictitiously. Other names, characters, places and events are products of the author's imagination, and any resemblance to actual events or places or persons, living or dead is entirely coincidental.

ISBN: 978-1-7321448-0-4

Published by Jocelyn Bates

Jocelyn@jocelynbates.com
Jocelynbates.com

To all the people who taught me to Love.

It was just like Sen had said it would be. All of a sudden, she just knew it was here. It felt like time was catching up to itself so she could be hurled back into her own world. Grace knew that there was no stopping it. She had just a few moments before all of the knowledge of this place would leave her, the Love, the Magic, the Pain, the Boy.

Her heart, even though it had been Uncovered and glistened with the essence of pure emotion, began to break. A small and life-altering crack edged along the perimeter. It made a quiet rolling gesture along the surface of her heart and then as time found its trail of breadcrumbs back home, the crack made for the center. It struck with the force of lightning. All it left in its wake was a single Love letter. A song he sang to her playing over and over again filling the void where her memory once was.

When she opened her eyes, she was alone in her bathroom again. The knife she held so long ago, was lying lifeless in the sink and all she could do was hum a strangely familiar tune, though she wasn't sure where she had heard it before.

Part One:

Grace

Chapter 1

It was one moment in particular. The moment that brought Grace to the Shadow World. It was the last in a series of twisted plot lines laid heavy in her lap. It was the sum total of crap moments that led Grace to do it. Grace was eighteen and those moments had been piling up inside her since she was six. She couldn't shrug them off anymore. At first, she could train her mind to forget them, she could write them down and burn the pages with defiance, she could tuck them away in the extra alcoves inside. But she couldn't do this anymore. She was full and it all needed to spill out somewhere, but there wasn't anything big enough to hold it.

Grace had spent most of her life alone. She didn't have any trusted allies, any confidants. She didn't have any friends. She was surrounded by people with whom her connection was dim. It wasn't that she was awkward or different on the outside. But on the inside, Grace felt things that set her apart from the others. She had trenches dug deep in places where there should have been rainbows and unicorns and sweet sixteen parties. Instead there were the faded footprints of a memory that trampled her, there were ghosts of un-lived lives and unspoken truths that appeared before her. There were layers of different that threatened the glue she held herself together with. All of this had placed her squarely in the center of a mystery that she was unraveling. An investigation that set her in motion downhill at high speeds to see what a crash really felt like.

Grace, was the epitome of cool. She was kind to everyone she met and it was easy for her to make people laugh. She didn't appear to take anything too seriously and that kept her safe from ridicule. She could have been friends with whomever she chose, but she kept most people at a distance. The only people she let in were those as mysterious as her own past, or those who might help her unravel her own mystery.

Grace had one relationship. She was fifteen when she met Austin. He didn't go to school with her, he was eight years older than she was. Austin represented a chance to know more and he played a very particular role in Grace's investigation. Being with Austin alienated most everyone else from Grace's life. He was the driving momentum that led Grace to the site of her crash.

The closer Grace got to her crash site, the more she was seeing and hearing things that others didn't. It was beginning to get hard to tell what was real and what wasn't anymore. Let's be honest, if you couldn't pick reality out from a lineup of insanity, would you tell anyone?

She ended up in front of her bathroom mirror, reliving mistakes, replaying other's opinions and actions and watching shame and regret battle it out on her skin.

She didn't start out like this. In fact, she was quite the opposite.

Chapter 2

When Grace was born, she was born into a brilliantly beautiful mind. One that needed no introduction to curiosity. A mind that thirsted for answers of all kinds. It was a mind that had a lot to learn and a lot to say. There was so much to do and to learn, that her little brilliantly beautiful mind couldn't wait to arrive in this world. She came early, in her own time, in her own way. In an ice storm, with quick labor. She was ready to initiate this world in the ways of Grace. When she arrived her first cry rung out. It was heard in the mountains of Peru, across oceans and among the people of her community. She stated her presence in a vibration of here-ness. She was loud and dramatic. That day, everyone just kind of knew. There were stories all over the world that were spun the moment she cried out, telling of the birth of a Storyteller.

In her first years of life, her mind had to wait for the rest of her to catch up. At four and a half years old, Grace was a young girl with blonde hair swinging curls at the ends. She had green eyes that held a sparkle. She liked all the typical things a girl likes, pinks and purples and dresses and purses and dolls and high heels and such. But at the same time, Grace's brilliantly beautiful mind was onto bigger and more epic plot lines. Grace's mind had found intrigue in bedtime stories, really any story at any time that anyone was willing to tell her. But Grace's mind liked bedtime stories the most. There was something to the quiet, the shadows, the costumed pajamas and the snuggles and pillows that accompanied these stories in particular. In her home, bedtime stories consisted of mostly fairy tales. Grace's mind thrived on fairies and kings and jesters and forest creatures and adventures. It swallowed down the harsh lessons of the Brothers Grimm. It spun out beautiful ribbons of Grace's imagination from the straw known to other children her age as books without pictures. She was far beyond her age in what was read to her and how she understood it. Her mind was insatiable. On nights that were later than usual and actual bedtime was closer than a mini-novel, her mother would read her tall tales and short stories. On nights when hours became just a few quick moments, Grace's mind would be easily held captive with a play by play of a workday. It liked to weave a spider's thread around each story, catching all the points of view, all the hidden meanings and all the lessons it offered in its web. To Grace's mind, stories were practice for when she grew up. And, in a way, her brilliantly beautiful mind saved her and would one day lay out a future to behold.

You can imagine, that for a child so versed in stories, her first words might just be 'Once upon a time' and 'Happily ever after'. And you would only be half correct. Her first words were 'Once upon a time'. But she never uttered the words 'Happily ever after'.

As Grace grew into her mind, she also grew into her compass of truth. Everyone has one, a compass of truth, a way in which the world is sorted into good and bad, truth and lies. But what happened with Grace is something truly incredible.

It happened when she turned six. Grace had caught up with her brilliantly beautiful mind. It was no longer satiated with fairy tales and short stories, putting on plays that relived the same lessons she read about at night. The imagination of others no longer quenched it. It began to quest in the world around it. Grace's mind, which had been born of the purest curiosity, now crept out from behind the fiction into Grace's everyday. It searched relentlessly for inner truths to expose in the rare beauty of a story told in tandem with a little magic. Her brilliantly beautiful or beautifully brilliant mind scoured reality for truth. In doing so, it was practiced at and capable of picking up inner truths. It did this by honing in on the crackling energy of the space between. The space between is where all the unspoken words, actions never taken and secret desires settle. Her mind was able to translate this energy into emotions that Grace felt and was then able to bring back to her heart in the shape of words that drifted along the cliff of a juicy story. Grace didn't quite know how she did it. She just did it. And the more she did it, the more intimate her understanding of human behavior became. And once Grace understood and recognized and heard all of the inner truths, the world wasn't so black and white after all. In fact, there was barely any black and white at all. So, one person's happily ever after was another person's hell. In turn, Grace could never utter the words "Happily ever after" without feeling like she was a liar.

Grace was an astute child, aware of everything around her. She wasn't the kind of child who asked adults 'Why?' all of the time. She was the kind of child who spotted a 'Why?' and then went after it like a starved dog after a steak. She had perfected the use of all five senses and trained them to perk up at a moments notice in order to investigate and expose those them, find those inner truths begging to be heard. Her natural tendency toward questions and curiosity found a fertile playground in everything around her. And this only stoked the fire of her beautifully brilliant mind. Combine this with a fearless sense of confidence and wild imagination that grew literary magic like weeds in a forest, and you had Grace, the six-year-old storyteller, and truth-sayer. By the time Grace was six and a half, she was a Master Storyteller. It was evident in how she approached her podium of silence and began her journey with whomever happened to be her audience at the time. It was the way in which the words wove around her tongue, spat out of her mouth and caught the breath of those who listened. It was the way that she formed thoughts into truths into lessons that stung people in the back but yet had them on the edge of their seat for more.

Grace would find inner truths in the corners of an adult conversation. She found truths hanging on the street corners and walking home from town. She found them in the space between her parent's arguments behind closed doors. She found them on the television, in the car, at the grocery store. When she had captured enough inner truths to find the commonalities between them and the umbilical cord of a major theme, Grace would begin to spill it all out into a story. The stories she told seemed to be somehow a part of a lineage of stories that began before time itself. They were sometimes archetypal and epic and sometimes simple and so very obvious. When she told her stories, it was as if time would stop. Allowing her to pick out the smallest of details and place it in the most perfect of places to hit just the right sound in her voice to call you in. She became almost mesmerized by the truths herself, like a monk in service. She was a speaker of, a speaker for, a conduit. And the stories she told, they were funny and silly and sometimes sad. They would be so entertaining that you would be caught up in the telling and it wasn't until the very very very last syllable was said, that you'd be hit, full on in the face with the truth. And she didn't mean it like that. She was just doing her. Grace was just doing what Grace did. Grace was just allowing her beautifully brilliant mind the freedom to be brilliantly beautiful. She was showing those around her, with pride and excitement what she learned. What's makes it even more of an unexpected twist was that Grace was a purely ordinary girl on the outside. There was nothing much special about her. She was average, to say the least. She didn't call out to anyone, 'Hey! Look at me!' Many adults were surprised to be so entranced by Grace and her stories. Though there actually were two things that did set Grace aside from other children, but many people didn't even notice them. Her eyes, as she began to tell more and more stories, sparkled brighter and brighter. And her heart was just a fraction of an inch closer to the outside world than most people. These she would learn were traits of her kind.

Throughout her childhood, Grace was a conductor of controversy. She would listen in on adult conversations, exploring for hidden truths. When she would hone in on a truth that called her to speak it out, she would interpret and articulate it with the sweet thickness of honey. Then she would direct and guide it gently into your heart with words that dropped like dew on a flower petal, disturbing nothing on the surface yet seeping into all the places that thirst for its magic.

Truths are important, but as adults, we often hide from them. Our flower petals curl under the weight of season after season, truth after truth. We are no longer able to hold onto each dew drop until it penetrates us, the truths start to roll off our backs. It was the same for Grace's family. They were only human after all. Grace would bring them story after story opening their eyes to the misgivings of humankind, she would bring them to tears with honesty and honestly, she would call them out on their own choices more than once in a while.

At first, they felt like the parents of a prodigy, and they encouraged her, uplifted her and supported her, and she thrived. What other child of six could look around the world, select truths like apples off a tree, peel their skin and weave them into a blanket of reflections that found you around a campfire with all your kin hearing the lineage of a truth? It was a true gift, just like there are children out there who can solve equations as toddlers and play Mozart on pianos before their hands are barely big enough to reach across the keys. Grace was gifted with understanding human behavior and the space between and then translating it all into the magic of a story. She touched people's hearts with her renderings. However, being the parent of a prodigy is never easy, and then add to that, having to be the subject of your daughter's human behavior interrogations and the likeness of far too many characters brought to life on her stage. Well, it can be a bit much for the average human, even when it's your own daughter. Of course, you want to support your child, but sometimes your survival instincts take over. Grace's parents fought off those instincts for as long as they could. No one wants to shut out or shut down their own daughter. It's only human to shut down eventually. It's only human to need a break from it, and a break is all it was supposed to be.

It started out with an innocent and simple distraction in their own heads, a to-do list, something that needed to be done, counting the piles of laundry they did last week while Grace told her stories. Then it graduated to whispering amongst themselves here and there while her stories were being told. Eventually, they would take their time coming to sit down and listen, they would get up in the middle of a story, or they would avoid her stories altogether by coming up with excuses why they couldn't make it today. Over time, Grace's parents began to lose their enthusiasm for her stories, and they forgot how special Grace was and how poignant and necessary her stories actually were. When they did sit down and listen to one, afterwards they would say things like "That was wonderful Gracie!" or "Wow! We loved your story!" but Grace knew what was happening and realized that even though they were saying these things, they didn't mean them.

Grace would ask, "What part of my story did you like best?"

And they would answer in vague terms, "The beginning!"

"Oh! I thought the ending was profound."

"You know, the main character and the way she figures it all out."

"I just love that you're telling us a story, it doesn't matter what it's about, just that you love telling it."

"I can't wait to see the sequel on the big screen one day!"

Grace was beautiful, and she was brilliant, none of this fooled her. So she slowly began to tell less and less stories to her family, and more of the stories were told to her stuffed animals, her dolls, her goldfish. Though, she still told her family stories, the only ones she saved for them were the urgent ones she knew they needed to hear. She told them with all of her, hoping that they would get in somehow. And sometimes they did, but most times, her parents had turned Grace's volume down. And so, Grace's fate was sealed.

It wasn't until one particular story, that her family turned the volume off completely, for good. I guess it makes sense to some therapist out there why it would be this particular story, but to Grace, it was the most important story she had ever told and no one heard any of it. When she finished, she decided she was done telling stories and here began a path that led her to the bathroom mirror at a dead end night a decade later.

Of course, there were also the kinds of adults who were more than taken with Grace, as she was quite unique. There are the perverted kind of adults who swallow down truths in big gulps, in hopes that if they swallow enough, it'll wash clean their actions. Like if they eat enough truths, it'll somehow make it okay that they were a perverted bastard. And any perverted bastard who saw a girl like Grace, made and designed by truths, seeker, and explorer of curiosities, magic maker... well, she's quite the main course. And this too sealed Grace's fate.

Grace made and designed by truths, seeker, and explorer of curiosities. Her words, her stories drove her into silence. Her very gift alienated her from those she loved and drew in close those who would take advantage of her. At six years old, her own story began to unravel into a pile of mismatched memories that waited twelve years to be picked up again. It was just one story, one truth, one girl that needed to be heard. And all she told was simply washed off the back of those she loved most.

And so Grace went silent. She started the process of burying, of compressing and of smiling on the outside.

Chapter 3

Grace's Final Story

Once upon a time, there was a girl who woke up somewhere she didn't fall asleep. Like she was transported by her dreams like she was beamed somewhere new, like someone waved their wand and requested her presence before the king. With her eyes still closed, she put on her beautiful smile then began to open them slowly, afraid that the light of the throne room might hurt her. Her eyes didn't have to adjust for very long. Dark was there. He greeted her like royalty; only she knew the Dark knew nothing of royalty.

"Hello princess," he began, and he whispered to her all the things they were going to do. He whispered under a heavy breath "I won't hurt you, I would never hurt you. It's just a game. You can open your eyes, let me see your beautiful green eyes, they're bright enough to light up a kingdom" So she flung them open to find she was in a place of shadows. Light and dark were dancing with each other elegantly in a tight space without much breathing room. They swept along each corner mapping for an exit, but only danced in circles. She figured it was day, but the light was so low. It was bright somewhere else, like in the King's castle, but not where she was and her eyes certainly were not lighting anything up right now.

Every so often she felt the Dark's breath reminding her she wasn't alone. "Princess. Yes. This. Here. " The Dark was laying down the rules of the game over her, like a blanket of skin and hair and sweat and tears. She found it strange that she only felt the Dark's breath when she craved the light, like the Dark knew she wanted something he couldn't give her, so he gave her what he could. It sent tingles drifting along her skin and between her legs. It sent tingles that the little girl hadn't ever felt before. "You like this, don't you?"

After a few moments and as her eyes adjusted and after the Dark quieted her with his open palm, she began to get scared, stuck beneath the weight of his rules. She decided she needed friends. And like magic, the moment she decided she needed friends, they were there! They came out of her brain bounding and jumping and filling the space with something more than the Dark. Today, they were playing fairies. And because they were playing fairies, every so often, she would see a sparkle to remind her of the light and the king's court and to let her know that everything was okay. Her friends, they chattered among themselves, and they blocked out the whisperings of the Dark until the Dark demanded to be heard and raised his voice in her ear. "You're not looking at me. Look at me. Listen to me. Tell me." Her mind swirled between what was happening as she tried to figure it all out and she couldn't help but wonder where the King was, where his throne was and its seat was the very same soft red velvet like she'd always imagined. She needed the Jester to make her laugh. Laughing always made her feel better. But then she would hear it again. The Dark and its voice would boom louder and then sink into a whisper then a breath caught in his chest. "I love you." Then her questions would turn back to why the light ran away. Where did it go? Why was he whispering and why was he talking of love, why won't he stop? And then she'd see a sparkle again and forget for a moment. She'd catch a glimpse of her fairy friends playing tag among the tight shadows and smiling at her. Her friends were so wonderful and buoyant and loud, but even they needed time to make sure everyone was playing the same game, and tag needs rules laid out too, so there were moments of quiet. There were moments of Dark, of questions, of tingles, too many tingles. She tried to do everything he asked of her, but she couldn't make the Dark stop worrying about her need for light. The whispering, the tingles, they were constant, darker and heavier. From the shadows came slashes of light across an ouch, or a stop, or a please that escaped her mind. She heard her own voice echo in the small space. Then suddenly the weight of his rules lifted and she looked down to catch a glance of own her hand as it did things she didn't understand and as it talked to the Dark in a language she didn't know. She couldn't really hear with all the laughter from her friends when they came back around. Her friends who had finally gotten the rules of their game straight, they were to play freeze tag, and the fairies would sparkle as they flew in different directions and before she knew it ... the whispering was gone, the Dark was gone, the safe was gone. She was wet and breathing hard, and her friends all said goodbye because they said she had to grow up a little and they wouldn't be able to help with that. You know, the dark comes every night, whether it whispers or not, whether it tingles or not, and being afraid of it doesn't help anyone. She couldn't be afraid of the Dark, it somehow needed her, and when it left, there was an empty space where it had been. The Dark had needed her. She knew it. She could feel it. Pieces of her even gave in to it, to try and help it. Her hand was writing a love letter in the air, taken with this new language the Dark spoke to her. So even though the Dark set itself inside her and planted the first little seed of fear and longing, she got up and wandered into the light looking for the King's court. And the tight space where the darkness played was only tiny in comparison to the world of light and the wide and beautiful path to the King's Castle that opened up to her. In her head, all her friends cheered with excitement for a good laugh from the Jester, for a hug from the King, a cuddle from the Queen and maybe a special minute to sit on the throne and feel the red velvet for herself.

*   *   *

This was Grace's story and unfortunately for Grace, though she told it out loud to her family, those who loved her most, not a word was heard. And she desperately needed it to be heard, so that someone, anyone could assure her that the Dark was indeed a perverted human being who gulped down truths as if it would somehow make things right for him. Because Grace was made and designed by truths, a seeker, and explorer of curiosities and she was quite the main course for this perverted human. She remained unseen and unheard by those who she needed the most. Here, she began her journey to heal on her own, which is the hardest of hard ways with the most mistakes and the most lonely as a traveling companion.

Chapter 4

As Grace went off in search of the King's castle and to follow the path of light, she was changed forever. It basically left her a woman and a six-year-old cohabiting in a pre-pubescent body not yet designed for such feelings. And in and of that Grace got all kinds of turned around, confused, and I might add, quite broken. I suppose one might call it being jaded like the green that crawls out from beneath a copper statue slowly over time. In an unassuming way, the jade took over Grace and the innocent flamboyance that once defined her, lay in wait beneath it. She was a changed person, challenged by a whole new set of rules, new truths to uncover. She was left with an amazing amount of questions that no one could help her answer because no one was quite comfortable listening to her story, which she offered up to anyone was willing to hear it. In most cases, they said, "Oh Grace! What an imagination you have! Where do you get such stories?" In rare cases they shut her down "Grace, don't make up lies. Go to your room, and I don't want to hear another word about it!" Grace would respond in silence and walk away.

After a week or two of being shut down and shut out, her beautifully brilliant mind went to work mending what had been broken. It sewed shut any open wounds and left just the tiniest of residual scars that played out in the occasional nightmare. Other than that, she had no memory of that day, and the whole thing was made more mysterious by its absence. Her mind had replaced it with a story. The most ordinary and boring story of the Dark it could muster.

What could not be erased or re-told however, were the traces the Dark left behind. The constant dance of anxiety that lived in her hands and fingers. The fingerprints all over her body of action that was taken on top of her. It had confused and excited her young body, and it awoke something deep inside that would not go back to sleep. She was able to keep it at bay for a few years, but it had cost her. She kept it at bay, by closing out the truths around her. She kept it at bay by denying the very thing that she was born to do. That decade in between was not easy for Grace. But in the beginning, especially, she often wandered down darkened streets, talked to many, many strangers, tried to find her reflection in the people around her in hopes of some recognition of what she was missing. She kicked up pebbles as she shuffled along, her toes digging into the well-traveled dust, all the while accidentally finding truths and hiding them away in her mind. Whereas, in the past, she might have woven those truths together into the most delicate and beautiful and haunting stories, now, she was silent and the stories traveled inside her, building up. Every so often a truth would find itself woven through a random moment and slipped through her lips and that felt good to Grace, after all, it was her natural tendency ... but for the most part, she kept it locked away inside her.

It's kind of hard to explain what exactly happened next to Grace. It's hard to explain because Grace wasn't like you or I, she was different. Her heart was a fraction of an inch closer to the outside world. Her eyes were just a little bit brighter. Her hands were plugged into the energy around her. She had a brilliantly beautiful mind that hungered for the truth. But, when the Dark visited her at six years old, it frayed something inside, like an exposed wire. A connection was either broken or made, no one knows, but it continued to spark inside of her. And the more she denied who she was, the more she starved her curious mind and the more stories that got buried inside, the more the space between called out to her. All of a sudden, the world was made of raw connection that she literally witnessed with her eyes. Whereas before, she sensed the truths and knew they existed and she heard the crackling of energy in the space between, now it was like the next iteration of a superpower. All of a sudden what she clearly understood before became actual space carving itself out from what surrounded it. The space between had a life of its own, taking shape, shifting forms to grab her attention. It sought out Grace so it could be seen. It spoke in tongues that Grace understood. She was in communication with the world around her in an entirely new way, and it scared her at first. Actually, it terrified her at first. It was something that she couldn't control. She thought she was going insane, but after a little while, she figured out that the world around her was passive, it wasn't going to hurt her or even try to touch her. It just needed to be heard, like Grace. So she developed an empathy for it all and decided to bear witness to all that went on around her. This, however, complicated Grace's existence. It inserted itself directly in Grace's path and became an everyday occurrence.

One time, Grace was walking down the street kicking up the well-traveled dust of lives past. She lifted her eyes as she heard quiet laughter and footsteps coming toward her. She saw a couple, beautiful and smiling as they walked, without attention for anyone else. They held hands, her head leaned into the space between his shoulder and his head, but it didn't quite touch him. He looked down at her, his eyes drinking her in. Grace thought to herself, "It looks so easy, the kind of love they don't have to work for … "Her thoughts traveled from there onto her own want for easy love and then to the question of what easy love was. Can love be easy, doesn't the actual thing of love deem it to be more than just easy? "love is epic, right?" she said aloud, not realizing she was speaking out loud. Then as the couple neared her, Grace witnessed the pulse of the space between them taking shape, and growing and swelling until it was pushed free of the two of them breathing life into itself. And there it was, the child she lost, in a heartbeat, color flushed all around him. His baby face contorted with tears and bloated with grief. He looked at the woman then spoke in tongues to Grace, which was vaguely translated into, "I is hers, I love more than hers, she loves to forget to have another,

I just need not forgotten, I feel love even here and she needs not forget but she forgets I needs love too." Then he faded back into the space like he was a balloon deflating and he was gone.

This kind of occurrence happened to Grace all the time, especially in the first few years after the Dark's visit. Grace would often learn a truth from the visitations. In this occurrence, Grace understood the story of the couple, and she no longer felt any pangs of jealousy or questions of love. This woman lost a baby that she carried around in the space between. The memory was so heavy that she thought she needed to have another baby to replace him when and all he needed was to be carried once in a while. This man whom she looked at with such love and laughter didn't know of this baby; it wasn't his, he didn't even know her then. She was on the hunt for a new life, a new someone, a new family. This wasn't love as much as it was compromising and compensating. Grace now knew the story, as if it was her own to tell and she felt the words rising to her lips begging to be released into the world. But Grace refused an utterance of it. She thought the remedy for her lay in silence, but the remedy was in the telling of the truths.

Grace was confronted with truths all of the time. Not all of the truths were sad or angry, some were beautiful and filled with joy. But all of the life she witnessed outside of herself made Grace feel like she was empty. She still had that missing something, like her own truth just left, gave up on her and so she was walking around with that crack slowly growing into a chasm. And every time she played witness to someone else's story, it sparked something like intrigue or curiosity in herself. Yes! She used to be curious. She used to be quite curious. And each time her curiosity was peaked, something responded inside of her. And before long, Grace was trying to get to the bottom of her own truth. This was a dangerous path that led in many dangerous directions. It propelled Grace to dig deep, deeper even, into an experimentation with pleasure and its many tendrils.

Grace began to seek out stories that resonated with her, that made her tingle. She was no longer a passive witness to other's truths. She used her gifts, her eyes, her heart and her hands to find her kindred stories in hopes of finding her missing piece. She became an active participant calling out the space between to quest for it. She called on it often. She became more aware of what happened between human beings, the static spaces, the echoing canyons, the emotions that filled everything in but were left unsaid. The more Grace learned and saw and witnessed; the more Grace began to become intrigued and curious about the limitations of control. Something inside of her was demanding to be played out over and over again as her memories tried to push through. Something inside of her kept putting her on the weak side of control.

When witnessing wasn't enough anymore, Grace, at nine years old, began to experiment with the physicality of pleasure and its dependence on control. It resonated deep, deeper even, within her. Like the missing piece of her was calling back each time she went a little further. Each time she pushed the limits of what pleasure could be under the hand of control. It became somewhat of an addiction, this wicked curiosity, this experimentation. And it invited characters into Grace's life that should have stayed in their own story. But one thing Grace knew from her years of reading, A true adventure leads past the reef, into the darkness of a limitless ocean, and so she adventured on in the name of Pleasure. Control. Needs. Control. Pleasure. She was onto something, and she wouldn't let it go. Her mind pushed her further each time, hungry for answers. And this exact interrogation is what led to the heartache, the pain and the misunderstanding. It led her into the arms of Austin.

Her interrogation would find her stained with blood in the name of love, it would testify to the nothingness from which she came and from which she thoguht she would always be made of. It would choose steel toe boots. It was from others and it wasn't her truth at all, it was theirs. Yet something resonated so she couldn't quite let it go. She couldn't stop, she needed her truth so still, she placed herself willingly on its altar and consequences would be doled out accordingly. And those consequences were more expensive than she could ever have imagined. They were her sense of self. They were her, they were her ability to Love and be Loved. Had she known this, she might have gotten help. She might have stopped, she might have let it go.

There was a separation that happened during the visit with the Dark and over the next decade of Grace's life, that separation which started as a crack would split into a chasm the depths of the grand canyon, eventually filling back in again right up to her reflection in a bathroom mirror at age eighteen where the reunion of all of her would overwhelm, drown and suffocate her very existence.

Chapter 5

Grace was older than most when her moment happened. What started out as an experiment in control and pleasure had deviated into an abusive relationship that took Grace down with it.

She had just been dropped off at her home by Austin, her boyfriend. At first, she was drawn to him because he dangled an element of danger in front her. He was the edge that she needed to go further into her obsessions and addictions and he would feed her insatiable need to find the intersection of pain and pleasure. In the beginning, Grace dared him to take her, every last piece of her. She fueled him on, she laid herself naked in front of him and summoned up his Darkness. On the outside, she handed him rope and handcuffs and she begged him not to take it easy on her, she begged him for harder. On the inside, she was practicing how to call on her fairy friends. As their relationship progressed, however, Grace began to wash herself clean of the need for pain and began to crave the gentle. She had pushed the door fully open, had sacrificed herself on the altar of Darkness and somehow, after years, a light began to beam. It was the first time; she craved the side of sex that stroked the forlorn and lonely parts of herself. She craved the kind, reassuring side of sex that told her it wouldn't

31

hurt, that showed her how to love him back.

This is where things got complicated. Austin had been versed in the ways of the Dark and Grace had handed his Dark precisely what it needed to grow bigger and more powerful than Austin could control. And for this, Grace began to blame herself. And it was this blame that started everything in a new direction. A direction in which Grace no longer heard her own beautifully brilliant mind. Its sounds had been replaced by the insults, the blows to her head, the lies, the terrorizing thoughts. Fear replaced the confidence she had in both for herself and for Austin. She no longer trusted anything that swelled up from inside her. She grasped onto a need to save Austin from his Dark and in doing this, she gave up on herself.

Austin had just dropped her off at her home. Grace stopped in the kitchen to find a knife, before walking up to the bathroom, taking off her clothes and looking at herself in the mirror. She saw the parts of her that he called fat, ugly, unacceptable and the parts of her that denied Love and held onto pain. She focused on her lip swollen and red. She thought about how this was all her fault, she focused on all the demons she called out in the name of curiosity. She focused the hatred inside of her on her body as she brought the knife up to her skin to cut out all of the bad.

*　　*　　*

Here. Here is her moment.

Chapter 6

This is when it happened. The knife in Grace's hand fell into the sink. And it all stopped.

It was as if the world around her became static, bits and pieces of who she began swirling all around, her existence began spewing random, and nonsensical facts through tight lips every so often until she could make out just a few words and memories floating in her peripheral vision. Nothing seemed to make sense. She would see a story someone told her once, a piece of advice someone gave her and a belief someone planted when she was young. These were the Shadow World's way of teasing her out of her earthly existence. It was meant to make her curious, like the Alice from Wonderland, teasing her into its world. As her curiosity grew and she started to come back to her body so she could reach outside of herself, those tight lips loosened and her grip on the moment shattered. As she placed herself back inside her body, it all happened at once. She felt the surge of her everything release itself into what seemed a moment of pure pain, pure joy, pure longing all at once. It was a waterfall of a universe running through her and every nerve ending, every blood vessel, every pore opened itself to the possibility of its own existence. They were released from her body to be reclaimed by a side of herself. The random spewings and nonsensical facts became obvious remnants of her, magnified findings of hidden secrets and desires she always kept under tight security. It was the finale of a long night of fireworks, soundlessly going off around her, and each sparkle had a bit of her essence, her life, her story, her. The random light show became every little piece of her life, and who she was, only it was all floating outside of her as she witnessed it, in a static state of Oh Shit! She couldn't exactly wrap her mind around what was happening. One minute she was standing in front of her bathroom mirror contemplating actions with unforeseeable consequences and the time to take action hurtling toward her. The next moment everything went dark. Shadows fell into the space around her, time and place shifted so quickly that all of a sudden she was suspended in her subconscious. She could only move the tiniest of movements, at the slowest of paces. As an outsider seeing this, one might call it beautiful, like the beginning of a new world, the kind of cosmos stuff that we take for granted. It is definitely something to be looked at with awe and reverence. But as someone going through it, it's best felt with full dissociation from your actual body and the knowledge of what is actually happening to you. All the pieces of a whole gathering into separate everythings and then expanding and bursting into two wholes, two yous; only each whole is missing the other half. Being torn in two is not an adventure that's easy to describe. There's the you that you are the you that you leave behind and the you that you become. That's three you's for only one you, and you can feel all of you, each fiber, each thread, each memory, each thing you ever did both together and separate. You can feel each emotion and each emotion being torn in two. Have you ever felt what happiness feels like being torn in two? Or what sadness feels like being torn in two? The pure essence of a feeling not even a whole thing in and of itself and yet it can be felt being torn in two just as your bones, your body, your spirit. It's ridiculously painful. It's emotionally painful as well as physically painful, and I'm betting that's why the majority of us forget it ever happened. Grace was a special child, and she would never forget. There are a few of these children, that never forget. They are special; their hearts can handle it without dissociating and forgetting, even if they wanted to, they aren't capable of it. They are special, and they have a job to do here. They need the knowledge of how it all works in order to save us.

Chapter 7

Grace opened her eyes. The lights were bright and filled the space. She found herself on the floor, naked, the knife she once held up to her waist, her skin, her own body, had fallen out of her hand. She felt an air of detachment. It was as if she was herself and witness to herself at the same time. Her vision was somewhat blurred, and it was doubled. As she lay there, still and almost numb she realized her heart was beating, no, it was racing, trying to make its way back to the present moment. But there was something odd about her heartbeat, at first, she couldn't place it and then she realized, her own heartbeat had an echo. She distinctly heard two beats for every one. But it wasn't far away, it was there, in her chest. When her vision had doubled, so did her heartbeat. But its rhythm hadn't changed, just within the kept time of her pulse, there was now an extra heartbeat gentle and deliberate and steady.

Slowly Grace began to feel the pins and needles of slight movement in her body and she felt a rhythmic trembling of her hands, fresh with the memory of holding that knife. Her hands that had done so many beautiful things in their eighteen year life, now trembled with fear for what they could have done, what they wouldn't have hesitated to do. "What happened? Had time stopped? Did I pass out?" These were all thoughts that swam through Grace's mind. Almost scared to find the answers, Grace slowly pulled herself up off the floor, back to standing in front of the mirror. Her mind was trying to put things together, searching for the pieces that were missing. The first thing she did was look in the mirror. She looked at her reflection, her eyes still seeing double, it was like they saw two of her in a shattered glass, but nothing was actually shattered. She could see the expression of loss painted across her face. What exactly had she lost? Would it come back? She looked into her own slightly brighter eyes and saw the truth she had so very longed for all her life; she could see that it was settling back in. She couldn't understand it yet, but she knew the truth was there somewhere in the green hazel swirls that were circling her pupils. It was as if her eyes were alive and breathing and letting her know that it was all okay. She looked in the mirror down her face, her lips, her chin her collar bone, her shoulders, and her eyes fell on the place where her heart was beating for two. She could actually see it flickering with life just beneath her skin. It was the tiniest movement, quick and beating and she listened to it. She felt like maybe the heartbeat would talk to her, tell her what was going on, explain the whole mess, but all it did was beat on with that deliberate, gentle echo of a second heartbeat, it was mesmerizing.

The heartbeat, just like a swinging timepiece, stopped her mind, stopped the questions and the chatter and her incessant need for answers. It brought her down to a place, a quiet, subtle place. A calm and resting place and it was here that Grace fell witness to a changing, to what she could only explain as a dream, but it wasn't a dream. Her feet were solid on the ground; here eyes transfixed on the place where her heart beat in the mirror. She was awake and aware, it was just that a calm had overtaken her and it was strange because it didn't feel like her own calm. It felt superimposed over her, but she wasn't scared of it.

As she stood there still and calm, the world around Grace shifted. It started with colors. All the colors that surrounded Grace in this world, they started to vibrate. Everything she looked at began to blur just the slightest with this vibration. Then one by one the colors of our spectrum, red, orange, yellow, green, blue, purple ... they were washed away. As one color was washed away, all the other colors would shift to release that color from itself, the same would happen with the next color. It created this effect almost like the Northern Lights, all the colors releasing, changing and releasing, changing and releasing, changing until all that was left was black and white and all the nuances of grey.

What happened next gave Grace's stomach a lurch, even through the facade of calm. A rumbling started from deep below her feet. Before her ears could hear it, her feet sensed it. It reminded Grace of what an earthquake would feel like, though she had never experienced one. The rumbling swelled with a need to erupt, but it remained contained underneath, like a caged monster. The floor began to shake, and the walls trembled. There was the sounds of everyday things knocking into one another. All the while the rumbling grew and swelled even bigger and louder and Grace felt a heat rise to the bottom of her bare feet. She heard cracks and the distinct sound of fabric tearing, it was right there, in her ear, threads crying out as they broke free. The cacophony of all of it crescendoed, and as it hit the frenzy of this fucked up shit, Grace was spun around. The walls fell back; the ceiling rose to alleviate the sky's need to be seen. The floor split open to find grass. Grace was no longer in her bathroom. Quiet broke in again, silent and still. Black and white, the colors never did find their way back in. She was still naked. Her feet were soaking in the soft, cool grass after feeling the heat of whatever just happened. She was outside. There were trees and rocks and grass; it took Grace back to realize how beautiful nature could be even without all the colors that she thought were what made nature beautiful. Grace turned around where she stood to take in everything that surrounded her and off in the distance she noticed a large building with a path leading to it. The building was enormous with large glass windows where the vaguest essence of color drifted free. She saw smoke rise from the building shifting shapes as it rose. The building had two large double doors. Grace could tell they were made of old thick wood, the kind from a Dickens novel, with a story written all over and from within them.

Grace looked around her again, taking in the trees and the large amount of rocks that surrounded her. It was interesting because she hadn't taken much time to look at rocks in her world.

Here, she took a moment to let them speak to her, and she was stilled by the life layered within them. She wondered if any of the rocks wished they were on a cliff, living life dangerously, then she laughed at her own thought. It was quiet, so her laugh echoed across the earth. Was this earth? Did aliens abduct her? Where was she? The questions rose up inside, but as soon as they did, that calm superimposed itself again, and she let it all go. Silent, still, no wind, no sound, no movement.

She looked around; this place was foreign to her. It was beautiful in its colorless depth. She wasn't afraid. Her heart still beat for two, her vision still saw double, but none of this seemed to bother her. Her senses in this world were peaked. Grace wondered to herself if it was because there was no color, her senses weren't distracted. Regardless, in this world, Grace could hear things she couldn't see, see things she couldn't feel and feel things she couldn't imagine.

This place didn't have incessant needs to answer. It didn't have constant reminders of shoulds, coulds and woulds, and it didn't speak to her like the world she came from. This world was more like a meditation. It didn't imprint on her, but rather for the first time since she was six, she felt like she was imprinting on something else. As this thought floated around in Grace's mind and made its way into her subconscious and below the calm that was superimposed over her, she felt a need rise up inside her. She felt this need with all of her. Her chest convulsing, her breath irregular, her eyes tearing, she sobbed as this need found its home inside of her. It had been there so long that it lay deep in her blood, her bones and in the chambers of her heart. How could she not know it was there all this time? She fell to the ground, knees catching her. Her hands pounded the grass as her eyes leaked a bright hazel green into the ground. As her chest convulsed with the power of needing to imprint, Grace let go of something, of a part of herself and as she did, a second Grace flickered into existence, naked beside her. Hands pounding the grass, on her knees leaking bright green hazel color into the ground. Grace's heart returned to one heartbeat; her vision was clear again, her hands stopped trembling. The calm was gone. And Grace felt confidence. Grace felt acceptance. Grace felt Love.

Chapter 8

Grace looked at this version of herself; it was identical to her. Everything about her was the same as Grace, even her bright eyes and the tiniest beating right under her skin where her heart rests. This version of Grace had skin that seemed a little more translucent than hers and Grace could sense the blood pulsing through each vein. It made her seem so much more alive and mysterious than Grace herself ever felt. On this version of Grace there was a large mark on her forehead. The mark could be described almost like a tribal tattoo that was centered directly in the middle of her forehead, it was black and white, like the rest of this world and it was a series of lines spiraling into a center point. The spiral had flecks of black that danced alongside it. It seemed like it was moving as you looked at it. This didn't surprise Grace so much though, because she always had an affinity for spirals, drawing them, staring at them, tracing them with her fingertips when she was anxious.

The two of them stood looking at each other and Grace for the first time looked at her own body as if it was someone else's, which it kind of was and kind of wasn't. For the first time, she saw all the beauty coursing through it, all the gentle curves and crevices that made up who she was. She could see the stories of her own life present in the body standing in front of her, and it brought her to silence. She felt a kind of awe at herself, and she was taking all of it in, each scar, each birthmark. Each part of herself that she once saw as a defect or a map of what disgusted her, she now saw with clear eyes as a map of her own heart, the sadness, the joy, the gratitude, the abuse.

Grace looked at this version herself in the eye and finally spoke. "Who are you?"

It spoke back, in the same voice, almost as if it took the same breath as Grace, "I'm you. Well, only a part of you, a part of you that's been needing to heal and to know our story for a long time now. In fact, we've been searching for the truth, haven't we? I've been inside of you all our life. I'm the part of you whose heart is broken and who needs to be heard and who isn't afraid to know the truth regardless of what it holds. I know you, I am you."

Grace stayed still, not moving either toward or away from this. God! She was so confident so matter of fact, She knew what she was saying, and it all came out so clear. Grace felt an immediate connection to her voice, a magnetic pull. She recognized something about it right away! She continued on.

"I don't understand, how can you be a part of me and yet, be in front of me?" Grace asked, confused and overwhelmed and awed.

"That part, I admit, is confusing, We're here in a world that's separate from our world, I have a job to do for us that can't be done in our world. We're one and the same. What you've experienced over the whole of your life, I've experienced. You can think of me like your emotional center; I remind us of our heart. I'm the part of you that feels without judgement."

Grace looked at this self of hers standing in front of her, awe still spilling over, but she wasn't putting it together yet. She went on trying to catch Grace up to the present moment.

"My memories are yours. Together we paraded through department stores trying on the life of mannequins to pass the time; we made up stories for everyone around us, including all the kids in sixth grade so they would leave us alone because our stories were epic and no one knew where the truth ended, and the lies began! We had our first kiss in a cluttered mudroom and it was spectacularly awful, but it pushed us to want more." She went on, as Grace seemed to show a flicker of understanding in her bright hazel green eyes. "I remember things that you've forgotten. I remember the Dark when you were six, and I remember calling for our fairy friends in to distract us. I remember all the spaces between that begged us to give them voice. My hand was your hand as we tested the limits of pleasure and control and I looked at us in the mirror with contempt and hatred just as you did, knife ready to cut out everything that made us so very undesirable. I was there. I still am. But right now, I have a job to do for us, and I need to do it on my own, so here I am, in front of you, instead of inside you. But I'm still part of you. We are still connected."

With tears beginning to swell in her eyes Grace asks, "How do you know about that all that stuff?"

She replied, "Because I was there with you, we went through it together. Don't you feel the pull toward me? I can feel the pull toward you ... "

"I do, I really do, it's so strange. I have this urge, this need to touch you to put you back inside. To know every single inch of you. And I just want to cry; I haven't wanted to cry like this since I was a child. I don't ... "

Grace tried hard to put it into words; this pull towards herself being outside of herself. It was like all of her feelings were reaching outward toward this other and it was hard not to be overwhelmed by it all. Everything seemed so tangible between them like there were seven dimensions of texture to each memory, each feeling. Grace was becoming overwhelmed with longing for this other of herself. The longing was rich and full, it smelled of the scent of playdoh and scented markers, its texture was smooth yet sticky, and it called her to it in a language of Love and playful gestures. It was unreal. This longing, so hard to resist and so malleable, she could see it connecting the two of them.

She was interrupted from her thoughts noticing that Grace was getting caught up in the details instead of trying to find the bigger picture. "You'll find here, in this world, things feel different, more, so much more than in our world. Feelings are magnified and have many shapes and sides to them; you'll learn more about it as we find our place. You can control it, and not get lost in each feeling by simply breathing the air, don't forget to breathe, deep and purposefully, The air here has just what you need to let it go enough to see it, understand it and explore it but not get lost in it ."

Grace took a deep, deep breath and slowly the longing that captured her settled down like a fire to an ember. It perched at her feet in wait and Grace was free of its control. But it was still alive almost smoldering, crackling with intensity. Grace was absolutely amazed.

"What is this place? Where are we?" She asked.

"Grace, you're special, not everyone gets to witness this world. You get to experience it along with me, and some others do as well, but only because we have a path, a job that has to be done when we leave this world. Pay attention to everything you see, feel and do here. This world is magical and so completely different from your world, so it may take some time to adjust. Just know, that while we're here, we're okay. Everything in your world is as it should be, your body will move through the day as if nothing has changed. No major changes in the everyday should take place. It's taken care of. We'll know if anything happens that needs us to attend to it as soon as is happens. And while we're here, that anxiety that dances between your fingers everyday, you can breathe it away, deep and purposefully."

Grace, looking down at her fingers winding in, between and through each other as she took another deep and purposeful breath. She noticed again, something settled right in front of her, she saw it with her own eyes. This time, it wasn't a fire or a smoldering, it was a flutter. And it didn't settle at her feet. Instead it spread its backbone into wings and lay across the air gently riding it down to the space above her left shoulder. It was more like an insect with many arms reaching out to test the air as it settled down onto her. And there it stayed, like nothing she had ever seen except maybe in a children's book a long, long time ago. "Fascinating," she thought, as she finally felt the space between jitters expand to more than a moment's worth of peace. She hadn't known that space since before she was six.

"Since we're the same person, my name is Grace too, but that could get confusing. So would you like to choose my name for our time here?" the new version of Grace asked her. "Choose your warrior name, a name that holds all you wish you were; I can be that here."

Grace thought for a minute. She always loved her name, she didn't need any other name, but Grace was kind of a passive and circular name, and maybe here she needed to be more angular and direct ... she let it sink it for a minute ... She thought of all the wild woman, warrior names in her memory and then it came to her. It felt sure, confident, strong and definite. She said "Anika".

"Anika, it is. I like it. It makes me feel taller and more in control, but deep down the Grace in me, keeps me honest and grateful. It works! Anika, imbue me with your superpowers!" she declared out loud with a gesture loud and silly, and both Grace and Anika laughed out loud. It felt good to laugh, and Grace let it go without a thought.

"Now, I have a name, but no clothes! Which is unfortunate in a world where everyone does wear clothes, believe it or not." She smiled at Grace.

"Where are we supposed to get clothes?" Grace looked around, not seeing anywhere she might find something to cover herself up with.

"I told you, this world is magic, and so all you need to do is imagine something on us, and it'll appear." Grace, doubtful at first, but then again, this entire situation was pretty damn ridiculous, closed her eyes and tried to think of something to wear. It was weird because all she could think of was colors that she'd like to drape her body in. She hadn't realized how she had let colors define her in her world. Here there were no colors. Or at least just the slightest hint of color and the only time she saw them was when she overlooked the building in the valley below. So she tried to direct her mind to think of materials and feelings along her skin. She wanted to feel free and strong and beautiful; it had been so long since she felt that way. Magically, as she honed in on that feeling, she became wrapped in the most luxuriously feeling material from her chest, around her waist, her hips and her upper thigh, it released her body at mid-thigh and graced down her leg from there. She felt gorgeous; her skin was cradled in a material she could only describe as silky satin cotton comfort. It held her where it touched her and released her where it flowed free. In it she felt powerful as if she had a superpower and were standing on a cliff with her hands on her hips overlooking a windswept ocean. Damn, she never knew clothes could do this for her. Or maybe it was just in this world?

She looked over at Anika, and she too was wearing the same as her. And wow, it was a powerful sight. The tattoo on her forehead swirling inward, dancing and her bright green eyes, her strong but imperfect body. Anika looked down at the clothes than up at Grace as she said, "Nice choice! I don't think I've felt this good in quite some time; I feel ready to befriend dragons and travel worlds." She winked at Grace. "But let's start with this one, shall we?"

Anika turned toward a building in the valley and started to walk in the direction of a path that led there, through trees, rocks and open fields. It seemed like a long way to walk, but Grace figured she had a lot of questions and that would require a lot of time for answers and this would give them plenty of that to reconcile it all.

Grace followed after Anika.

"Before you ask me any questions, which I know you have many, I want to explain something to you. When you first saw me in this world, I saw the flicker of recognition. I saw that you saw me as you. And as you saw me as you, I saw what I can only describe as reverence in your eyes. You recognized my beauty through all of our imperfections. This is something we haven't felt about our body and ourselves in such a long time, in a decade at least. And there's a reason you felt that way here, looking at me.

Our body, has mapped out on it every experience that we've had, the beautiful, the ugly, the tender, the violent, the soft and the hard. Our body has a memory too and that memory imprints on our skin, in our bones, runs through our blood. Our body has been the canvas on which our life is painted. Everything shapes us. And you were able to see that, to find the human in that and the beauty in that, instead of only seeing the marks that some may consider something other than beautiful. In order to come to this, you needed to see this body from outside of yourself, from a different perspective. You've been lost in the experiences and haven't had the chance to see the trails of beauty they've left to remember them by and to remind you of your journey. It took seeing this body without the complication of your feelings for it, to fall in Love with it, to cry for it, to get on your knees in front of it. See, I'm your heart, your feelings, your gut. So when you were able to see yourself or rather our body without the attachment of past feelings, you made that connection whether you realized it or not. You could see us for what we are. Beauty Infinite. This world will make these things happen. There are many beautiful, wonderful and powerful truths to be discovered here. It's your job to find them and to integrate them. It's my job to heal our heart from the past." Anika stopped talking and gave Grace a moment to put it all together; it was a lot that she laid before her.

Grace was following along; she was on the outer edges of understanding it, looking in, just about ready to take the leap of believing. She had felt the reverence when she first saw Anika standing in front of her. Her impulse to weep from gratitude for her own body was intense. To kneel at its altar, to bow in its presence. It sounds ridiculous, but at that moment she somehow knew that every part of her body, every scar, every bulge, every wrinkle and every imperfection had a story and each one was important. She could see and sense the stories surging through that translucent skin of Anika's. It spoke to her it told tales of her courage and strength, her weakness and addiction, her innocence and intrigue. She innately understood her human being-ness, her humble worth, was worth as much as any human being could be worthy. But also at that moment, she felt the shame and guilt for having denied this very body love in all form and figures. It was like she had opened a door for grief to enter. But things moved so fast that the grief hadn't had a chance to find a home inside her yet.

Anika went on. "So, you can understand why you felt such reverence toward my body and not yours even though they are one and the same? It's really so much in such a little time, but I need to catch you up and quickly in order to get to my job. I need to tell you about how our bodies are created, how the ridges are formed, the edges are molded, the expanses are poured, but you need to process, so let's just walk for a little while."

Grace and Anika continued on their journey toward the building. Grace took the time to look around her, to experience this world. This world was full of subtle changes, the air she breathed had a sweet smell to it and the magic to contain feelings.

"Amazing," Grace thought to herself.

"It is," Anika thought back and smiled.

As they walked down the path, Grace noticed that her feet made no sound on the ground. Nothing crunched beneath her feet, even though she was definitely walking on a dirt road full of tiny pebbles and loose gravel. She couldn't hear the sound of Anika's footsteps either. The silence was clear all around her. She also noticed the way the trees made room for her and Anika, even though she felt no wind. The air seemed to be still without a stir, and yet the branches and leaves of the trees moved to open up the path and the sky before her. It reminded her of how the anxiety that danced between her fingers spread its wings and rode the air down to her shoulder. Was it that the air was thicker here? It didn't feel any harder to walk through than in her world. Was the air alive? Questions. So many questions. What was missing was any other kind of life, there were no animals, no birds, no insects.

Grace asked Anika, "Are we the only ones here? Are there any animals, wildlife, insects? Does anything else live here in this world?"

Anika replied, "Oh Yes! There are many things that live here, but as you'll see when we get to The Hall, emotions are the most fascinating creatures that you'll witness here. This world is very magical, and right now, it's guiding us to where we need to be, and no wildlife of any kind will interfere unless they're called in."

Anika continued on, "And of course there are many of my kind at The Hall. There are the few that are guiding their selves to understanding like I am, but for the most part, once they get here, they start working."

The two continued on in silence again as Grace pondered what she just heard. Others, like herself. The thought comforted her, and secretly she made a very clear and humble wish to meet someone like herself.

Anika heard it, felt it and something burst open inside of her, was it hope? She couldn't contain her smile, and she was glad that Grace was looking away from her for the moment.

They got closer to The Hall, but it was still quite a ways from where they were. The dirt path became rockier. The pebbles seemed to get larger and create a path of footsteps for both Grace and Anika. It reminded Grace of when she was younger, and she used to try to find stones to walk on to cross brooks and streams. She always loved jumping from rock to rock, like it was a challenge to cross and the water always seemed so alive, like a formidable opponent in the game. It was the same here, it was like the rocks stepped up to meet her foot, to guide her over the ground and the ground almost seemed alive if Grace looked closely. The space between the rocks was breathing, rising and falling in a steady rhythm. It didn't seem to scare Grace. Instead it filled her with excitement and a playful energy. She began to jump from rock to rock like when she was a child. She was really enjoying herself when Anika stopped her. She pointed to the rocks at their feet and the rising and falling of the earth at their feet.

She began, "The earth, this world, our world, each human being, they all have something in common. I want you to think about what you learned in school about layers of the earth. Picture the diagram we were shown when we were younger of what the earth's layers look like."

"Okay, I think there were like three or four layers, a really thin one on top and they got thicker as it went to the center, where there's a ridiculously hot center. I don't know; it's been a long time!"

"You're right," Anika continued, "Do you remember how the land we walk on is formed, how water chooses where to occupy and the land rises from beneath it? The land that we walk across, the continents that we call home that is the outermost layer, and it shifts with each heated occurrence in the layers below it. We live on these plates that aren't really solid ground. They float along on a layer of molten lava. When the lava gets extra hot and bubbles beneath our layer, the plates we live on shift, collide and grind against each other. These create earthquakes, and volcanos and such. When these events happen, the shape of our lands change, often very subtly, we don't even notice, though over the years and decades and centuries it becomes more and more apparent that things have changed.

I want you to think of each human being, each animal, each living creature as an earth all to themselves. This includes you. Think of the outermost thin layer of the earth as our skin. Think of that ridiculously hot center as our heart and the layers in between as our bones, organs, and muscles. When I say heart, I mean the center of our emotions, not necessarily the organ of our heart, though it beats through each and every emotion. I mean our emotional center. It's the place where our emotions reside and have their roots. Our emotions grow out from here. They shift, take shapes, they speak to us from here. I am that emotional center. I can't exactly see the shape I take inside of you, I just am. But, I can feel it. I know that I am just like your name, circular and passive, inviting and humble, strong and gentle.

As our emotions grow, they sometimes build up, get pushed down, they can erupt and explode too. When this happens, it's like the lava of our earth bubbling up from the heated center. On our earth when this happens, we have earthquakes and volcanos, and the continents shift. The same is true for our bodies. When our emotions get pushed down too far and erupt and explode, things shift in our bodies. Sometimes it's sickness, sometimes our face changes, sometimes, it's in a nervous tremor we develop. These little eruptions and explosions can keep us in balance, releasing pockets of unexpressed feelings, so they don't build up too much. As adults, this is how we calibrate our emotions and get through the really hard stuff in life. But, as children, our bodies aren't as versed in how to balance all of this out. Often times, we're taught how to deny some emotions and take full advantage of others to get our needs met. We learn from a very early age how to manipulate them, without learning how to understand them and express them. Well, because of this, when we're kids, especially when we're teenagers, we have a big build-up of feelings that have been pushed down and misunderstood. We hit our emotional limit. This creates a vortex of heat at our center and it's this vortex that leads us to a moment or an event like the one that just brought you here. Usually, it is a moment in your life when it all bubbles up at once and the plates shift and collide so much so, that it allows your shadow self, that's me, to split from you and heal your heart. That's what this place is. This is where I go to work it all out, to free your hearts from all of the constraints others and yourself have put upon it. This place is magic. Watch, I'll show you exactly what happens."

At this Anika pointed to the rocks beneath their feet. As Grace looked down, she could see the earth below the rocks breathing, inhaling and exhaling like a river that keeps the rocks afloat, but Grace couldn't feel the movement under her feet. She became lost in the rising and falling as the magic began. Grace could see inside the moving river beneath the rocks, in it was the call of emotions. She saw them all swirl and dance and connect and then start to occupy each other's space, be pushed down and be burdened. As the call took on voice and got louder and louder and the emotions built up like a solid wall, the waters rose until suddenly at her feet rocks began to cluster toward one another, colliding and as they did, just a few rocks were lifted and displaced to a new home. As this happened out came a wisp of black and white smoke released into the air. The black and white smoke took on the shape of Grace and then dissipated. The ground was itself again.

Anika began again, "Here's where it gets confusing and I'm going to leave you with this thought to question on your own. Just as we are all a little earth unto ourselves, so to are our relationships, our social circles, our communities, and cultures. They all have their own layers and plates and lava. We are part of even larger earths with collisions and eruptions and earthquakes. This is why it's important for all of us to be clear with our own hearts, because we play in fields much bigger than our own. It's in these fields where the eruptions and explosions are the size of genocides and war. It's in these fields where we create laws that govern and closet and harm in the name of broken-ness and denied emotions. We need to be clear in order to make change. So, you see we are more than just ourselves, but it's important to understand ourselves as the first point of change.

I know it's a lot. I'm asking you to shift in how you look at your world. But you're here because you're special. You have a big job to do when you get back to your world, and you need to be ready for it. I'll do my part. I'll Uncover your heart. But you need to use this world for all that it offers, find what's lost and find the magic so that when you go back to your world, you're prepared. You have nothing to fear in this world. Nothing."

Anika looked at Grace who had a somewhat faraway look on her face. She was breathing, she was blinking, she was looking about her and Anika wasn't worried, she knew Grace would get there, she didn't want to push her too much right away.

This was, at last too much information for Grace, her mind turned off. It was so many words, so many ideas, so much information in just a short while, her brain was spinning from the amount of it all. She just looked down between the rocks. She reached down and put a hand on the ground below, she felt it rising and falling, steady and true to what Anika said. She could even feel the heat from under her palm. Grace looked up at the sky from between the leaves of the trees. She wasn't sure, but she thought she could hear it whispering to her. She thought her ears caught pieces of words sweeping past them, but she couldn't make out anything in particular. Instead, she just felt a wave of peace wash into her and all of a sudden she knew singularly that Anika was right. Everything she said was correct. And she was all of a sudden filled with a sense of purpose and a sense of adventure. She got up, and she started off in front of Anika, almost leaving her behind. She needed to see what lies ahead, she understood all of what Anika had said, and now she knew that her truth was waiting for her here. And she knew, without a doubt that she was going to be given a second chance at everything, just as everyone was when they split in two and shook free from the world she came from. She had a desire to drink it all in at once, to go, to be, to do. She hopped, rock to rock, rock to rock, rock to rock, Anika following behind.

Anika shouted, "Wait up!"

Grace stopped for a moment, looked back and shouted, "If

we really are one and the same, I should be able to lead us once in a while too. Catch me if you can!"

Anika, glad to finally see this kind of life in herself, and secretly somewhat relieved to be able to follow for a little while shouted back, "Are you sure you want to race me?"

And they both took off past the rocks, into the grass, through the fields, laughing and out of breath the whole way to the path leading directly to The Hall, where they stopped.

As they made off, a breeze kicked up in the air for the first time since the Anika had arrived bringing with it a sparkle, like a raised glass, and the tiniest of rainbows played hide and seek among the leaves of the trees, landing softly on the head of a beautiful red fox that peeked out from behind a tree as it watching the two girls intently, low and quiet.

Part Two:

Kai

Chapter 9

It seemed like it was days or even weeks ago now that he had arrived in the Shadow World. He felt at home almost immediately once his body and mind adjusted to the change. He found a comfort among the black and white landscape and a recognizable whisper in the wind that played like a memory. He'd always felt a connection to somewhere other than where he was, and he guessed that this may have been the world he felt connected to. He didn't have to try very hard to understand the language spoken here, which was one of feral emotion. He expressed emotions and feelings. He was more than adept at identifying these emotions for others; he was an artist with them. It was only when he tried to do the same for his own emotions that he felt like all he spoke was gibberish.

Thinking about it, he had always felt cursed by the language he spoke. It seemed to single him out, to stake claim to him and to cordon him off from others assuring a kind of alienation from his generation. What irony, to continually feel other's pain, loss, excitement, joy, grief, desire, guilt, happiness, greed, embarrassment, and yet not to have a single thread of relationship with them. To know they'd never spill it over willingly. To be so connected and intimate with someone that he lived their feelings, literally and yet to be so fucking separate and almost invisible to the people whose hearts usurped his. Cursed. Or rather he *had* felt cursed by it. Since his journey here, and having felt the emptiness of the others at the moment of his split, he no longer saw it as a curse. Since coming here to the Shadow World, he saw it as a most spectacular gift, a gift that he was trying so hard to retain and to use to revive himself. Now, he saw it as a second chance, a heaving breath of possibility, a vibrant life that was waiting to be lived.

When he arrived here, it had been the most pain he had ever experienced, and that was something truly insane because he had known pain like an old friend since the time he was born. When he finally got here, he hadn't needed to be guided or directed by his other self, though he still was. For him, nothing seemed so out of the ordinary about this journey at all. It just was. That's kind of how he lived his whole life moving with what was in front of him. Working with what each moment presented to him. It was the opposite of Grace, he didn't question everything, he took everything that was handed to him, and he played it through his instrument, accepting it all. He didn't have much of a choice in this; he was consistently being presented with the moments of others. He needed to stay in the here and now in order to process it all. The memory of his passage here was vivid in its detail still days later. He had been in bed. He had decided that he had had enough pain, that his heart couldn't take it anymore. That he would do something to stop it before the world he lived in placed itself squarely on top of him suffocating any happiness that still resided inside. No. He would do it on his terms. He was determined to feel something other. Something more. Something, anything but the pain of others.

Chapter 10

His name was Kai. He was born into a family that loved him, but he was the youngest of four children. The only child, in fact, that didn't follow the rules of existence. These rules being, to learn skills on schedule, to go to school, to get good grades and to eventually make lots of money to spend on things that others tell you that you need. No, he didn't follow these rules. Even as a young child, he didn't play the part that his parents expected of him. He was late in walking, talking and generally anything that people asked him to learn. He cried a lot, and he was often found hanging out on the floor in a corner where there were loving moments, heated arguments, long goodbyes, and such. He was quiet, but he hummed to himself all the time. His parents didn't exactly know what to do with him. And they fucked up, just like all parents do, not because they were trying to fuck up. They were genuinely trying their very best to raise their child to be a successful adult. They just didn't alter their definition of success to fit Kai and his gift of empathy. So, they left him alone. It was the very opposite of what he needed. They didn't push him, or question him. They didn't engage with him as they did with their other children because they didn't speak his language, to be honest, not many people did.

When they did engage with him, they spoke of goals and mistakes, success and failure, they spoke of his brothers and their accomplishments. They spoke of anything other than Kai's feelings, and the world of emotions. They spoke anything but the language that Kai was born to speak. Since his parents didn't provide Kai with a vocabulary of feelings, he became lost and overwhelmed by what he felt everyday. He needed to learn how to understand and process everything that was going on inside of him, and he needed to do it fast, in order to make sense of what was happening. Kai was so young, and his heart was so gifted in the ways of empathy, but instead of holding him up and teaching him how to understand his heart, his parents let him drown under the weight of it all. Maybe his parents were afraid of the feelings, perhaps they knew they fucked up, no one knows, but Kai grew up quiet and alone in a family full of people, misunderstood and full of emotions that weren't his and that he didn't understand himself. He became a child who spoke little, retreated from big gatherings and whose heart flickered with emotion between feelings of anger, sadness, joy as quick as the wind changed direction.

Kai had never found a way to turn off his gift or to direct his gift in ways that would allow him breathing room. He only had to be around people who were holding emotions inside in order to feel what they were feeling. Only, when Kai felt it, it wasn't something he could turn off or bury, it became a very real, very tangible emotion for him, that often took control of Kai's body. This complicated his life in ways that were incomprehensible to his family. It pushed him to the margins, hiding from people. He found friends in those who sought to either express everything they felt when they felt it or dulled everything down with substances. As he got older, he didn't care much about the paths set before him by his parents because he was too busy navigating the water of the emotions people around him were busy suppressing.

After years of this, Kai found himself chest deep and unable to swim in waters that rose each and every day as his ninth year approached. More and more he found himself on the sidelines of life, trying to recover from the onslaught of feelings that pushed up against him whenever he was in public, let alone in his own family of six.

Chapter 11

It was when he turned nine that Kai was given his first guitar. His oldest brother found it in the corner of a shop window, and he instinctively brought it home to Kai. The first time Kai put his fingers to the neck of this instrument he felt Love. It may have been the first time he felt Love that was purely his own. Unadulterated Love. It was over his ninth year that he taught himself how to play. By the time he was ten, he could play anything asked of him. He understood music, and its language, which was very similar to the language of the heart. If you had placed sheet music in front of Kai, he would blink, blank of recognition. He cared nothing for reading or following along with music. He wanted to befriend it, dance and play with it, mold and stretch it, discover it. Music was not meant to be on a page, it was meant to grace the space between.

Kai had the natural instinct to bring together all the emotions he was feeling and the music he was playing and therein he was truly born.

What happened when the guitar and Kai were united, was incredible. Kai found that he was able to translate all the feelings that he perceived and felt from others, into music and in doing so he was able to let them go from himself. But it was his effect on others that was his true gift. When people would listen to a piece of music he'd written about something he felt, they could feel it too. They could understand it and see it and it would play itself throughout them, vibrating the resonance on their heart. In a way, Kai brought them home, and in that, he saved quite a few relationships, talked people off edges, gave them back a voice, infused them with the courage to be still with themselves, heard the unheard and saw the unseen.

With the arrival of the guitar, Kai was able to venture out into the world without the fear of being consumed by all of the unplayed emotions because he had his own instrument. He had a way to express without being controlled by it all. The more Kai played his music and spent time composing feelings, the more the waters began to recede from around his chest. He created works of sound that embodied exactly what feeling wrapped itself around his heart, and as the sounds left his strings, Kai felt just a little bit lighter each time. In this way, Kai needed the guitar; he developed a relationship with the guitar and the music it allowed him to create that was a lifeline for Kai.

Empathy is a truly needed and amazing human feature. Less and less people in our world have been practicing its art, but it'll never go away, it'll find its path into people like Kai, whose heart is always open and doesn't close, who hears the hearts of others even from great distances, who can feel for an entire generation, even though it may kill him in the end. Kai didn't have a choice, he was an answer to void that was getting bigger and empathy found its path into his veins, pumping through his heart. He was imbued with this ability to feel others sorrow, pain, joy, sadness, anxiety, frustration, but he was never given the tools to sort it out, until he was given his guitar. He had a way with it, one that would seem almost inhuman except for the songs of humanity that bled from him. It was a gift, a superhuman gift. And it was just like it is with Superheroes. Each Superhero that has a Super Power has an equally powerful villain that's constantly plotting against him. There always seems to be an equal consequence on the other side of a gift. It was the same with Kai. He needed to grow up with his gift, but his world became too big too fast, he couldn't keep up and didn't know how to adjust. It started with high school.

With all of this going on you might imagine how hard it was for Kai to concentrate at school, where he wasn't allowed to use his guitar in class. Where he had to sit naked and exposed, his heart soaking in everything around him but void of a way to release it back into the world. Each day he had to sit like this in class, and each day he dreaded it.

He often found himself at the nurse's office or sneaking out to the bushes behind the fields to find space and escape the tension of everyone around him. He certainly wasn't succeeding at his education, at least the education that school was providing for him.

High school introduced a broader world to Kai, a larger picture of life. When Kai was younger and his world consisted of only his community, it was easier to use his guitar and play what he was feeling, but as his world opened up, his heart began to go global. He wasn't able to put it all down, to play it all out. He hurt from the inside in ways he couldn't understand because he was no longer face to face with the the feelings.

He learned of War, of Genocide, of Greed and Hunger. He learned the ways of Power, and he felt both sides of it, the need for it and the epic consequences from those that abused it. Knowing both sides is what seemed like the worst part of it all. He hadn't wanted to know both sides. He felt dirty because of it. He just wanted to feel it and give it sound and release it all. But he got caught in between, and he needed desperately to learn how to shift his perspective, but he was alone, there was no one to help him. His family had given up long ago.

As he neared his seventeenth birthday, things came to an unavoidable head. When he placed his hands on his guitar, all that came out was chaos. Overwhelmed was an understatement, he became paralyzed with grief and fear and hatred, that wasn't his.

Life had become unbearable for Kai. It was here that he turned to certain drugs, to try to right what he felt was wrong. It was his way of trying to hone in on the simple feelings again. The everyday feelings of the people that surrounded him. He thought if he could just feel what was in front of him he might be able to lessen his burden. He might be able to lighten his heart just a little so he could breathe again, so the waters would recede. But it had the opposite effect. Instead, When he was high, he made music, but it was the music of his heart, and it spoke the same chord over and over again. The chord of his own loss. It sang of past friendships never forged, of a child on a floor in a corner, of death and dying, because that was what it felt like now. It was a record skipping over itself replaying, replaying.

He was made for more than just his own feelings, and as he composed the refrains of his own echoing sadness, all of the rest of the world pounded incessantly on the floodgates until they opened. The waters flooded in and flooded in and flooded in. They washed up among his chest, his shoulders, his neck, he tasted the salt of endless tears raging in rivers of torture and inequality. He gasped for the sweet air of a silent heart. He didn't yet understand that his answer was in telling this story through his fingers with persistence and truth. The answer was in connecting all the experiences to the same branch. It wasn't in the fractured definitions of different feelings but rather it lay in the base root of one emotion and he needed to find it, fast. Instead he found the false hope of denial and trudged forward looking for more ways to calm the storming sea from drowning him.

He went looking for another way to try and focus his heart's attention. He found small razors in his dad's bathroom cabinet. He would hide in his bedroom with the door locked, not that anyone would come looking for him, and he would make little shallow cuts with swift movements all up his forearms. Then he would concentrate on the blood welling to the surface. But this too, failed Kai. And it's here that he found himself at his moment. At his event. At the point of drowning and losing his battle.

To the world around him, Kai was the picture of addiction, depression, anxiety. No one knew what was actually happening inside of him. That he was trying to take action, to control it, to make it better. But the outside world wasn't able to look in. Addiction, depression, and anxiety, these are things that our world doesn't like. Our world, our people, they choose to ignore these things, pretend they don't exist, even when the vehicle for them is a person who has the potential to heal a generation, like Kai. In our world, addiction, depression, and anxiety are seen as weakness, as false feelings, as a defect, and so the world pretended that Kai didn't exist, even as he was the only one feeling for everyone around him, even when he actually opened his mouth to cry for help. Our world failed him because of our own fear of our hearts and what they may hold inside of them. When his SOS fell deaf, he made a choice. A choice that would certainly lead to regret.

Chapter 12

Kai was eighteen when he made the choice. He'll never know if it was his choice or someone else's choice that coursed through him and brought him there, but the choice was made, and so it happened. He was laying in bed, his blood pounding inside of him with a fury that he knew wasn't his, but it got him thinking how unfair it all was. How unfair that he should have to feel these feelings of others and yet they got to shrug them off and do whatever they like. He felt cursed, and it added to the fury that was already boiling over. He was sweating profusely, his covers wet with rage. It was here that he decided he had had enough. He had felt enough of others. He had lost his own feelings among those that spun inside him like tornados. He, who had been spurned was no longer going to give his gift to anyone else. He wanted his heart back, on his own terms, in his own body. And so he grabbed his guitar. The one thing in his life that had his back. He got out of bed and picked it up over his head. With all he could muster he lost his lifeline. He brought it down as hard as he could on the bare floorboards at his feet. The crash shattered all around him as the wood, warped and split, the strings popped and flung wild in the air. As they were freed from the instrument, they sang out one last chaotic chord, full of pain and sorrow. A call to the other side. Kai felt a piece of him shatter as well. It happened all around his feet, like he shook his head while it was full of glitter, sparking down in a slow motion of reflective light, but he knew they were pieces of him. And it didn't stop him. He raised the neck of the guitar one more time; he had to end it. Pieces of wood dangled from it, bent and broken, random strings holding on tight trying to keep anything it could together, but still, Kai raised it above his head ready to slam it, burn it and bury it.

As he began to heave in the broken breaths of someone overtaken by rage and the reflex to destroy catapulted his arm forward and down toward the floorboards, the lights went dim. They began to fade away. Kai felt his body lurch backward almost like he was a rag doll pushed back on his bed, with no muscle to fight back let alone hold him up. As Kai watched, unmoving, his guitar fell gently to the ground. Like it was laid lovingly by the hands of an angel. It lay there motionless among the floorboards as still as Kai himself, who realized now that he had no control over his body. He could not move it, though he could feel the tiniest of pulses rushing in his veins where his skin was scarred with determination.

For the first time, he felt nothing. He felt empty. His heart was clear of all of it. It occurred to Kai in this very slow moving moment that this is how others felt, others who weren't him. This is what was present instead of feelings, this nothingness.

This void, this blankness. It felt so disconnected. It felt, No, it didn't feel, it just was. And for the first time in his entire life, he wished for the feeling back. He saw the gift that was his heart and yet he could do nothing. He figured he should have felt fear or longing or sadness, but nothing came to him.

He watched with blank eyes as one by one the colors of our spectrum were sucked out of his bedroom, his home, his world into each and every crack of his broken guitar. As one color was sucked in, all the other colors would shift in their hue and tone until the next color would let go of its hold around Kai and be sucked in. As colors filled the cracks and holes of his guitar the spaces where broken once lived were healed. Kai couldn't help but wonder if he too would get sucked into his guitar. All he could think of was the strangeness around him and the ridiculous notion of getting sucked through a guitar. He laughed, only it was so slow that only the tiniest of creases started to penetrate his cheek right above his lip. He wondered without feeling if he finally went crazy. Did he finally lose his mind? Would he ever move again?

As the last color swirled around and into the guitar and every-thing surrounding Kai took on a shade of black and white, slowly the air, the ground, the sky above started to spin. Everything blurred as a speed beyond our understanding was reached. The bed Kai was sitting on dropped out from under him, the walls of his bedroom tore open exposing black and white streaks trying to make sense of a new world. Trying to find their new place as floorboards disappeared and out from beneath Kai sprouted blades of grass and edges of rock. The roof of his house lifted into oblivion and into focus came a beautiful and poetic grey sky.

As the spinning began, Kai felt his insides rip open to receive his feelings back. Like the Hulk, his body accommodated to the size of an entire generation of feelings struggling to be heard. His everything stretched and grew and swelled to the cries of both pain and love, happiness, and sadness.

Imagine, just for a second, what this felt like to Kai. He had finally rid himself of all emotion, he was empty, only to find himself craving to have it back. Then all at once, in a shock wave, it rushed back in. All at once. It was at least a hundred times the size it had ever been, holding the vast opposites of who we are as a generation, because who are we really, without our feelings. We're just robots. So Kai embodied all that makes us human, across nations, across oceans, across cafes and beds and cellblocks. All of it, at once. And it ripped him in two, literally. Shards of who he was pulled free of his bodily flesh, and found themselves suspended above him reflecting the cacophony of design that was once Kai. As a final chord boomed him back into a moving existence, Kai found himself on the ground heaving from the pain of it all.

Chapter 13

Kai's body was shaking uncontrollably. He looked up from the ground at his hands. Next to him was himself, naked with a guitar strapped over his shoulder, his hand laid gently on his own back trying to calm the resonance of it all. Kai felt for his chest to make sure he was alive and there, where his heart was, he could feel the slight beating beneath his skin. His heart was just the tiniest bit closer to his chest than most and Kai was sure the journey to this place had inched it forward just a little bit more. He opened his mouth to say something, and he found nothing came out, not even a whisper. His voice had been lost among the pieces between worlds, severed by the shards of his own screams. His other self-lifted the guitar off his shoulders and handed it to Kai. Still shaking he took it, understanding that his guitar was to be his voice here. Kai simply accepted what was happening in front of him and allowed himself to move forward into it. He didn't have a choice, and somehow Kai knew that everything was just where it should be at that moment. As he looked around, he saw that he was in a different place, one brushed with all the nuances of black and white and everything in between. He saw the shore, the path, the forest, the rocks. He felt the quiet, the thickness of the air and the gaze from behind his own eyes looking back at him.

As the reality of this other world settled inside Kai and the shaking slowed down a little, Kai looked at his other self, who knelt beside him with kindness and compassion in his bright blue eyes. The blue of his eyes almost dancing, like a morse code around his pupil, ever still, and yet constantly shifting. He was still naked, and Kai noticed his skin looked more translucent than his, especially in places where the skin was pulled tight. The size and shape of his body was the same, but Kai saw that all along his skin there were marks where veins were, they looked like the marks left on top of a running river where the currents would meet and join. The marks had a life in them, they weren't like a tattoo but more a living picture in his skin. Kai's eyes fell on his forearm where all the marks he had made with his dad's razor blade now formed the paths of resistance in the rushing river that flowed under his skin. It was these marks that foamed up past the surface into beautiful reminders of Kai's own pain. Reminders that Kai did have his own feelings, that they were just under the surface, needing to be lifted up.

As Kai was taking everything in, he suddenly realized that he was completely naked as well. It was as if his clothes couldn't stand the pressure of the broke open-ness that landed him here. And before anyone could say anything, Kai instinctively placed his attention directly on what he wished he was wearing and before he knew it, he found himself in jeans with a gentle flare at the bottom and a silk-cotton shirt with embroidered edges and a velvet trim that buttoned up to his mid-chest, exposing that small mound of beating heart right at its center. Kai looked down in amazement. His body relaxing from the comfort of it all, the shaking all but ceased. His other self was dressed in the same. What he changed for himself would change for this other self as well, they were connected, one and the same.

Kai realized that he didn't know this place or understand it, but he felt at home here and trusted most anything that occurred, It had been so long ago that he believed in magic, but there had always been a part of him that knew. He knew there was something different about him. Kai thought to himself; maybe this was a journey that was only beginning.

His other half spoke

"Hello."

Kai nodded

"You probably don't understand what happened. I can feel that you're not afraid or full of questions, but understanding is a different matter entirely."

But Kai knew precisely what had happened. For some reason, he felt at peace with all of it. He didn't need any explanation. But his other self knew differently, he knew Kai needed to hear it. He began just as Anika began with Grace.

It came to the point where Kai's other self asked him for a name. Since Kai couldn't speak, and he didn't know yet that he could think thoughts and his other self would hear them, he just picked up his guitar, and he began to play "All along the Watchtower". He was hoping his shadow self would understand that he wanted his name to be Hendrix.

His other self nodded in complete understanding and said "Hendrix it is."

Part Three:

The Hall

Chapter 14

Grace and Anika arrived at a footpath leading to The Hall. They were both heaving from the long run down, feeling the air of this world penetrate their lungs with curiosity. As Grace placed her foot on the path, it was like someone wiped off all the fog surrounding her. Her mind cleared, and there was a pearl of serenity settled perfectly within her gut. She stopped and waited for Anika to join her on the path, with a knowing that she didn't have to do this alone.

Together they walked up the path to the clearing where there stood The Hall. It was a gigantic stone building, like an old factory, though not rundown. It raised to the sky and challenged the tops of trees. Immediately Grace understood that each stone was placed with care and cooperation among a people that built it out of necessity. That necessity was of utmost importance, and so this building echoed that. It straightened your spine and gave you purpose. It inspired greatness to simply look upon it from the path.

The stones of the walls were laid with precision and a quirky kind of pattern that adjusted itself depending on who was standing in front of it. It was like a dance that happened so subtly that you didn't even know quite why you couldn't stop looking at it. There was a thick and lush moss that cascaded down from the side of the building, and it was here that Grace spotted her first wildlife of this world. They were small birds that could fit in the palm of her hand gathering along the moss. They were fluttering in and out of it. The birds were far away, but for some reason, Grace could see every little detail of their faces. Their eyes seemed to hold the wisdom of a hundred years at least. They were large for their small bodies and each eye welled with tears, a wetness that didn't spill out. Grace innately knew that their job was to hold. They were vessels of empathy. Why Grace knew this, she didn't know, but it had something to do with their eyes. She had known exactly what it felt like to have tears that couldn't spill over, that she held in her own heart. They were magnificent creatures.

The Hall was not only tall but long. And Grace noticed that each stone laid in the foundation of this building was etched with pictures. They weren't exactly masterpieces, more like hiero-glyphs. There were lines and shapes and artistic gestures. Some were barely visible; others couldn't go unnoticed. It seemed like each stone spoke to the other with its picture. Was it a language? Grace assumed it wasn't because there were no repeating images. Each picture elicited a guttural response in Grace. She took her time looking from each stone to the next. As she looked at one, her left hand curled into a fist and sparks flew out from between her fingers. When she looked at another, her chest rose and fell heaving a heavy sigh, with it a word swam out into the air, the letters of the word alone spelled out in wisps of breath that disappeared as soon as it was seen. Yet another stone crossed Grace's eyes literally until all she could see was her nose. And then she sneezed and out came a liquid laugh, gurgling from each nostril. Each time Grace looked closely at a stone, her response was new and different. She began to realize that the pictures on each stone were feelings, because each time she had a physical and emotional response, it somehow matched with the picture on the stone.

Anika, watching Grace turn her attention from brick to brick, being overtaken with emotion after emotion, finally said, "If you stop looking directly at each brick with focused attention, it'll stop. The key to the magic of this world is focusing your attention, so when you drive it into something, that something can start to take on a life of its own. But, when you take your attention away, it all calms back down."

Grace heard this, and so she stopped, and instead of looking so intently at each brick in front of her, she let her eyes roam from brick to brick, taking in the larger picture, and she was able to see it for what it really was, a symphony of the heart. Each brick spoke to the next in tones of feeling, and they all played together in the landscape of the building. It was magical. When Grace was able to step back from it and take it all in as one, she could hear the music of it all and it laid itself down directly in her heart. Grace put her hand over her heart allowing it in. It just may have been the first time in many years that she allowed anyone or anything access to her heart.

There were seven steps leading up to the two huge wooden double doors to the entrance of The Hall. Each step was the same size and shape as the next. As Grace walked up each step, she could swear she saw a glimmer of each color of the rainbow play beneath her feet, but it was fleeting and only an echo of the opaque colors from her world.

There were two huge wooden double doors that almost leaned into the stone wall beside it. Grace looked at Anika and Anika said, "All you have to do is put a hand on the door, and it'll open for you, as long as you're meant to be here."

Grace placed her hand on the wooden door in front of her, and it opened up to a room. A spectacular, amazing, busy, beautiful, quiet yet screaming loud room of incredible sights. Grace walked through the threshold.

Inside the doors, The Hall was an open room with floors that ran along the perimeter of the building but left the center of The Hall open to the reaching ceiling. There was an aisle right up the center of The Hall, and this was where Grace and Anika stood as they both took in the sight in front of them.

This was new to Anika as well as Grace; She had never been here before, she had always resided inside Grace until the shift that separated them brought her into this world. Anika knew of this world, she knew of this place, she knew exactly what she had to do here and how very important her work here would be, but she had never seen it before. She knew the directions, the instructions, the history of all of it. She was able to see in her mind what everything was to look like, but she had never actually seen it for herself. All of this information had just come to her when she separated from Grace. It all happened at that exact moment in front of the mirror when she was birthed into existence by the earthquake that shattered them. It was like knowledge was placed inside her as she became this self. It was the knowledge to guide Grace and to do her part. As Anika looked around, she thought to herself, "What a wonder! This is amazing!" Anika knew what to expect but had no idea how she would feel when she actually saw it and understood the depth of it all. She had never seen anyone like herself, and here she was surrounded by others. They were busy working, moving, creating and Uncovering. That is what she knew it was called, Uncovering. For that moment on, into Grace's long life, Anika felt true pride for what she was about to embark on. She felt the importance of what she was about to do, the significance for not only what she was about to do for Grace but what she was about to do for an entire generation of young people. When Anika shone with this pride, Grace too felt it, and the two of them literally lit up, an aura of brightness peeking out from beneath their skin. As they shone, standing on the aisle in The Hall, everything stopped, just for a quick moment. There was a nod of recognition from each and every person in The Hall and then everyone went back to work with a little more joy than usual.

Grace asked Anika, "What are they all doing?"

Anika replied, "It's something called Uncovering, it's what I'll be doing for you while we're here. It's funny because I know exactly what to do and how to do it, but I've never done it before, and it's so much more amazing than I could have ever imagined! And we have an imagination that is like no other, as you well know, or rather used to know before we let it slip away."

Anika began to walk up the aisle, leaving Grace to explore on her own, she looked back and said to Grace, "I'll catch up with you later, I need to find my place, look around, be amazed, take it in. Remember there are awesome things to discover here and nothing to be afraid of."

With that, Anika was gone, and Grace was left alone in the center of The Hall as her brightness began to pull back into itself and she was back to her present moment. Grace took a few deep and penetrating breaths feeling her anxiety flutter out of her. She could feel the stillness at her fingertips and the curiosity that sat directly in her mind's eye. She repeated to herself, "There's nothing to be afraid of."

Chapter 15

Grace stood alone in a room full of bustling movement, wonder, and curiosity. It was the curiosity that came so naturally to her that she recognized immediately. It was like an old friend that came to greet her and pull her inside for a cup of tea. It was a friendly and kind sort of curiosity, and it was so welcoming to Grace. So welcoming to her, that even in a room full of strangers and strangeness, in a world she just arrived in and never knew before, she felt like she was at home. Yes, she knew this curiosity. It wasn't the kind of curiosity that made kids torture small creatures in their backyard, like worms or lightning bugs. It was a genuine and humble curiosity. One that drives children to want to know about the games their grandparents played when they were kids so they could have the chance to relive it with them. A curiosity that lives among pages of a journal streaked with ink and tears to understand all the whys. A curiosity that allows wildlife to become friends with human beings and trust their ways. This is how Grace knew that she was safe. The curiosity that lived within the walls of The Hall. And this is why Grace felt comfortable enough to take a few steps along the center aisle and look in on what was happening all around her. She knew there was nothing going on that couldn't be seen in the open or known by all.

Grace was also keenly aware of how many noises were puncturing The Hall. It was comforting for her to hear the noises that lived here, and yet there was still a blanket of quiet that lay over it all. It wasn't until she turned her full attention on something that the volume of it was naturally turned up. She couldn't help but think she needed some of this magic in her world. Imagine if she could simply turn someone's volume down by taking her attention away from it. That would have saved her a lot of grief in her eighteen years in her own world. She thought to herself, "That would be a game changer!" The same could be said of what she saw in The Hall. She saw it all just as she saw everything she looked at in her world, but when she brought her attention to something, in particular, it became that much more in focus. She could see things far away as if they were right in front of her, even the smallest of details. Grace felt like she had been given some sort of superpower.

Everything that was going on around her seemed so different than anything she had experienced in her world, though there were some elements that reminded her of bits and pieces. She could sort of place the activity she was witnessing as experimentation. There was intent focus on the relationship of observer and subject even though there was more going on than simply observing. What made it all so hard to place, was that in Grace's world this kind of activity happened inside white walls, sterile environments with lab coats and Grace always pictured people with rim glasses, which always made people seem more intelligent to her. Here, the air wasn't one of a sterile environment, it was closer to a place of therapy for children, paper hung on walls with etchings and drawings, there were couches and bed and chairs that ranged from bare to luxurious, no one space looked like another, they all had their own unique flair. The Hall was still black and white though, and Grace had the distinct sense that if this world was imbued with color, each space in The Hall would be a different one. It would be a far cry from the white that pervaded the medical fields of her world.

Each unique space had some of the same features, a bed full of pillows, a chair, a table, a mirror, instruments both musical and mysterious, a box of tissues, frames, some of which were filled with pictures while some were blank, and a computer screen like Grace had not seen before. Grace assumed it was a computer screen. That was the closest guess she could make with her current knowledge. It looked like they were at the very least made of four dimensions. The screens swirled inward and outward at the same time like they were made of particles from space, a little milky way in each screen. And people interacted with the screens differently than they did in Grace's world. Sometimes they touched them or talked to them, exactly like in Grace's world. At other times the people reached in and grabbed things from the screens or literally stepped inside them. The screens even billowed outward in shapes and faces. In one space, a screen delivered what could only be described by Grace as a living memory. It was more tangible than a hologram or a movie played on a screen, but not exactly present in the here and now. It was marked like time had already stamped it delivered and edges of the memory seemed to convey that. Grace looked away as if it was all too personal to witness and she would soon realize how right she was.

Along with these things that were in every room, each room had their own unique items that surprised Grace, from umbrellas and parachutes and old-school typewriters and chocolate fondue to more out of the ordinary items like 7 pronged tongs and large sewing needles with thermometers attached, molds of body parts hanging along walls, fabric that looked like it belonged in the closet of an elephant.

In every space, there was a person working. A person that was not dressed in a white laboratory coat but rather a their own stylized kind of outfit, like the one Grace and Anika were wearing. Grace assumed that these people were just like Anika, pieces of others that came from her world after a moment they almost lost to regret. They all looked just like people in her world, except for the fact that they each bore different markings on their person and their skin was just the tiniest bit more translucent than hers. Some of the people had tattoos that swam on their skin like Anika's, but all the tattoos had different designs and symbols. Other people had what looked like scars or burns. Some of the markings paid homage to the animal world; they were nuances of the wild that stretched across a back or a face or a hand. Grace would learn later that all the markings were specific to each person working there and that the tattoos, in particular, were marks of the artists. This is why Anika had the tattoo on her forehead instead of a burn or raised scar.

This is where it gets hard to describe. The Hall was a place with an air of investigation, experimentation and healing. The question raised in Grace's keen mind was "What exactly are they investigating, experimenting with and ultimately healing?" As she looked from space to space, she saw that with each person there was a collection of what she could only call 'things' for lack of a better understanding.

If she understood better, she would most definitely not use the term things. These 'things' were living breathing emotions, the life-line blood of the hearts of young people. They were fears that spanned years of sleepless nights. They were sadness that had flushed itself of salty tears and spewed out course grains of sand. They were Love that imprisoned itself among broken beer bottles stained with blood. These 'things' were feelings in need of freedom from all the boxes they'd be put into, definitions they'd been written into and rules they'd had to follow no matter the consequences. These emotions and feelings were dying, and the people here were saving them by any means possible. Grace didn't know this yet, so she called them 'things'.

As she looked around at all of these 'things', She finally saw the color that she didn't even realize she had missed. There really was no color in The Hall, except. Except for the bright, the low light, the neon, the pastels, the primaries and secondaries, the rainbows of infinite shades of all of it pulsing from within these 'things'. The colors weren't filling The Hall, they weren't part of the building or the people, and they weren't lighting up the place or infusing anything else with color. They just resided in and exposed each 'thing'. They came in different shapes and sizes and textures, and they all seemed like they might be made of different materials. To describe them would be foolish, because each one was completely different. A lot of them contained color within, but not all of them. Some were made of light, some were made of stone and other's were made of a gooey kind of substance. Each 'thing' seemed to be in a different state of repair. There was no one way to categorize them, but Grace innately knew they all belonged together somehow. They came from the same sort of place. These things were shifting and changing as she looked from one space to another. They each had a story to be told. They were interacting with the people working with them in ways that were completely unexpected. In one space it seemed like the thing was hugging the person working with it as it grew outward and upward toward its person with softness and a pillowy bounce. In another, a thing looked like it was suffocating its person, masked on its face while its person blew a bubble into its mass. In still another space, the thing seemed to be dancing to music that a person was playing for it and as it danced, it began to glimmer and dissipate into a rainfall in the space. How truly odd it all seemed to Grace.

This place was a beautiful and strange laboratory. She wasn't able to place exactly what was going on, or to understand how everything fits together with her journey here, but she had the recognition of Love and tenderness with which every act was performed in The Hall. It was in the way that the people here held and touched each thing. The gentle look on their faces as they worked. There was serious reverence for each thing; the care was so apparent, so tangible it could only be fueled by Love. The gentle, affection that flowed from their hands was so thick and loving that if their hands had eyes, they would mirror the birds she had seen outside. And it was because of this that Grace continued further into The Hall, feeling called to a destiny, pulled to her place.

Grace moved further down the aisle into the Hall. She saw one woman nestled up beside a large and looming thing that was the color of nightfall. It had the sharp edges of shorn metal, and it was bigger than her. It was twisted and it recoiled into itself, Grace thought it had to be at least two times the woman's size when it was stretched to its maximum. Every few seconds it would disappear, almost like a picture on a television screen might disappear into white static. It felt to Grace like panic and fear. But here was this woman, her arm around it, reading it a story in a quiet voice like a child at bedtime.

There was a boy that held in his hands the weight of grey matter barely breathing. Even as Grace watched, the grey matter sprung holes that seeped nothing. As holes sprung its center deflated until little round band-aids appeared to stop the hole up, almost magically. It seemed like an endless cycle that happened over and over again, a repetitive dance between space and filling the space, only these band-aids covered it; they didn't fill it. So, slowly this 'thing' shifted smaller and smaller, almost undetectably.

In another space, there was a man with the handful of pulsing purple. As he held the purple, Grace saw a thousand little arms extending up and reaching to clamber up the man's arm. She could see he was struggling with containing it in his palm, but he didn't get frustrated, he remained calm and loving. Every time he would carry one arm back to his palm five more would escape up his own arm. Finally, the man allowed it to crawl about him, and when it stopped right over his heart, it got still, and every arm sank into the man's skin resting there with the rise and fall of his breath.

In another space was a man who was feeding his thing. It looked like it was refusing to eat though. It was emaciated and tiny and a dull kind of white. It had no brightness to it whatsoever. The man was trying to feed it slips of paper with affirmations on them, like 'I love myself.' When that didn't work, he wrapped the affirmations around it like a blanket, turned to his computer screen and projected scenes of a childhood onto the wall in front of it. The thing sat back wrapped up and watched, but nothing changed.

All around Grace people were working with their things, in unusual and loving ways. Love was what called to her from every corner of The Hall. Empathy, caring, tenderness, true beauty. It all had its place among the people here. Maybe this was why Grace had such a reaction to seeing Anika for the first time. Maybe this was why she wept over the beauty of seeing her own body. "Was Anika made of Love? Was she her Love personified in front of her?" Grace wondered. Grace began to list all the questions she had in her mind as her body so naturally walked through The Hall on its way to a destination unknown. Among her list of questions was, "If human beings that were total and full in and of themselves, could they express this kind of pure Love and tenderness toward something outside of themselves without anything else interfering?" These people were only pieces of people. Maybe that was how they could be do their job so humbly and lovingly. Grace tucked it all back in and found her presence in The Hall again.

Grace walked down The Hall purposely. As she walked, she noticed one space in particular. She placed her attention squarely in the center of it. There were two boys, they looked the same, edging out past boyhood into the years of men. Grace immediately wondered if one of them was like her, the other half to her half. One had just a touch of translucence to his skin with markings all along where veins might be on his arms. The markings rushed past one another like water over rocks in a small river after the rain. On his forearm, the water bubbled up into formations that the flowing water wound around. It was mesmerizing, she stopped and watched the inside of his forearms as he held a 'thing'. Its color kept shifting from a blue to a reflective surface of some kind. It seemed mechanical and at the same time ethereal.

She watched the veins; she watched the river spill over into this boys skin as he held his thing and then her attention turned to the other man in the space. He sat on a small stool with a guitar in his hands. He made no sound. He was poured over the body of the guitar The fingers of his left hand were winding up and down the neck in gathering storms of chords. His right hand keeping steady the time, like a lifeline. The music that came from him was haunting and gentle and it called to her. Grace could feel it building up slow and steady though it was anything but calm. The music had an intense edge to it, the kind of edge that begged to be pushed further. Grace honed in on the sway of the strings as he spoke through them with his fingertips.

His hair was long, like Grace's, but darker and not as shiny or well kept, his hair had a wild weightlessness to it, and it hung full of life, across part of his face. She could tell that he was tall, even though he was sitting down. His back was the slightest bit arched over, and he was ordinary, average looking, just like Grace. But when he looked up and caught her eye, she saw the blue. It was just a little brighter than any other blue eyes she'd seen, and that made him beautiful, unearthly beautiful. She immediately lost herself to him and had to find it quickly as she moved along the aisle to the place meant for her, her feet insisting on making up the time she spent with this man.

Chapter 16

Kai was with Hendrix. He gave his other self this name because he thought it had the steady strength and musical inspiration he needed to heal from what he came to call 'the separation'. This left him physically vulnerable. He didn't have complete control over his body, not only had his voice left him, but he also had random convulsions that traveled through his muscles that left him weak, he would soon learn that these were his own feelings coming back home.

All of the people working here belonged to another self from his world. Hendrix told him that he was special and had to pay attention because he had further work to do in his own world. But even though there were people everywhere, and of course, there was Hendrix who knew him better than anyone, Kai felt so alone, and it made it hard for him to concentrate. It wasn't even just that he had no one to share this with, but he was so used to being full of everyone else's feelings and inner thoughts, that the emptiness was overwhelming at times. Here, it was just him; he wasn't used to this. He didn't know how to fill the space all by himself.

Hendrix had told him there were others like Kai here, but that there were only a few of them and they also had jobs to do.

When Kai heard this, he secretly wished, a wish that became a booming echo in his silent mind, to find someone here, to have the chance to meet someone like him. To find someone to share this with, someone who might understand. His wish rippled through all the parts of him and wisped out through parted lips soundless and tethered to his breath. Hendrix, of course, knew what was happening although he couldn't see it or hear it. But he was connected with Kai, and could feel the need for an altogether different kind of connection rising in him. Hendrix allowed for the magic to be released out into this world and he too, secretly hoped to feel what might be sparked by it. Over the next few days, Kai would see a few people of his kind in the Hall, but by then Kai had lost interest in meeting anyone. He became very involved in Hendrix's work. He saw them walk past his space into a room; it was a room Hendrix called the Room of Lost Things.

Not being able to speak here had been an advantage for Kai, it allowed for him to co-mingle with all the people effortlessly. For, even though this world had a particular bustle and groove and its own variation of noises, it was a place of work and solitude and quiet. He fit right in without a voice and often the people that worked around him shared their knowledge and understanding of this place with him.

Currently, he was helping Hendrix with his work. As far as Kai could make out, the work that was done in this world was called Uncovering. Each person in The Hall had their own space to work. As they found their place within The Hall, they would also find their person's alterheart. An alterheart was a place where all the emotions from one's life in Kai's world were kept. Each emotion was placed there in the alterheart in its own unique way and found in a state that mirrored how that emotion was treated in Kai's world, by its person. When the emotions were released, they were separated and one at a time they were Uncovered to their original state and placed back in the alterheart. This was the delicate work each person was doing in The Hall.

Everyone's alterheart had a different shape and colors to it, this is what fascinated Kai. It was like a fingerprint, all its own. He wasn't sure what the shape, color, and size of each alterheart meant, but he was sure that it said something very poignant about the person it belonged to.

What Kai hadn't worked out yet, was why this all happened or what the end result of all the work was. He just knew that it was important. He also knew that he needed to help Hendrix with his own alterheart, afraid that his own emotions were too far gone to be Uncovered. He hadn't been shown his own alterheart, but he could see each emotion as Hendrix worked on them. In fact, this was his job right now. He was to be with the emotion that Hendrix was Uncovering and try to give it a voice through his hands, the strings and a song.

His fingers were finding their footing on his newly healed guitar. Kai was searching for a basic rhythm with which he pulsed as a starting point. Here, in this world, Kai was able to separate the feelings from others from his own feelings without the help of other substances. Though he was finding it hard to translate anything into music. It was like his music left him with his voice, and he had to start all over again learning how to use his instrument. Only this time around, he was learning to play the sounds of his own heart, which was unrecognizable to Kai since for so many years it had been imprinted with the feelings of others.

He sat there leaning over the body of his guitar trying to relax and allow his hands to play with the beat of his heart. As he was doing this, he was studying what Hendrix was working on. So strange and foreign to him. He was told it was Hope. At first, Kai questioned Hendrix with a look of incredulity. "Is hope even an emotion? Isn't it more of a verb?" It was only a thought, but Hendrix answered it with a voice that Kai recognized as his own.

"Hope is a feeling."

Kai looked down at what was resting in Hendrix's hands. It was a tiny ball with the smallest little light blue pebble in its center. All around the center was a thick grey cloud-like substance that was immovable. Nothing Hendrix did would displace the grey matter. On the outside of the grey matter was a slick mirror-like layer of glass that slid back around anything that touched it allowing the grey matter to fend off any enemies.

Kai was concentrating on what was in Hendrix's hands when all of a sudden he felt a longing. A real and true longing. A longing spiked with a call and response kind of curiosity. A longing spiked with warm coils that snaked up his spine. A longing spiked with a clear conscious to move toward someone. He gripped the neck of the guitar, feeling the weight of its curved back lean into his palm and without a thought his fingers thundered across the strings with the longing that possessed him. What came out was heavy and full at the same time that it was playful and ... Kai thought to himself, "What is this?" All at once it was as sensual and serious as poetry and yet it tasted of the marshmallows and chocolate chips of childhood. It was deep interrogation, and at the same time, it was the trace of fingertips along his scars without question. He looked up to find himself looking directly into Grace's eyes from across The Hall.

For a moment, time stood still. Then the moment burst through whatever was happening between Grace and Kai. Grace continued down the aisle by herself, and Kai brought his attention back to his guitar. And that was all that happened. The day moved forward, though there was more than just a recognition that placed itself directly between the two of them and soon their search for one another would begin.

Chapter 17

Grace continued on down the main aisle of The Hall a little shaken by the boy. She couldn't help but wonder who he was and what his story was about. She could tell he was like her, a visitor here, though it seemed like he was doing work along with his other self. Would she work with Anika as well? She was able to feel the truth of him, his vulnerability. She sensed a fear within him, but not the kind of fear that holds you back, more like the kind of fear that propels you forward into life. She also sensed the very beginning of a young Love, like a tender shoot fighting for light in a crowded garden. So how did he get here?

She wondered what kind of event brought him here.

And then it started again, her round of unanswered questions making their way back into her brain. "Where is Here?" She thought to herself. The questions seemed to want continue even though her anxiety had all but been alleviated while she was here.

She made her way to the back of The Hall after quite a long walk. At the end of the aisle there was a room. This space was the only space in The Hall that had a door. Its door was dark. It held the darkness within it somehow. Grace swore she could see, deep in the black of the door, all of the other colors calling to be freed. The door scared Grace, but at the same time, it called to her. It almost mimicked her fear of it, swirling threateningly. She stood in front of it, at the back of The Hall. She stood in plain sight of everyone in The Hall going about their work. There was never a moment where she was told by anyone to stay away from anything, and Anika said she was safe here. It was strange, the pull to move closer and open the door and the paralysis that held her back. Grace had always been mightily curious, and here, that curiosity was peaked even if it was laced with fear. As she made up her mind to open the door, assuming it wasn't locked, she took a step forward. As she moved closer and her curiosity overpowered her fear, the darkness of the door lightened, almost like light shooting through the clouds of a passing storm. The dark was replaced with a light grey streaked with white as she touched the door and pushed it open. It wasn't locked, it didn't even have a latch, it simply pushed open with hardly any effort at all. It seemed like a lot of suspense for barely a creak as it swung open and Grace quietly laughed.

As she walked into the center of the room, which was enormous, there was a red velvet chair, right in the center. The red velvet chair was more of a throne, and it was just as she had imagined the King's throne had looked from so many years ago. It held a deep red hue of fierce power. It was royal in the most royal of senses and being right in the center of this enormous space; it just begged Grace to sit in it. Grace walked over and slowly with intention and the full attention of her senses; she placed her hand on the back of the throne. Her fingers memorized every fiber of the velvet as they ran across it. The palm of her hand studied the rise and fall of the back panel of the throne. She gripped both sides of the chair from behind, to feel the strength that it held in its wood and to connect with the very forest it came from. She felt safe. With her hands holding onto the chair, she felt the full armor of protection from any and all around her. That is the kind of potency something has when it's been infused with childhood belief and trust. Never taking her hand from the chair, still running it over its edges, she walked to the front of it. She knelt on the ground and placed her head gently and purposefully in its lap. And there, held by everything good, she beckoned the fairytales that birthed the trees that welcomed the people that gave to the kingdom. She called on her friends the fairies. She invited the freedom of a moment into the room unknowingly, and before she knew it, she was sitting upright on the throne, looking out at all the fairies as they played hide and seek. They ran in between trees in and our of the shadows, from the grass to the sky and then back again.

Grace was watching with what can only be described as awe. Struck by feelings of familiarity, disbelief and the realization that it was real all along. Her mouth was raised with a wide grin. One of the fairies called to the others; she had gotten bored of hide and seek and insisted on a new game. They all gathered to decide on what game to play next, and their chatter faded.

Grace realized they had all disappeared into their fairy gathering and yet something still seemed so familiar. This anticipation that they would join soon in another game. Something seemed so damn familiar, but Grace couldn't put her finger on it. So familiar, fairies and games and thrones and forests and shadows. She couldn't put a finger on it. And then in the darkness, as if it was happening right in front of her, she saw herself, age six, knees to her chest waiting in the Dark.

Grace blinked for a moment trying to stop time while she placed the memory but she couldn't. There was no stopping time, and there was no placing this memory. The memory was actually trying to drive itself back into her, but she knew nothing of it. At the time it happened, Grace's beautifully brilliant mind made a choice to push this memory deep inside her. But here and now, it was time to unearth it and give her the answers she had been looking for ever since.

Grace watched as her young self remained alone in the Dark, shivering, afraid to move, afraid to stay and afraid to leave, though she couldn't imagine why? Was it a game of hide and seek that she was forgotten in? Was she stuck? Did she do something wrong and was afraid of the consequence?

And then the small rickety door was pushed aside, and Grace was able to place where she was. She was in a closet, but there were no clothes hanging, only the space with small wooden shelves up high and a wooden rod up top, abandoned and sad. When the door was pushed aside, and the some of the Dark escaped, Grace was able to see the shadow of a person, a man. He seemed so much bigger than her six-year-old self, but he knelt down to her level. He sat down on the floor next to her and began to talk. He sat, legs crossed next to her, leaning in toward her. He placed a large hand on her arms that were gathered around her knees in defense.

Grace couldn't hear the words he was saying. It wasn't until she focused her attention acutely on what the man was saying that she could hear the words and understand the intention that he entered the room with. It was here that Grace's body convulsed with the tiniest remembrance of the memory. She took hold of the arms of the throne, and she pushed her back hard against the red velvet back to brace herself for what might possibly come next. And to give her the strength to bear witness to it. Somewhere within this space, Grace knew she needed to see what came next.

As she focused in on his voice, she heard him speak of games and of loneliness, she heard him speak of the Dark and company. She heard him speak of good feelings and imaginary friends. He spoke of bodies and apologies. He spoke of needing help and how she might help him. As her eyes were focused but not focused on what was happening in front of her, and his voice punctured her twelve years of denial, the blood rushed in her ears and drove through her veins with abandon, but she continued to watch. She watched her own little six-year-old body do things. She watched herself try to make things right, try to take away his loneliness. Her hands reached out and felt for his wounds, wrapping him in her compassion, in her gentleness, in the palm of her hand. Before she knew it, her little, six-year-old body was underneath him and exposed. Her six-year-old mouth was biting itself tightly closed, and wetness stung her face. She was witnessing the rape of her own innocence. She felt pieces of her six-year-old self-bubble up through it all into her body. It returned to her just as it was in the moment she witnessed it. She felt the pride of making someone feel better; She felt his hand on her body. She felt his gentle touch on her; she felt the prickle of curiosity smolder and flame inside of her. Then she felt the pain of him enter her, the weight of him on her small chest and the suffocation of his hand on her mouth. She felt the fear creep in again when his voice changed and he slammed her against the corner. She felt his apology and the tears he shed fall on her face as she lies motionless underneath him. She heard his voice say, "I love you" and a shudder of ran across every inch of her. All she wanted to do was wipe it all away, but her hands, they would no longer move, they were paralyzed by indifference and fear and the decision being made inside of her. She felt the quiet that would eventually silence everything that had happened to her. She felt it all. She felt all of it. It came back.

The tears were streaking down her colorless cheeks as she sat in the red velvet throne. She had the hiccups, and her lungs were failing her as they seemed to be stuck open receiving all this information at once. Her hands were still gripping the arms of the throne, unable to release it for fear that it would leave her here in this memory, stuck forever. Before she knew it her hair was wet with sweat and tears and strings of mucous. Three hours later, she was still sitting on the throne; the same scene paused in front of her. It was her six-year-old self, alone again in the dark. Her panties gone, her dress pushed up by her elbows, her eyes looking off in the distance seeing Grace in a throne with fairies dancing around her in a game of tag.

They connected. The memory had found its home and all the pieces were finding their way back. It began to make sense; only there was so much to place in order to really understand the path this led her down, so she stayed there, unmoving while everything put itself back in order inside of her.

She must have been in the room all day stitching the memory back up inside her. She didn't want it, she wanted to forget it the moment she fully remembered it, but she knew she couldn't. She knew this is what she was hunting for all her life. It all made sense now. In some kind of perverted way. Looking back, to realize that this was the memory that spurred her into the discovery of her sexuality, that spurred her to examine domination and control, that spurred her silence and the end of her storytelling. Her parents, they didn't listen. The shame and the guilt of it all were too much. The anger and the sadness and the grief, there were so many feelings wrapped up together. Grace forced herself to stay still until she could bear its weight. There were so much confusion inside. Grace tried to force herself to understand how very strong and self-preserving her six-year-old self was, so she could stand up and walk out of the room, so she could leave the safety of the red velvet throne. After about five hours, Grace's hands released the arms of the throne they gripped so hard all day. The pain of releasing them and straightening her fingers felt good, a reminder of the present moment, bringing her back to her body. She shifted her weight into her feet touching the ground. And slowly stood, shaky at first and off balance, but her body remembered rather quickly how to move. She got up and all the images before her faded into nothing.

She looked at the red velvet throne and thanked it, then lifted her head and scanned the room once more. She realized the walls were made of wood. All around her, was beautifully grained wood, with texture and natural patterns of growth. As her eyes scanned the walls she could see pictures in the patterns, she played a game with herself trying to see images in the knots, like how she used to try to see things in the clouds when she was younger. Grace silently admitted to herself that she still did this when the clouds were big and fluffy.

As her subconscious went to work looking for images in the wood grain knots, Grace realized that when she focused her attention on a specific knot she could see an actual picture inside. Not just one she imagined she saw but a live living picture. She walked up to a knot in the wall and focused in. She saw an argument. A young boy, maybe ten and his mother. They were in a house, and his mother was yelling at him about his school work. The boy had a look of fear, and the mother seemed to be trying very hard to get her point across. Grace focused in on what the boy was saying and heard him pronounce that he tries to get good grades, he really does. She heard him say that sometimes he just can't concentrate, he can't focus, it's all so very boring at school and by the time he gets home, he forgets, he just forgets. The mother's voice gets louder, she doesn't want to hear about forgetting or trying, she wants to see good grades, and she hands him a medication bottle full of pills. Grace stepped back and realized this is all too much for today. She decided to leave this living room, this Strangely Living room. She scanned for the door noticing the crack of light coming from The Hall outside.

As she steps into the light of The Hall, she's all but forgotten the two men in their space. Her mind is busy trying to wrap itself around everything that she had been witness to. Graqce wasn't sure exactly where to go, she was hoping to see Anika and be led to a place of rest. She walked back along the aisle toward The Hall's entrance.

Chapter 18

Kai couldn't get Grace out of his mind. Each time he closed his eyes, he saw her eyes. He had a sense as to where she might have disappeared to, though he himself had never ventured there. He looked back to see her heading in the direction of the room that Hendrix called the Room of Lost Things. He knew of the room and the magic that was held inside of it, but he hadn't any desire to enter it himself. He was too focused on his work with Hendrix to be sidetracked into that sort of magic. Hendrix told him the room would call to him if he needed it, and he hadn't felt any major urge to go there.

What surprised Kai was how willingly Grace had walked toward it. He hadn't seen her before and here she was already drawn in by the magic of the room. After they had locked eyes and both had turned back to their before, Kai could feel Grace's presence pull him in the direction she walked, his eyes followed her pull. They found her in front of the door, a swirling black storm of fear present on the outer panel. He had turned away for a second, and when he looked back she was gone, the black was replaced by a grey panel streaked with white across its surface and all but a crack between the door and the wall remained.

He went back to his work on the guitar, but the longing she had awakened inside of him wouldn't let go, it was all that came out. In a way, it made Kai happy because at least he was playing something that belonged to him, but it also was not the Hope that Hendrix had cupped in his hands.

Time passed and Kai pressed on in his place with Hendrix as Hendrix tried to Uncover the Hope. At first, he just held it, hoping it would sprout in his hands, having been held and supported by him. When this didn't work, Hendrix began a full examination of the Hope.

First he placed it on the table in front of him. He began measuring it, poking it gently, speaking to it, rubbing it, massaging it, playing music for it. He made notes on a piece of paper, collecting all that he discovered. And, in fact, he had discovered something exciting. When he touched it gently, it pulled away from him, but when he pushed into it firmly with purpose, it pushed back into his fingers. It actually responded to him. Hendrix continued examining the Hope using the instruments all around him.

In Hendrix's place, there were a large variety of instruments hanging and leaning against things. There was bubble solution and a bubble wand, a stack of materials of every texture, a stack of screens that had different sizes and spaces between, There were also virtual thought bubbles hanging in the air and models of his own hands hung along the wall cupped in different depths and heated to different temperatures. There was a wall of water that played its sound over the background of The Hall, and there were a variety of plants and herbs planted in small pots all along his computer screen. There was a dark corner at Hendrix's feet under his desk that had a small red velvet pillow to sit on. There were earplugs and duct tape and mouth guards. There was speakers all around the place, and of course, there was usual stuff, tissues, picture frames, chair, bed, etc.

After a few hours and having fully examined Kai's Hope, Hendrix began to put what he learned about the hope into play. He squeezed it like a stress ball concentrating on not hurting it, and he noticed that as he squeezed it, it pushed his hand back open and the weight of it seemed to change. It seemed to get heavier. The mirror-like substance that shifted along the outside of the grey matter accommodated to this new flattened shape in the palm of his hand. Progress! The mirror-like substance on the outside of the grey mirror had come together on the top of the flattened Hope and was one single piece altogether. Then Hendrix held up the Hope to Kai's face and he asked Kai to breathe on the mirror like he was going to write with his finger on a window. Kai did as he was asked, his warm breath fogging the mirror substance up. As it began to fog up , Hendrix asked Kai to think only of Love and of taking care of someone as he gently but firmly pushed a finger into the fogged up mirror.

This happened to be a very easy thing for Kai to do at this moment, as the longing for Grace was unfolding out from between his fingers into a trail of breadcrumbs that lay in wait for her. He had, in fact, already begun to feel feelings of caring from the moment his eyes met Grace's. So he pictured her eyes staring back at him as he laid his finger gently and purposefully into the fogged up mirror. As he did so the mirror and the grey matter parted allowing him to touch the light blue pebble at its center. Kai's fingertip glowed from the blue light the Hope possessed. More progress! Hendrix was beyond himself. He let out a small yelp of excitement and quickly placed Kai's Hope in one of the outstretched hands at the exact temperature of 99.9 degrees. Here the Hope would sit for at least another day, as Hendrix planned out his next move to Uncover it completely.

Kai went back to his guitar. He tried to translate the Hope he just felt. He tried to play it into his song, the light blue essence that for a moment he began to care about as it lit something inside of him. He could feel the inspiration and then tenderness penetrate his instrument as he looked up and saw her again. She was walking away from the door, down the aisle toward where he sat.

He could tell by the way that she walked, by the careful and direct steps toward the entrance of The Hall she took, that she came out of the room a changed person. He could smell the faint sad scent of the salt water as she passed and it reminded him of the vastness of an ocean, the mere width of which could engulf her in a second flat if it chose. As he had this thought his attention went from his own Hope to her very real, very tangible, very mixed up state of mind. He tried to block it out but something had burrowed inside of him, and all he could feel was the loss, the monotonous sounds and rocking of grief above everything else. It was getting tangled up with shame, and then anger would sweep them all away in a flash until grief freed itself from the grip of it and coasted back in again. He felt seasick from it all, a cycle that completed itself over and over again, his heart banged from one side of the ship to another, Was she hurting herself? Could he help her calm the storm? Was it the Rage that needed to be heard or the sadness, or none of it? The confusion and questions were brought in by the girl; he instinctively knew it wasn't his questioning as it twisted around everything. Kai felt the tension grip him and swing him forward and back, closing in and somewhere underneath it all there was also a glowing ember of heat that turned him on, that prickled incessantly inside him until he grew to the size of a man. "My God!" He thought Is this really happening? He didn't seem to have any control over his body, let alone his thoughts. Then, all of a sudden, as quick as it came in, it settled down and it perched right in his gut, he could feel it, but it wasn't a bad feeling, it was just perched there, waiting, longing.

This all happened as Grace passed by Kai, No one noticed anything different, they all went about their work, including Hendrix, until he too found himself raging the storm. Because Kai and Hendrix were connected, not much got past Hendrix when it came to Kai's heart. The two of them were trying to coast through to the other side of Grace's heart as she walked by, both of them drowning from the sheer mass of it all. Had she not walked by so fast, they both may have ended up shipwrecked and barely breathing on the floorboards of The Hall, in need of resuscitation.

Grace had walked past Kai, not even realizing Kai was still sitting on his stool. She was lost in her own world, her own memories and her own retrieval. Yet, in a single moment, as she walked soft and steady toward the entrance of The Hall hoping Anika would catch her weight at the double doors, she let a piece of herself go and it fluttered, landing directly on top of Kai's shoulder. Whether she meant to or not, no one will ever know. But this piece of herself melted the minute it touched Kai. It was almost like it sank into his skin or it was sucked in by Kai himself. Whatever went down, it happened in the time that Grace walked past Kai, and it was settled by the time she passed him and found the front double doors. Though it felt like a lifetime to Kai and Hendrix, it was less than a minute to Grace.

As Kai came back to himself and was able to place the piece of this girl to the side, he looked after her in awe of all she carried. As he was looking after her, she looked back, and he could see the bright green of her eyes peek out from behind her long brown hair, that was tangled wet in knots, and he knew she would assimilate any information she was given in the room. But he also now, had an idea as to the depth and weight of what she was given, and he longed to walk through it with her. He longed to touch her, to make sure she was real. He longed to be alive with her.

Once Grace had left the building Kai's thoughts found themselves lingering back at the room with the door. Since his time in this world, which he approximated had been about three days, he had seen some people just like him walk through The Hall. They all had some things in common; they had bright color to their eyes, there seemed to be a confidence and a strength that rose from them. Sometimes Kai would catch a small flicker from under their shirts where their heart beat steady. Yes, he had seen others to whom his essence called, but it wasn't until he saw this girl that he felt a need to know more. Some of the others he had seen, had come to the room that the girl just came from. They would go in with the same bright eyes, the same confidence and strength but when they came out of the room, their eyes were drained of color and something else. Their journey into the room, into the magic, took something from them in return for what they lost. But not Grace. Kai hadn't cared to understand it anymore than the simple curiosity of what lay beyond the door for each person because he knew he would never go there. But this girl, she held onto her bright green hazel, she was still smoldering inside. She left nothing behind in the room; she brought it all out here into this world with her. She was special even by special's standards.

He thought back to her body as it came out of the door, the way she held herself, She had come from what Kai had known as the Room of Lost Things. What had she found in there?

The Room of Lost Things was a place where people from this world went to find answers, to find people, to find things, memories, objects, thoughts, reasons, all sorts of stuff when they needed it. Generally people were drawn to the door when there was something for them to find, People didn't naturally just go and open the door on their own, it called to them. Kai wasn't sure what exactly lay beyond the door, he just understood that the concept of the room was different for everyone who entered. And that to each person who stood in the room everything appeared different and unique. He also knew that once your thing was found the room went back to a generic room, wooden on all sides and quite large. He knew this because if there was nothing to find for anyone in a day the door opened itself and anyone who walked by could peer in. He had looked over there one day during the week he'd been here to find the walls lined with dark wood. It was the kind of wood that told a history, with layers and knots and its own landscape. It's said that if you pay close attention to any of the knots in the wall, you can see living pictures that show you things that are in the process of getting lost. Kai never was quite sure why. He never assumed much, and so he just let the thought of it float gently down and out of his mind, he had other work to do. But since seeing the girl walk out of the room, his urge to know more grew.

Kai thought to himself. It had been a strange and good day. Progress was being made. His curiosity was peaked. He found the girl so interesting, and it gave him something to think on. And the Room. He hadn't ever wanted to know too much more about the Room. His thoughts were collecting themselves as Hendrix interrupted them.

"She's one of you, only she's just arrived here, and yet she's already been to the Room of Lost Things. I hear her name is Grace. She has work to do as well. She needs to find Sen. She's in need of some integration and Sen can help her with that."

Not being able to speak Kai thought, "Grace ..."

And then abruptly his mind settled on the thought, "Who is Sen?"

Hendrix heard this thought, but he let it trail its away out and about the room as he continued on with his plan for Hope.

Chapter 19

Grace walked back out of the Room of Lost Things. She began to walk down the aisle toward the main double doors of The Hall. As she walked down the aisle, steady and in forward motion, she had a moment. It was moment when she thought for a second she might be forgetting something. In that moment a small flutter of herself freed itself from her body and laid itself on Kai's shoulder as he watched her. As it took leave of her body, Grace sighed. A beautiful and long and resting sigh. One that put a period to the end of story that had been waiting to be told and heard and believed.

Grace walked out of the double doors. She was present within herself but had no room for anyone else. All she wanted to do was find Anika and rest. The moment she found the open air of this world, she stood there, looking up at a beautiful black and white and grey sky filled with the magical and thick air. Then she took a deep and purposeful breath. The lingering edges of all the emotions rattling away inside of her stilled and dropped and made space for Grace to find sense in it all. She was able to think, for a moment, clear of all of it and she heard a whisper of something forgotten. But before she could place it, she saw Anika, waiting for her outside. Her eyes were streaked and swollen just like Grace's.

Anika took Grace's hand and led her on the path into the forest. As they walked, Anika said, "I've known all along what you had forgotten, but I couldn't force you to remember. I don't have control over your mind, I only speak through your heart. I tried to guide you to places that would spark your remembrance, but everything was buried so deep in your subconscious. I'm so sorry."

Grace didn't need Anika to apologize. When she walked out of that room, everything in her found its rightful place and she understood what had happened over the last twelve years. And though she was full of unfamiliar grief and curiosity and anger, she knew it was just a part of her that she had long ago dismissed.

She said to Anika, "I understand. I completely understand now."

Anika replied, "Follow me. I'm going to take you somewhere that I think you could use right now."

They walked in silence into the forest, off the path. They walked on pebbles, on rocks, on dirt on grass, over tree roots and dried leaves. They walked deep into the forest until they came to a large willow tree. Grace looked up to the top of the tree where all of the branches then cascaded back down to the ground.

Anika said, "This is the Willow Tree. All the wildlife here in this world, have made their home in this tree. I like to think of it as the Tree of Life in this world. You have nothing to be scared of here. Nothing will hurt you."

Grace walked closer to the tree and began to hear the low wild voices of different animals.

"How many animals live here?" she asked

"Many, but I think you should meet one extraordinary creature."

Anika grabbed Grace's hand and led her straight into the billowing branches of the Willow Tree. Once inside these branches, it was as if a whole world of the wild opened up to her. Grace saw animals and creatures of all sizes and all shapes, some familiar, and some not so familiar. Anika led her into the very center of the tree where there was an opening in the trunk of the tree.

Inside there was a large circular pillow and in the center of the pillow lay the most beautiful red fox Grace had ever seen. But it wasn't a usual kind of fox. It was larger than an average fox of Grace's world. It had a large eyes and a kind face. Its fur looked like it was laced with sleep. It lifted its head toward Grace, and it called to her. Its large brown eyes beckoning her to come and lay next to her. Grace walked right up to the fox and then laid herself down next to it. Curled up inside its soft, warm body. And she slept, protected. She had the most beautiful dreams in her sleep that day. So much so, that when she awoke, She was able to breathe deep again. She knew there were things to do and she knew that she would be able to do them.

Part Four:

Magic

Chapter 20

There's a magic to childhood that is not understood. It's not meant to be understood. If you try to understand it, you'll only travel the labyrinth of illusion. But this magic creates worlds, calls to fairies, dreams in dimensions that exist only for children. This magic teases at the edges of our peripheral vision and pulls open the curtain to a most magnificent stage show of truly ridiculous and amazing proportions. Grace had always been able to tap into this magic as a child until her trust waned heavy with the stuff of adulthood. This magic can't withstand the anxiety and worry, the fear, the sadness that persists in the life of adults and Grace, unfortunately, was baptized into it all when she was only six.

This magic is the very oldest of all magic. It's older than the dirt gathered beneath bare ancestral feet. It's older than the rocks stacked high along the ocean's edge.

Its the very strongest of all magic. It's stronger than the gale winds of a god's fury. It's stronger than the brute strength of a peoples army.

Its the most beautiful of all magic. It's more beautiful than a pale moon gazing over its reflection in a dark lake. It's more beautiful than a single star burning through its last sparkling essence.

This magic is a child's magic. It is born with wings of flight and horns of protection. We're all born with it, some of us have known all along how to collect more of it and how store it inside and protect it. We're all born with the knowledge of how to use this magic too.

Oh, we were blessed. This magic spelled Love across our view of the world in wisps and wonders. It whispered long sentiments of Hope into our ears as we fell in and out of sleep. It showed up in dreams of wild creatures kneeling at our side and being nestled under the care of Life Larger. It nurtured our understanding of More Than This.

This magic is something that, as long as it's heard, it maintains its integrity, it keeps open its doors to the impossibly possible. But once it's questioned and forgotten or denied it closes itself off, turns out it's light for you. It can't take the risk of misuse. It's that powerful that nothing would survive if it was used by someone who didn't fully live in its light.

It's still present; it's always around. Children can see it all. They can see where the Love and Hope have gotten lodged into crevices and forgotten about. Its the children who can still see the crumbs of its existence and they gather and collect it. And those that gather and collect it, they know of its power, and they waste not a single precious thought of any of it. No amount of it is inconsequential. They use it for anything they like. This includes, rainbows, unicorns, robots and spaceships, family pets, winning contests, and yes, creating whole entire worlds to save humanity from their own heartbreaking mistakes.

The Shadow World was born of this magic. It taps into this magic to keep it alive. Everyone present in its world has the potential for highest of highness in the name of Love. It hasn't always come easy and to be honest, the magic used to create the Shadow World was forged from the fires and metals of war. It was the dream of a boy who could only see fear and hatred around him, who couldn't comprehend humankind's choices. He believed, he believed in something that could be bigger than just us. And with his belief, and a sacrifice so very humble, he made the Shadow World out of his Love for us.

And so, the Shadow World, at its perfect center holds the essence of Love. It's this Love that allows for the magic to ripple out and be tapped into in whichever way you choose in the here.

There are those here who have learned the ways of the magic and use it to protect the Shadow World. They understand the balance needed to continue the work there. They understand the fibers that connect the worlds, the way they knit into one another and how both worlds rely on the other. Sen is one of them. She straddles both the world she came from and the Shadow World.

Chapter 21

Sen had heard the silence of Grace calling to her over the past hours. She knew the Room of Lost Things was pregnant with Grace's lost memory and so she knew Grace had arrived. She had dreams of her arrival, so it was not a surprise to Sen. The walls of Sen's space were filled with pictures that told of Grace's arrival. Sen had marked the space just days before in anticipation. She had burned incense and read the smoke. She threw cards along the floor and had been stepping around them since they fell in the particular way they did. She had hung beads and charms and wind chimes and ribbons and flowers, and she had draped the room in the scent of childhood. She had spoken to the birds about Grace, and she had rummaged through all of her books, collecting words and sentences and images and colored clippings and fabric ends and scraps of what others might see as useless edges. She had mixed the liquid with the solid and was waiting for it to gel to the consistency of glue that would create the magic Grace needed to put it all together, it was simmering in a white iron cauldron over a green hazel flame that sparked from a drawing Sen drew just that morning. Yes, Sen had waited for Grace to arrive for at least a few days and the preparation was just about finished, and just in time too, as Grace's silence stopped calling to her. The silence had been replaced by a chatter of questions and thoughts that weren't cohesively tied together but that were thrown together jagged and restless against each other, like a mosh pit of recollection. Sen knew Grace had received her Lost memory and she knew that once Grace had rested, it was time to bring her in.

Sen was different from most of the people in this world. She had witnessed the changing guard of people working during her time here. Most of the people who work here, they are here only for the time that they are needed, and then they Merge and go back to the other world. New people arrived everyday to do their work and find their place. It's a constantly moving carousel, that doesn't stop. There must always be movement between the worlds to keep the connection open and greased. But Sen, she straddled the worlds at all times. She lived here in this world, but she had an open connection with the other world. No one knew where she came from and exactly when she arrived here, but when she did, her space opened immediately to her, full of everything she needed.

Sen was a woman, full and natural with wild hair, feathers, and stones. She looked like she was channeling the fire of Janis Joplin in all that wore her and surrounded her. She had hands well worn with all the candles lit and snuffed out, pictures drawn and erased, cards thrown, oils prepared, papers cut and paints washed in her life between worlds. Her skin was smudged with charcoal and pastel and marker. She was a mix between an artist and a toddler that got loose in an art closet. Sen always had a soft spot for messes, making them, finding them, collecting them and making sense out of them. She felt right at home here in this world, and here she had everything she needed to tend to those she loved in the other world. She played a hand in their destiny, she altered courses and helped those who called to her by name from the other world.

She decided to call to Grace. She opened the palm of her hand and whispered a chant into it, blowing it out into the air and watching it wisp out of her place down through The Hall. Then she sat and waited, her eyes closed, her large and well-worn hands slowly, smoothly and deliberately working the knots from each palm. She was clearing herself, preparing them for the magic she was about to create. She was tracing the lineage of her soul along the lines of palm, heating up, waking up the wisdom that resided within so that it was at the ready when Grace arrived.

Chapter 22

When Grace woke up, she was in the fox's den in the center of the willow tree. Her body was warm and relaxed up against the fur of the fox. Her mind was nestled in between sleep and waking. She had hesitated opening her eyes because she wasn't sure what was dream and what was not after such a deep rest. But she distinctly heard her name called in the wind. She heard the long vowels of her name whispered among the trees of the forest. She sat up slowly as she heard it. It was more than a call, her body ached to follow it, and the more she sat in stillness, the more her body ached to go. So she thanked the fox quietly and gave into the call, following her feet, as they found the path leading toward The Hall. The call was so insistent. At first, it was her name. She had heard all the syllables and consonants and vowels of Grace dance across the branches and leaves and thick healing air, but as she got closer to the origin of the call, the sounds became louder, and they shifted to something she couldn't understand. Had Grace actually heard her name called, or was it her own mind playing a trick on her? She heard it, but she wasn't able to understand it. Now, it seemed like another language entirely. It certainly wasn't English. It had a melody to it, just the barest of melodies that jumped from syllable to syllable. It was almost hypnotizing.

Grace arrived at the double doors of The Hall. When she walked up the steps leading to The Hall, she opened the double doors, and this time she didn't walk straight down the center aisle. She wove in between spaces following the melody laid out in the call. It almost looked like she was dancing, the way she glided from direction to direction. Grace allowed herself to be led and by doing this she had released some kind of freedom within herself. As she weaved down the aisle, she smiled.

She was led to a curious space. One thick with the smell of incense and the fabric of a memory from Woodstock. There were door beads, shag rugs, candles, hanging lamps, books, so many books with all different covers and bindings. Each book was a different size and shape and thickness, and they all called out to Grace, Read me! Find what you're looking for here! Just a peek? I have what you need.

She stepped inside tentatively and felt a cushion of comfort nestle inside of her. She looked at the floor covered in cards with pictures staring up at her. Pictures of swords and pentacles and cups and wands. She found a square table in the middle of the space with two chairs inviting her to sit down, so she gently walked around the cards on the floor careful not to touch even an edge of one, getting a sense that they were part of a more serious business, and she sat down at the table. It felt so natural for Grace to take a seat here, at this table. Like the chair was made for her body fitting it perfectly into its cushion. As she sat down, a veil was lifted from the table surface and coming into view, into focus, Grace saw all the elements needed to make a collage. She saw scissors, and paper, and fabric and glue and cut images. When she placed her hands on the table to try and touch these things, to see if they were actually there, she heard a voice behind her.

"Well, I see you heard my call." Sen let out a chuckle of pride at her own work.

"My name is Sen, I live here, in this space. This is my humble home, welcome!" She gestured largely to all that was around her, and took a deep bow; her arms swung up behind her.

Then Sen continued with a warm smile cast across her face, "I love to have visitors, it's something special to make my home yours. Would you like some tea?"

Grace, not entirely sure of this woman and yet afraid to disappoint her, replied, "Sure."

Sen walked over to a counter that ran along the walls of her space and picked up some white pieces of scrap paper and a paintbrush full of a sticky glue. Directly onto the counter, she swiftly and with what looked like not a thought at all, swiped and pasted the tiny scraps of white into the shape of tea cup. She did this with the ease and flow of a true artist. In no time, there was a collage of a teacup in front of her. Then Sen carefully chose a word from a large jar, appropriately labeled "The Word Jar" and pasted a single word in the center of her collaged tea cup. Grace couldn't see exactly what word Sen pasted in the center, but before she could ponder what was going on, the collage grew up out of the countertop into a steaming hot cup of tea, sitting on the counter where the collage had once been. It was a beautiful white porcelain teacup.

Sen asked, "Do you take milk or sugar in your tea? My feeling is that this tea is best all on its own, you may want to taste it before you decide. But I have both in case you need." She handed the teacup to Grace.

Grace put her lips up to it, in utter amazement of what she just witnessed and she took a sip of the warm liquid. It was subtle. It wasn't floral at all, more of a citrus kind of flavor, spiked with a warming spice. It felt good going down, it seemed to ground her back in her body. She could feel any anxiety held over from the day before quiet down within her. She looked up and said, "Thank you, you're right, it's just fine like it is."

Sen went on with wide and inviting eyes, "I especially love when people join me in my space and are willing to create."

Grace looked at her questioning, when did she ever say she was willing to create?

Sen answered without an utterance of the thought in Grace's mind, "My supplies wouldn't have shown themselves to you if you weren't willing to create with me." She winked at her.

Grace felt a motherly vibe from Sen, but it was so much more than that. She felt the power contained in this one body, in this one space and she couldn't quite grasp what kind of power it was. I mean, collage? Could that possibly be a power? Was there more to it? The questions swirled as Grace looked around again, the cards, the wafting smoke from the incense, the jars of tea leaves and herbs and words, the books. She realized what wisdom this little room had living in it and for a moment, Grace felt completely content, like being here satisfied each inch of her. She had always been a believer in magic, even if her beliefs squatted inside of her darkness for years. She had always believed in the witches of fairy tales and the fairies and gnomes and wishes on stars that spoke through the pages of books and childhood songs. She had always believed that the energy contained in our world could be tapped into in ways that mirrored the soul. Grace innately knew that the soul was full of light and that magic was its language. Being here, in this place, right now, with Sen, Grace's soul felt the beginning of what a happily ever after might feel like. There was a part of Grace that found a small and beautiful piece of home.

Sen began to pick up small pieces of paper and fabric brushing glue along their backs placing them down on a new piece of linen paper. As she did this, she began talking.

"I know you've been to the room, to the door in The Hall. The room has a name, it's called the Room of Lost Things, and it calls to those who have something missing when that something shows up in the room."

Grace listened as Sen went on, taking in each word Sen spoke.

She continued," I know what you found, and I know what it's done to you, come here baby." She put down her craft and grabbed Grace with her full arms. She brought her to her chest, and Grace felt the rise and fall of Sen's breath. Sen, in fact, did not let go of Grace until there seemed to be a drop-in Grace's weight. Something that was tight around her throat and her chest had dropped and fell to the very bottom of her belly, lower even.

Sen let go and said, "Now you should be able to breathe deeper, the desires found their chakra in the right place, this is something that's been off since your lost memory. What happened to you upended any desire and placed it squarely between your heart and your voice when it really belongs down deeper, in your root chakra, as they call it."

It was true, the moment Grace felt the weight drop, it was as if she sat straighter, the lump in her throat disappeared, the space in her heart was ready to be filled with Love instead of desire. The wrongs were righted, and the desire that she so wanted to uncover, was in wait just where it should be, calling out to be test driven in a strange and yes, curious longing to be touched. All of a sudden her gratitude for Sen was overflowing, her eyes teared, her pulse quickened in realization of the weight of the last ten years, the forgiveness that she felt for herself coursed through her mending all the leaking veins and she could feel a gentle spinning right at her third eye. Grace brought her finger to her forehead, where the spinning was its strongest and could feel gentle grooves in her skin, her fingers tracing the mark of a spiral. It was just like the mark that Anika had on her third eye. The only word in her mind, flashing in white neon was the word, Integration. Grace let her fingers linger on the newly formed spiral feeling, the life behind it, and in that gesture, broken pieces of herself began to gather together again.

"Honey, we can't change the past, it's been lived, things have happened, they've changed course and set you on new coordinates. You've been driving in directions without knowing why." Sen went on, "You've been chasing tornadoes, and you've done quite a good job at landing directly in the eye of them." As Sen was talking her fingers were moving across the table grabbing pieces and clippings sharp and small and pasting them into a spiral cone on the surface.

Sen continued, "The problem remains, that if you do not know why you chose to chase tornadoes, then you will never learn what you came here to learn." As she said this, the collage of the tornado that Sen had pasted together on the surface of the table grew up into the air right in front of them, casting an actual small tornado across the table upending all the scraps, the clippings, the paper, the fabric, the scissors, even the glue. Then it disappeared. In its wake it left a picture of a little girl on the ground in a dark corner, holding her knees her head bent low in the shadows, and the word Love.

Again Sen let her hands comb across the images and clippings rearranging the picture that the tornado had left picking out new pieces and pasting them together while she began to speak again. "Your journey has brought you here, You and Anika, both. You're special; you aren't like everyone else, you have gifts that course through you. You see truths, the spaces between who we are and what we present to the world, they speak to you. They show themselves to you in many different forms. I don't know if you know this, but you are a storyteller. You are the rarest form of storyteller. You've cultivated yourself into the kind of storyteller that truth seeks out."

As Sen spoke these words, Grace looked down at the collage on the table in front of her; it was beginning to form into a picture of a campfire, surrounded by a tribe of people. Sen's hands worked furiously until the collage that was pasted together on the surface grew into the entire space. The table disappeared, the shag rug, the cards, the books, the jars. And Grace found herself with Sen around a campfire at night with an entire village seated under the stars listening to a man marked in paint and cloth. He was telling a story, and the village was rapt in his tale. Grace listened as he told of creatures of fear and creatures of Love, he told of the dance that married the two and how they must always choose a side. He told of a bird who tried to choose both as he perched in a tree. He so loved to sing, he so loved to sing so the world below could hear, but he also was afraid of heights. On days when he chose Love, he flew to the highest branch and his song sang out wide and free touching those near and far. On the days he chose fear he walked as man, his feet on the ground, his beautiful sound thumping against the earth echoing back to him, and him alone. Then, one day in the heart of winter, this little bird, who had longed to share his songs with the world, but who also had become taken with hearing his own voice wanted to both give his song to the world and hear what it sounded like at the same time. He strapped his fear to him like a backpack. He allowed Love to lift him higher, and as he inched out to the highest branch of the highest tree he began his song, he felt it echoing in the silence of those listening but he could not hear the song he sang and so he unstrapped his fear and held it tightly in front of him as he looked down hoping that his song would echo back to him but instead the weight of his fear tipped past the edge of the branch and brought the little bird down, all the way to the ground, his fear was too heavy for his wings. The fall was too much for his little body.

As the storyteller finished the story, the campfire, the village, the man, they all faded out of existence and Grace found herself back at Sen's table, the pieces of collage scattered once again.

Sen began once more, "You are a storyteller, you always have been. Truth seeks you out, and your job is to sew it into a story that people can digest. A story that people can listen to, a story that people can see in front of their eyes and witness. A story that people can ultimately learn from and begin the chain of change. You used to know how to do this. As a child, you were the one who decided to follow this path. Though things have happened that have changed how your path has laid itself before you, you still have a job to do. You can't deny it. It's time you learned how to own it."

Grace was perched somewhere between dumbstruck and exalted. She was still reeling from the magic, it was kind of dizzying to say the least, but she was taking it in, and there was a part of her that was nodding enthusiastically. It was as if she knew precisely what Sen was saying and she just needed a gentle push in the right direction to make it all happen.

Sen continued, "I want to introduce you to someone first, so you understand more clearly, where you are, who we are, how we all got her and any other questions that might be answered better by someone other than me. I don't mind questions, but I'm better at showing the answers."

Sen's hands went back to the collection of images and clipping and scraps and her big paint brush slick with glue on the tip. This time it seemed she was more careful about how she chose to design her collage. Her eyebrows danced along her forehead as she hummed under her breath seeking out certain shapes or textures. When she was done, she asked, "Are you ready?"

Grace answered, "yes."

Sen replied. "I brought a little surprise along for you as well; you can thank me later!"

And before Grace could even think of what Sen might be talking about, where she sat at the table was pushed up and away as a new scene took its place. It was a bare room, wooden walls. Grace placed it immediately as the Room of Lost Things.

"Great. This isn't the kind of surprise I want, I've had enough of this room for one day." Grace thought to herself.

She looked around and saw a chair. It wasn't the red velvet throne but rather a wooden chair, made of the same ancient wood as the walls. In the chair sat an old man, he was looking down at her over his glasses. The man had long thinning hair, and a long narrow face but large cheeks that held his smile up. He was full of wrinkles and spotted skin, and he motioned to Grace to come and sit with him. Grace looked him over; she didn't feel any fear. Even though he was full of the signs of age, he was joyful, and it read from his eyes to all he looked at. She felt an urge to do anything he wanted, she immediately trusted him, as she could feel the Love that came from his center. Just his presence alone, made her feel like a child who was asked to take her place on the circle rug, and she did so eagerly. Grace took a seat at this feet. She sat cross-legged waiting to hear the story, to put things together, waiting to understand this place finally. As she got comfortable on the floor, Grace heard a sound coming from behind her where the door to the room was. She turned around and saw the boy from The Hall with the blue eyes. It was Kai. She felt an urge, a longing, a desire flitter inside her, it was warm and inviting. He walked up and without a word, he sat next to her, silent. He was actually quite caught in the same desire wondering how he was ever going get to know Grace without a voice. So he just sat next to her, and then prepared to listen to the old man for he was drawn here just as Grace was drawn to Sen's space.

Chapter 23

When Grace and Kai saw the old man they both sensed that he would bring them their destiny. They were more right than they could even imagine. With both Grace and Kai sitting on the ground at his feet, the old man opened his mouth and began almost as if he was already in mid-conversation,

"You are guests here. You're welcome to work and witness and heal. Your shadow selves will do their work and then you'll Merge back together and return to your own world. You'll forget all about this place and what goes on here and that's the way it has to be. I'm not sure what would happen if your world knew we existed. I'm sure it would be chaos in both places. The separation of the two worlds is necessary for the the work here to be done.

Just as you'll leave when the work is finished, most of the people working in The Hall will leave when their work is done. There are also some of us that live here permanently. They call this world their home. These are the people whose other self in your world didn't make it past their moment, their event. For them it was life-ending. Do you understand what I mean, when I speak of the moment or the event?"

Both Kai and Grace nodded yes. They both knew that they had both come here after a choice that was made, an action that began to follow through on itself, one that would change the course of their living. They both innately understood that this was when they finally gave up on themselves.

"These people didn't make it long enough to find the solace and the Love that was waiting to be acknowledged inside of themselves. They never got to breathe space into their hearts and be given a second chance. Their Uncovering never started because they got lost. The magic of this world catches these people and cradles them in its palm, gently leading them here. Only once they arrive here, they cannot leave. There's no work for them to do and no place to go back to. They arrive here broken and whole at the same time with no shadow self birthed. They're often in shock, motionless and stagnant. But it's their time here that breathes new life into them, a different sort of life. As their time here passes, they begin to find the Love that eluded them in your world. They begin to find purpose and they stake a claim to this world and all it represents.

The old man paused to let what he just said sink in. "Are you still with me?"

Both Kai and Grace nodded, aware that he was talking about people who had decided to take their own lives and who had succeeded.

The old man continued, "This world, it was created by such a person. It was someone lost to their moment. It was a different moment than most. He was only ten years old, though he felt as if he had lived one hundred years at least. It was during a time of brutality in his world, a brutality that played out over his ten year old body in train tracks of inequality. In order to escape the brutality he decided to wrap a thick musty rope around his neck. He saw no other way out. For him, no Uncovering was needed, nor was there any world that existed yet, to help him Uncover anything. This was need. Pure and simple. He prepared to end his life.

Because he was only ten, there laid inside him the Hope of Entirety. The Hope that there was something more, a place where brutality and hatred and war and famine did not exist. It was a tall Hope, one only a child could fully possess. He called out to it and he hung on to it so desperately, trusting like only a ten year old boy could. As he jumped from the chair, rope cutting into his neck, a light blue lit pebble of the tiniest fraction, appeared in his pocket."

At this, Kai took in a sharp breath, and thought to himself, "Had it been the same pebble that Hendrix was working on in his space, were all emotions the same at their core?"

The old man paused and said, "The very same Kai, my friend."

Grace lit up at the sound of his name. Kai, she smiled at the poetry of his name.

The old man continued, "As the boy's breath got choked in his lungs, and as the pain subsided and his body stilled, something released from it along with that tiny blue lit pebble. As he floated through the nothingness that pebble shone and before his very eyes, a world was cast in front of him. It was magic. It was beautiful and serene and flush with color that thrived in everything it touched. And he found himself on the shores of this world, alone. The first voyager to a world created by his own incredibly real and tangible and desperate Hope for a place that honored Love above all else.

The boy spent his time exploring this world, and finding out all its secrets, learning its magic. He learned that here most anything was possible. As he grew older, Yes, I have aged; I began to think more clearly about how to share this place. I began to focus my intentions and attention on saving others from my world. And just as today, intentions and attention are the keys to creating anything you want here." At this he looked Grace directly in the eye. Both Grace and Kai understood that they were talking to the ten year old boy who had created this place out of need and Hope.

"As I focused, more people began to arrive, often broken and whole at the same time, riding on Love's back to this very place. I would bring them into my world, and over time I found that the broken parts of the people here would heal with the Love that was present everywhere. I found that the people became infused with care and tenderness and a Love that expanded. I found that the more people this world saved, the more purpose they found and the more called we all were to work for others. I suppose it was the natural progression of a world created from Hope and Love.

It wasn't long before I gathered my new community and taught them my ways. I taught them how to use attention and intention to create anything they wanted here. I taught them how to use the magic that was present in the very air they breathed. We studied as one, challenging the edges we ran up against. It was together that we, as a community created the magic that's called the Uncovering. It was our answer to healing the world we came from, so that no one had to end up on our shores, broken and whole at the same time. It was a way to unmask the truth of our emotions and give the people of our previous world a second chance before their hearts hardened into adulthood or they took their own lives.

We supported one another in journeying back to our old lives in order to learn and collect information from our pasts as a way to hone in on exactly what was needed. We put it all together to unearth, to try and find a center of it all. We studied the fault lines of relationships and families and the differences between those of us that thrived and those of us that didn't. We studied the children and their hearts and the states of their emotions. We studied how they traveled with their hearts into adulthood.

Through all of our research we began to understand the root matter that could change everything. We began to understand how the language of the heart had become a language lost over generations. More and more the language of the heart had been replaced by a vocabulary of right and wrong, black and white.

Our suspicion was that fear had placed itself in the shadow of Love and as each generation birthed another, fear's grip became tighter.

To put this in simpler terms. People began to become afraid of the feelings of our children. Not because the children are frightening, but because the very same emotions in themselves were uncomfortable and defined by the adults in their own lives. They were imprinting their own desires, fears and emotional habits on their children who weren't able to decipher these imprints from their own hearts' truths.

We noticed a deep set pattern happening in the children. A pattern of denying them their feelings in the name of right and wrong, in the name of 'supposed to' and 'should of'. Children were being taught to deny some feelings and over expose others. As these very same children became teenagers and then adults, their hearts became so confused with all of it that often they fell into depression, made decisions that weren't from a clear place and often placed themselves and others in harm's way. They gave over their free will to people in power. Those very same people in power began to abuse that power. And of course, more and more children took their own lives, and landed here on our shores.

We watched it all happen, all the while learning and researching. It was almost a decade later when it all came together. When we were able to see the ecology of what was before us, we learned what we needed and had found the vulnerability in the design of the worlds. So, with Love filling our hearts, we began to create the constructs for our magic and the Uncovering.

As we began the work for change, we understood how we could change everything. We started to think bigger. We decided if we could do this one thing ... we could change the course of an entire generation. We could create a world where hearts are honored and revered, where emotions were looked to for guidance and inspiration, not something to be feared or dampened or closeted. A world where the connections between people were alive with compassion. What a difference that could make."

He paused to let this all sink in.

Then he began again, "The community's magic created a door to this world, the Shadow World. It only opens for a short time when the vulnerability between worlds is present. It opens in that time when children are in between being a child and an adult. It's a time when the shadow selves come here to work at un-defining each emotion that's been imprinted by others. Each shadow self leaves this world with a clear heart and free will to offer each person from which to begin their adult life.

We collectively created the net, the dimming, the spinning, the Separation, the path here and the Merge back. The Hall was created brick by brick for the work of the Uncoverings, and the information the other selves needed was given to each shadow self who journeys here. We thought of everything and it was thought of with the highest of intentions and the wholeness of Love.

The vulnerability I spoke of is a time between child and adult, when a person hits their bottom, teeters on a choice that's leveled with regret, feels loneliness that harbors on hatred, when contemplation turns to action against themselves, when they essentially give up on who they are. They give up on Love. This is the moment we were able to exploit to open the door to the shadow world. It's like an internal earthquake that happens, where the space between inside of them, the molecules that make up their very body, shift into a new existence, a new understanding of loss. It's when their choices are so big that the landscape of who they are must change in order to hold them. And when it changes, there's an opportunity for the shadow self to escape. The part of each person that stays in your world is none the wiser, they feel lighter for a short while and then as the Uncovering begins here, there's an emotional adjustment that happens in your world. As each emotion is Uncovered, hearts often get broken, emotions unwind and sometimes repeat on an endless loop until clearness is reached. Sometimes, as memories associated with an emotion are released, a person in your world can experience bursts of anger or rage at letting go. The adjustment is different for each person. It's basically an unwinding of feelings that have been held onto so tightly and when they breathe for the first time untethered, there's no telling what the person connected to them will feel. So, if you ever wondered why teenagers can be so unpredictable, now you can cut them some slack." He smiled with this and then continued.

"We had to create the split in each person. We needed to have no attachment to the judgment, the analysis, the original imprints. We needed the work to be done with Love alone. And so the part of each person that comes here holds no judgment, only Love in their hearts. They can clearly see what each emotion needs and they innately know how to heal them. All of a person's emotions travel to this world in an alterheart. It's different from your physical heart. It's a carrier created out of what it needs to hold, which are all the tangled emotions from your childhood.

It's a truly amazing kind of magic. It took us over a decade and all of our own hearts to create it. This kind of magic is prehistoric. It's wild and untamed and so beautiful. So beautiful indeed that when the community put it into action, the Sun met the Moon and they danced along that place where the sea meets the sky, and you couldn't tell which was the Sun and which was the Moon. Then as quick as it met, it parted, splitting itself, the Sun traveling to the world we all came from and the Moon placing itself between the branches of trees here. But it wasn't bright enough to light this world, so it borrowed the colors from across this land. It drew all the colors into it and as it did, it grew bright enough to light this world. That's why every so often you'll see a little color dancing in front of you or in the shadows. It's still here, just not in front of us. But now the only dependable color is the color that lights up as each alterheart is opened here. Each feeling that gets freed from the alterheart has its' own colors and hue that shift and change depending on the state of the feeling. It was a surprising turn of events to become a world of black and white, but what it did was highlight the work that was to be done here. The colors call us to what's important for each of us. And it allows for each person's shadow self to truly see the color of each feeling without the shade of any other colors. The design is perfect, it is flawless because when done with Love in your heart, even the mistakes make sense.

Have I gone too fast? Do you have any questions?"

With all the information both Grace and Kai were taking in, their questioning minds hadn't yet caught up with their listening minds, so they both nodded and the old man went on.

"It's complicated magic and not everyone finds their way here for various reasons, but those who do, receive the opportunity to be Uncovered. It wasn't intended for people like yourselves to find your way here, you came of your own magic and inner knowing, your own special kind of gathering that called you in. But your presence here is celebrated and honored. You and your kind are always welcomed and you're brought into the ways of this world so you can bring your magic to the other side of life."

Grace and Kai looked at each other. Grace allowed her eyes to travel down from Kai's eyes and settle on his open bare chest peeking through his shirt. She could see the tremor of a beating heart, just a little bit closer to the outside world, just like her own. Her eyes worked their way back up to Kai's eyes and she saw the bright blue shimmer of them. There. Right there. It was a moment of honesty. A moment of honesty between them. But still no one spoke a word and so the old man went on,

"So, that's the story of who we are, why we're here, how we

got here and what we do. I hope it helps you understand. See the design is perfect. People come and their shadow selves work on Uncovering the feelings brought here to be healed in each unique and amazing Alterheart. When those feelings are clear and bright and untethered from the lofty ideals of your world's culture then they are Merged back with their other self. It is then that each person can begin the journey of defining these emotions and feelings for themselves, without the imprint of others. When they are fully Merged, the sense of Free Will that resides inside each person is woken up and a true sense of purpose, responsibility, justice and inner strength can be received. It's then that they are truly an adult. Once the selves are Merged back into the world, no one has any remembrance of the journey here, that's a quite important part of our magic.

Like I said, it is a perfect design." The old man looked away, like he was looking out a window watching the children play across the street hearing a distant sound of laughter.

"We had focused our energy and our intention on helping the children become adults with clear hearts and free will. We hadn't considered the possibility that fear could create a world where emotions could be so buried that children never get to the point of vulnerability. We didn't foresee a time when our shores would be barren of shadow selves. Adults have always been afraid of letting their children feel certain things. Whether it's from the fear of their children hurting, their fear of failure as a parent, their fear of the unknown... parents have always grappled with fear. But something has changed. We never took into account that fear could be manipulated and used by those in power. We didn't consider that there might one day be mechanisms in place to control the ecology of the heart. We didn't consider that one day children's feelings could be buried so deep they were virtually erased by medications and therapies.

I don't know where the root of this lies. But it is more than the family, it is more than the individual. There's more to this than simple fear alone. From what information we've gathered, our children are being deprived of a primal need. A need to feel all the corners of their hearts. Their anger is quieted, their sadness is wiped clean. Their feelings remain unexercised inside them. Even their memories are being altered and reprogrammed as feelings try to resurface. But when we erase anger and anxiety and sadness, the joy and happiness become diluted too. And if a child doesn't feel, well they never make it here to be Uncovered. Because in these cases, there's nothing to Uncover.

It draws on the reservoir of my own sadness. I'm not sure what the end result of all of this is. Where does it all stop? We no longer have the answers. I'm no longer a ten year old boy, I'm many years his senior and a doubt in humanity and the reach of Love has landed itself in my lap. It's caused some glitches in our magic.

I just can't seem to understand why in your world, people want to deny children their own hearts. Why are people so scared of the pain?

All of this has led to an increase in people like myself who have been rescued into this world. There are so many more of us...each day. We think it may be the equal and opposite effect to what we've been calling the conditioning of children's hearts. We think it's an innate response in those of us that are prone to listening to our hearts, who are picking up on all the feelings that aren't being expressed and being drowned by them. Kai, you should understand this."

At this, Kai's heart fell.

The old man continued, "We don't know for sure, but something needs to change, something needs to happen ..." The old man trailed off, his eyes faraway.

With that, the man faded. Kai and Grace still sitting on the floor alone, in the Room of Lost Things. It was so much to absorb.

They both wanted to speak but Grace couldn't think of where to start and Kai, well, he just couldn't speak; as much as he wanted to in that very moment. Maybe the moment was meant to be made of silence.

Chapter 24

Before they knew it, Grace and Kai were left alone in the Room of Lost Things. The absence of the Founder was replaced by silence and longing. They spent a long silent moment in a room pregnant with Hope and Love and Loss and History and War and Confusion. The need to speak was present, but neither of them could penetrate it. They looked at one another, both of them searching for that moment's honesty. In doing so, they ignited the fire between them.

It was a minute more and then as if by magic, the room decided to make the first move, tired of waiting for Grace and Kai to do it themselves, they were edged forward in front of one another, just inches away. The wooden walls retreated back, and there was air to breathe as they found themselves outside at Dusk, the light falling behind the trees. They were sitting on a soft Grey blanket. They could hear each others breath catching itself up to the moment. The quiet loudly banging inside their heads as they both chose to get closer. They chose to close their eyes and move forward into each other.

Grace gently bit her lip, her tongue sliding across a fresh cocktail of anticipation and anxiety as she let go and leaned into him.

She caught him with her lips parted. Her hand not yet knowing what to do with this man in front of her. His body, foreign to her. Who was he? Why was she so damn attracted to him?

Her mouth met his, their lips in slow motion as if they were trying each other on. Not exactly tentative or delicate in their approach, they came to one another with a longing that had been in wait of this kiss, and the weight of this kiss was heavy with history even though they'd only just met.

Kai had been with girls before; he had kissed them and messed around with them. He had played the games of cat and mouse and hide and seek, but he always had to stop before he was able to feel what it was like to be with someone else. He often stopped short of having sex with them. Kai's gift of empathy had always made it hard to get close to anyone physically, even though he had plenty of chances. Girls often found themselves attracted to Kai, sometimes because of the guitar he carried everywhere, sometimes because of the air of indifference he tried to put out to the world or the fact that he couldn't hide anything, ever. Sometimes it was just how he looked, with bright blue eyes that sang songs of sadness. And Kai would answer their calls, he would accept their offers, he would find himself in a car or on a couch when he would suddenly be swept up by rushing feelings, and he'd be unable to decipher what was his and what wasn't. He could feel the pull of intentions that didn't play nice with his. He would know when a girl wasn't really into what was going on and he couldn't continue. Sometimes it was the embarrassment of finding tears streaked across his face during the games they played. Often he would leave. All of this gave him an understanding of what sex really is, a reverence for the coming together of two people, a sacred kind of respect for anyone who chose to show up physically with him. He had seen and felt first hand the kind of battles that raged in girls to bring them to the moment of sex. He completely respected the act itself and anyone who found themselves at its doorstep, understanding that the journey to get there isn't always easy.

But here, in this world, he wasn't overwhelmed by any feelings, he already had a taste of what swirled inside of Grace, and he felt the addiction for her eyes like the voice of a siren soaked in longing.

Grace shifted on the ground from sitting crosslegged and awkward to her knees, crawling closer to him, something building up inside her. Something wild and untamed like the magic that brought her here and it was beginning to speak through her as she found Kai's lap and sat on him wrapping her legs around his waist. They held on. Her hunger for him at a low growl as both their hands were finding the familiar between them.

As they spoke in tongues and lips and hands and fingers, Kai pulled Grace in with a strong and steady desire, his body closing in on hers, their chests colliding and two hearts, quickened beats, raging to meet at the surface. Their bodies were negotiating the curves and valleys. He felt himself push up against her, trying to grow up into her as he held onto her so she wouldn't fall.

Grace's tongue was tracing every gesture his mouth made with intention. Sucking in gentle punctuations of excitement and expectation as she imagined what his voice might sound like, how his words might feel when he spoke them. He tasted like comfort and addiction and Love. She distinctly tasted Love; it was wet with a slight sweetness that glided all over her lips. She mouthed questions of more, and he answered back yes with his kiss to her.

She held his face, his chin, her fingers discovering him. Her hands were spreading across the sides of his neck meeting behind his head as she pulled herself down on him again, to get her fix. She could feel him trying to hold back, trying to keep it for a little longer but she also felt his body beg her to go further. Still, he said nothing.

It was here, she stopped and noticed that the blanket they were sitting on had turned red velvet and that she wasn't outside anymore as if the walls grew to contain them. As if, in the walls, she was safe to explore him. She looked around the room, full of questions. What was the next move? It was her move. She knew this, or the blanket wouldn't be red velvet. She leaned in and kissed him again, hard. Harder, allowing herself to be present with this moment. Present with this day. Allowing herself to be present with this person, in this room, with the reminder of her memory. She allowed herself to feel and pour over Kai. She poured it over him in hard and rough kisses, tender touches, traces of sadness left on his skin in trails of blood where her fingernails held on too tightly. She gave herself over to him as she laid her body into his, feeling him between her legs.

She felt like he had entered her a hundred times, penetrating her over and over again, yet still, she sat on his lap, his mouth on hers heaving breaths of everything, all of it. She found his hair with her hands, and her fingers rolled over the tangles gently before taking hold of a handful and pulling his face off hers just an inch away. Her hand was gripping his hair tightly.

Grace's green hazel eyes looked into Kai's, and he could feel her need. For a moment he was brought back to when she walked past his space, and he felt the piece of her inside him wake up. He too, knew he was safe here now, and that this was only the beginning. There were centuries between them that were opening up.

Grace let go of his hair. And stood up, Reaching down to help Kai stand up in front of her. She unbuttoned his shirt her palms trailing down his chest and up again, pushing it off his shoulders and allowing it to fall to the ground. She stood there. Then her hands reached out to his jeans, unbuttoned the top button and zipped them open, bringing her hands to his waist, open palmed, she ran her hands down from his waist to his hips to his thighs, his knees and his jeans found their way off his body, Kai stepping out from them. He stood there naked. He was exposed and naked as Grace looked down his body and up again, her hands navigating around all of him, holding him.

Then she stepped back, sliding the soft, fabric of her wrap off her own shoulders as the beautiful cotton silk that covered her fell to the ground soundlessly and she stood in front of Kai, inviting him in.

What happened next was more than any tornado, more than any investigation or exploration. It was more than any game played, or therapy session. It was two people giving themselves over to each other. Each of them fully aware of they what they were doing, honoring everything that came before and remaining open to everything that was yet to come. As they reached heights and orgasms and resonated to the tune of Love, the room shifted to accommodate their every need. They found soft when they needed soft, hard when they needed hard, restraints when their demons cried out to be let free, candles, water, whatever their need was, it came when it was called. They continued in this room until both Grace and Kai fell asleep, naked and still under a soft blanket surrounded by pillows.

Both Kai and Grace would realize later that the Room of Lost Things had helped them find each other. And not only had they not realized they lost each other, but Grace found a lightness in being with another person that she forgot existed completely. She had forgotten how to give herself over to someone completely without her head sorting and filing away the moments. Kai found freedom in Grace's presence. He didn't know if it was because they belonged to the same sort of tribe or if their destinies had just chosen each other, but he found the freedom he lost when he got older, and his gift began to overwhelm him. It was the freedom to ride the wave of another's emotions without being drowned by it, but allowing it speak to him, to speak to the moment he was living, and it was such a rush.

Hendrix and Anika found the two of them sleeping, naked and hungry on pillows under a soft blanket on the floor of the room, they were tipped off by Sen where they might find the two lovers. Both Anika and Hendrix were connected to Grace and Kai, so they understood what was happening, but they still needed to get work done. So when the waves of wild abandon calmed, they went together to retrieve their other halves.

Chapter 25

When Grace woke up, Kai was still asleep. Her eyes opened lazily over the scene, the two of them still naked from the hours before, under a blanket, tangled in each other. She was comfortable there, her head nestled into the inside of his shoulder, her body tight with soreness from all its excitement. But it was quiet, and she could let her mind wander over everything; the memory, Sen, the Old Man, the room, Kai. Nothing seemed to overwhelm her, it just sat in her mind, squatting there as Grace picked through it all one by one, feeling the safety of both the room and Kai's presence. She hardly knew Kai, but she felt safe with him like she could tell him any story and he would hold it along with her.

First, she allowed her memory to rise to the front of her mind. It was like a beautiful and ugly diamond turning on its edge holding her six-year-old story. She had encased it and compacted it into just the smallest picture of what happened without having denied anything, and now it was there. Grace shuddered a little and leaned back into Kai as she thought about it. "Why now? Why was I given this memory back now? What does it have to do with anything?" Grace thought to herself. As she thought about it, the beautiful and ugly diamond seemed to actually appear in front of her. She reached out to touch it and found that it was there, a solid piece of her thoughts. It was hard and smooth, and when she laid her finger on it, it turned just slightly on its point. She reached out her fingers, she turned the diamond like a top, spinning it in front of her. As it spun the memory replayed inside the clear stone. She watched, knowing that somehow everything that happened in the last day was a part of a bigger picture and she was trying to fit in how it all related.

She thought to herself. "I know this is the Room of Lost Things, I lost my memory years ago and have been searching for it unknowingly for 12 years. This memory has haunted my entire life, it pushed me down, broke me, scared away my family, it tied me up and choked me, it screamed at me and called me names, it sent me out in the world to discover truths that almost killed me, and I had no idea it even existed." Grace's mind was reeling from thinking how this memory had touched every piece of her since it happened. She was trying to think how her life might be different, but she got stuck when she realized it was useless to think about what would have or could have or should have happened. She didn't want to feel the hurt anymore because she was tired of it, she had tortured herself with it unknowingly for years. But she was still curious how her memory played into everything. She thought about how everyone around her reacted when she tried to tell her story. How some people said she was creative and yet others called her too creative. She got warnings and laughter all at the same time. "Had they known? Could they have known?"

Grace wondered. She didn't think so. But it was here that Grace realized that at six years old, after this happened to her, and she tried to tell her family the story and no one heard it, she realized this is when she stopped telling others her stories.

Grace thought back to Sen; she had said Grace was a Storyteller. She had brought her to the campfire where Grace had been hypnotized by the storyteller. Thinking back, she could remember how she used to find stories, how she used to pick up the truths and twirl them in her hands and spin them around until she could pick out the strands of story that wanted to be told, or until something else happened around her that brought it all together. Then she'd weave it together into a tale that held captive whoever was listening. "Maybe I am a storyteller," Grace thought to herself. In the back of her heart, a feeling etched itself inside of her. She hadn't known this feeling before, so she couldn't name it, but it was something like feeling part of something bigger. It was as if she had a place at the table, her very own small cubby in the world that was all hers and right next to her was the cubby of someone else who was born of the same star stuff. Was it a feeling of belonging? Was it a feeling of pride? She couldn't place it, but it felt right.

She started to think about Sen again and all she had seen from the cup of tea to the collages that she made to the old man and the way Sen winked at her. Sen's magic was beautiful; there was no other word for it. The way that her hand conversed with the pieces that scattered across her table, the quickness with which she brushed the paste across. The way that everything converged into a reality, Grace didn't know how she worked her magic, but the only word for it was beautiful. Grace sat for a moment, cradled in Kai's shoulder and letting her mind wander to the possibilities of Sen's magic and wondering if magic like that existed in her world.

Her mind, wandering again, glanced over to all that the old man had said. The old man, the person who created this world out of Hope. He created an entire world out of Hope, and Grace added her own two cents to the thought, "And his sacrifice". Would it have worked without his sacrifice?" As this thought bubbled up to Grace's mind, she got a familiar tingle that she was onto something. There was a story to tell and a truth to tend to. The word sacrifice had always stuck out to Grace; she liked how it sounded, it had the weight of the verb attached to it. This word would eventually lead her to her next investigation, she knew it. As she thought the word sacrifice, it appeared just as the diamond had, in front of her, she reached out to it, ran her fingers along the letters. There was something so very familiar about the word. Then she blew on it, watching it disappear before her eyes.

As she blew on the word, Kai began to stir. He moved his body against Grace, and she could feel his warmth and his breath on her. Her mind shifted to Kai. "Who was this boy, this man? Who was he?" She slowly turned her head trying not to wake him up. She wanted to find the poetry in his face. She started to go over the hours they spent alone and together, how the room had shifted along with their needs, how the blanket turned red velvet, how she had kissed him and he had answered her back with his eyes, his lips, the weight of his body. She could still feel the hours they spent rolling across her skin like a fog rolling over the hills on an early morning. It was all still so present. She was finding the familiar in his face, while she was thinking of how her name might sound coming from his lips. It was here that she realized neither of them had even spoken a word to each other, that she only knew his name from hearing the old man say it. Did he even know her name? She couldn't remember him even uttering a sound during their time together. She distinctly remembered the sound of his breath, the gentle inhale and exhale as he lay asleep right now was a testament to that. She couldn't think of one time over their time together that she heard his voice. She was sure that her own voice had freed itself over their time together, though it may not have said anything in particular. "God, he's so beautiful, so perfect. "Grace allowed herself to think.

She looked toward the door of the room, realizing that the Door was open and she could look out on The Hall. Quickly, Grace got up to close the door as she saw two people walking toward it. It was Anika and Hendrix, and they were walking briskly in the direction of the room. Grace assumed the person with Anika was the other self of Kai, since it looked just like him, in the same clothes that she had, hours before, taken off Kai. Grace went over to Kai, she silently nudged him, not really wanting to wake him up, he looked so beautiful and peaceful laying there, but Anika and Hendrix would be there any minute. She figured he'd want to be woken up by her, not himself staring down at him.

Kai's eyes opened just a little, and he saw her. He saw Grace, her face so close to his, whispering to him. She whispered, "I think your other self is coming with my other self, at least I think it's your other self, he looks just like you, and I recognize his clothes. Isn't it weird to always be looking at yourself here!' Kai instinctively opened his mouth to tell her how amazing she was but then realized he couldn't speak, he had no voice. He looked at her trying to tell her with his eyes what he was feeling. He hadn't even really heard what she whispered, all he was concentrating on was Grace and how she looked leaning over him.

Anika and Hendrix were approaching the door to the Room of Lost Things.

Grace wrapped herself in the fabric she chose to don herself in here, which was conveniently folded right next to where she was sitting. She didn't even have to struggle with the long fabric, she just held it and thought about how she wanted it on her. It had a life of its own, slithering around her body dressing her with its luxury. It wrapped itself around her shape perfectly. Kai didn't even move to get dressed; he had been here long enough now and he knew he just needed to put his attention on what he was wearing for it to find itself on his body.

Before Anika and Hendrix got to them, Grace said playfully to Kai,

"Well, aren't you going to say hello? Good morning? Maybe?"

Caught off guard and unsure how to explain anything, especially since he himself had no clue why he had no voice, Kai just shrugged his shoulders. He pointed to his lips and shook his head trying to tell her that he couldn't speak, that he didn't have a voice. He mouthed the word 'hello'. Then, as she remained silent taking in the fact that he had no voice, he mouthed, "you are as beautiful now as you were beautiful last night."

Grace stopped trying to understand what was happening; she was tired of having to understand anything.

Here was this boy, this man, next to her, whom she shared all of herself with, willingly. Here was this person, to whom she placed a small, insignificant looking but rare and most valuable piece of herself in. Here was someone that she actually felt a destiny begin with, someone who rocked her world, layer by layer by layer. It wasn't an earthquake, it was the rumbling of a volcano, the plates had shifted between them, and for once, nothing shattered, but it smoldered, and it heated, and it was building into something. All she had wished was hear her name in his voice. To hear her name escape his lips, talk to her and tell her secrets. She asked him,"You can't talk? I don't understand, do you have a sore throat?"

Then she thought back again to the fact that he hadn't uttered a word over their time together. Not even a sound. She had freed her voice from its shackles, but he had remained silent.

She wasn't understanding at first. As she sat there looking at him, and he was looking at her, Hendrix ran up to them.

"Sorry to be so late, we meant to get it here in time to explain. I knew something like this could happen and I was meaning to help Kai ..."

Grace looked at Hendrix, in a moment of confusion on many levels. First, here is man, who looks exactly like the man standing next to her, who might very well have begun to have her heart. Second, Kai's other self, he had a voice, and Grace was hearing it. He was speaking. Grace had to think back quickly and decided Anika had her voice when she spoke. Third, Kai himself wasn't speaking, Kai had not spoken. Grace interrupted Hendrix and spoke directly to Kai, "Is this some kind of joke? You're other half, he speaks, his voice is fine. What's going on?"

Kai looked at Grace, wishing for his voice back.

Hendrix started, "Grace, ..."

As Hendrix said her name, he stopped. He began to see the tears well in Grace's eyes from the mention of her name in what could possibly be Kai's voice. It was a gut reaction; surely she didn't want to be crying in a moment like this! But hearing her name.

Hendrix continued, "My name is Hendrix, I'm Kai's other self, we're working together here. I can understand where things might be a little confusing right now, but we came to find you both because I need to help Kai in this world. Here, Kai has no voice. It was lost when he came here. We had split from one another, and somewhere in the center of the pain that sliced through him, his screams died, and he was left without a voice.

We had split before it happened, so I still retain our voice. I imagine when we're Merged, we'll be able to speak, as I still have our voice. But for our time here, he can't speak, he has no tone and no sound. We can talk through our thoughts as we're connected and Kai often speaks through his guitar. It was also destroyed in his event, but realizing that his voice was gone, I reached back into the world to retrieve it, and I repaired it for him to use here. As he said this, he handed Kai the guitar that was stepped on his back, and Kai took with a shy smile. His hands wrapping around the neck as if its loss would end him.

Grace thought about it a moment and how she had just wished to hear how her name sounded in his voice. And how she had just heard her name in his voice, even though it wasn't him, but it was him, just a piece of him that was separate from him for now. It really was all sorts of confusing and trying to keep it all straight was proving to be too much, so she let her questions go and accepted it. She remembered the sounds she heard from his space in The Hall when she first found him on the stool playing. She remembered catching his blue eyes and hearing the song of longing playing from his strings.

Hendrix interrupted, "Grace ..."

There it was again.

Hendrix continued, "I think Kai needs to come with me now, I've found something very important that he needs to see, but the both of you need time to process everything, to make sense of it all and on our way here Anika was telling me that Sen needs to see you as well."

As he finished, Kai turned to Grace, he leaned in close to her and breathed a silent breath into her ear hoping that she caught the Love that rested upon it. As he did so, he squeezed her hand three times, trying to tell her that he would come and find her in three hours. Grace knew exactly what he was doing, and she knew it would be the longest three hours she would wait in her life.

When Hendrix and Kai had left, Grace looked around the room as it was and she walked out with Anika, not bothering to put any pillows away, she knew the room would take care of it once she left, just like it took care of the red velvet throne.

Grace had a few questions for Anika as they walked. she said,

"So if we're connected, do you know everything that happens to me here? Can you feel it? Do you know where I am?"

Anika replied, "I feel everything as you feel it, just as Hendrix feels everything that Kai feels". Anika gave Grace a naughty look, one that perfectly described the night before.

"Well, that's embarrassing."

"But why would it be embarrassing, I'm feeling everything you're feeling, so I understand why you do things, you don't have to do anything alone here, while I'm separate from you. I'm your truest ally, and to be honest we can work things out together. You'll understand things better here than anywhere else and any other time in your life. You can ask me anything, and I can tell you the truth from inside of you. I hold no judgement for your choices. The judgements come from your mind, not your heart. While we're separate, there remains no shame, no guilt. This is something incredible, an opportunity beyond anything imaginable in our world. Do you get it?"

Grace nodded, "I do! But I'm not quite sure what to do with that information, now I feel like I need to make up a list of questions to ask you. I mean it's like getting to interview your own heart."

Anika said, "Exactly."

"So, I've been trying to piece everything together, and why it's all happening. I got my memory back from when I was six, I learned about this world, I found someone who makes me want to let go into him. It's so much in such a little time."

Anika nodded

"I wasn't sure why I got the memory back when I did, but while we've been talking, I'm thinking maybe now is the perfect time, because we're separate. We can work the whole memory out. The same with my heart, maybe I can let it go because there's that freedom from the guilt and shame and judgement."

"Sounds about right."

"It feels right when I say it out loud, I need to let it be for a while."

"And Sen wants to see you."

"I do have a quick question though. Was I feeling Love last night? With Kai? Is that what Love feels like? Did I give a piece of myself over to him? Was it safe to do that?"

"Well, that's more than one question. Last night was so much more than Love, it'll show itself when the time is right. For now, I need to bring you to Sen. And I also think it's important for you to meet the rest of your kind that are here right now."

"Okay, how many of us are here? Do I know any of them?"

"I don't know; I just sense that's it's very important for us to find your community. Maybe Sen has more answers for you."

Grace and Anika walked the rest of the way to Sen's space in silence, for the most part, until Anika broke the silence with a final "Well, that was quite a way to knock out our first days here!"

Grace smiled

"Yes, it was."

Chapter 26

As Kai left the Room of Lost Things with Hendrix, all he could think about was Grace. How she felt next to him, on top of him, holding him. His skin was still swept with her scent. He hadn't known anyone like her before, and apparently, she hadn't known anyone like him, as they were from the same tribe, whatever that meant. There was something between Grace and himself that he needed to touch again, He needed to smell again, he needed to taste again. There was something between them that placed an absolute need inside of him that he couldn't let go of. He had no control over it. In his mind, he replayed the night.

Everything that Kai did as they made their way to Hendrix's space was a reminder of Kai's night before. From the reverberation of the ground beneath his feet as he took each step to the force of air on his face as he walked on, it all brought Kai back to Grace. It brought him back to how she tied him to the bed at his wrists and ankles to gather her courage to play without pretense. It brought him back to the way she threw his body down to bring him along with her. It brought him back to the way he walked toward her in her most vulnerable open sweetness and how he lapped it all up.

Not one thing happened on their way back to Hendrix's space that didn't call up a physical response to the night he had spent with Grace. By the time they got to Hendrix's space, Kai's body was heated and sweating from living through it again.

Hendrix was also sweating and hot and said to Kai, "I get it, man. It was good. It was better than good. But you have to find a way to separate it, for now, I had a revelation about your alterheart and specifically about Hope. And it was all thanks to your night last night." Hendrix smiled a huge smile at Kai and Kai just laughed at seeing himself wearing such a big grin.

Kai and Hendrix entered Hendrix's space, and Kai lifted his guitar from around his shoulder placing it against the wall at his feet and took a seat on his stool.

Hendrix immediately got to work in the space looking for something. As he was looking, he began to speak again. "While you were in the Room of Lost Things with Grace last night, I was sitting here thinking about how to Uncover the rest of the Hope that was left being supported in my hands over here. I thought maybe I needed a break from working on it so I decided to take a look at what other emotions needed Uncovering from your alterheart. I took some time to set them all out.

It's a general rule here that we work with one emotion at a time to prevent any further collusion between emotions, so I kept them in their separate containers, and I moved them around and changed the order they were placed in. I played around with putting some closer to each other and some farther. I formed groups with some and I completely isolated one. It was then that I began to feel your pull from the Room of Lost Things. The longing and desire that palpated inside of my chest was on fire. It was starting to burn just to breathe so I had to sit down. While I was sitting here in the quiet of this space, trying to cool down from the inside, I heard it. I heard it! I heard the isolated emotion calling out to me. It was begging not to be left alone; it was calling out to be freed somehow. I ran over and got it out from isolation immediately and sat down with it in my arms. Unintentionally, I was sitting right next to Hope. As I twisted open the lid, this emotion that I thought was dying, began to breathe into the tiniest of heartbeats. It began to glow a radiant green that pulsed in a rhythm similar to Morse code. My instincts told me it was trying to communicate somehow, so I looked around, and there was Hope at my shoulder, doing the same. They were communicating with one another. We don't have to Uncover these emotions one at a time, at least not your emotions. They can help each other. And to add to that, I also realized this might be happening because of what you were going through. It all happened at the same time. Look at the label on this container. Hendrix pointed to a row of five large glass containers on the counter. Each container had an emotion that needed Uncovering in it. They were all different colors and in different levels of need. Then Hendrix knelt down low and got eye to eye with one emotion in its glass container, and he whispered, "Hello."

"Look at what emotion this is."

Kai looked down and read the label. Love. Kai shook his head out. He certainly did not fall in Love last night. He thought to himself, "You don't just fall in Love over night. Love is something that's fostered, that grows. Love has substance accumulated over more than just one meeting, one day, one incredible night. Right? I mean, Grace is amazing, and I've never given all of myself over to someone like that before. I've never let my guard down like that. I allowed her to see all of me." His thought process was moving so quickly as he processed all of what he was being told and what he was seeing.

"Kai, you're special, we already know this. You're here, and you're experiencing things, and your emotions are going along for the ride with you. They're going to shift and turn and untangle themselves as a you figure it out too." Kai looked at Hendrix, his eyes beginning to well with tears.

"I didn't think Love was possible for me. How can a person find Love and know it's true when all they feel all day long are other people feelings? How can I put someone else through a relationship with me, Who would they be falling in Love with? But it's here?"

Hendrix answered, "Yes."

Kai put his head in his hands and sobbed. The realization that he could know Love that was all his own, that he could have allowed himself an opening for Love was overwhelming. Hendrix stopped talking and let Kai release all that had been held inside for years. The little atom of unconditional Love that planted itself inside of him grew just a little bit more in those few minutes as Kai sobbed and his heart made its way just a little closer to the outside world, reaching for Grace. It was calling out to Grace. With each heave, he proved to himself that he was capable, even worthy of Love.

When Kai's breathing had slowed down, and he lifted his head to look at up. Hendrix took the glass jar that held his Love, and he twisted open the container. As the container lid opened a green, octopus-like moving mass crawled out and up Hendrix's arm. Every move it made was fluid and un-ending. Even the heartbeat that pumped through the middle of its body seemed circular and spiraled from its center outward vibrating along each tentacle. There were so many tendrils moving and snaking around Hendrix's arm. Kai looked down at the green tendrils. They were full of what looked like black dots and out of each black dots there grew a sharp spike. At the end of each sharp spike, there was a tongue that slithered in and out of the spike. It wasn't a gentle emotion, it had all kinds of harsh edges and spiky tips but it didn't seem to be hurting Hendrix. It looked like it was in complete control of every last tendril. At its center was a head, but it looked like it was dying, the green was faded, and there was burnt skin curling back from its round head. If Kai looked close enough, between the movements of the tendrils, he could see a glowing green center. As Kai was looking the octopus came up close to his face, and he thought he could smell the scent of Grace wafting up from the center of it.

"Interesting isn't it?" Hendrix said.

Kai thought, "This is what Love looks like?"

Hendrix responded, "No. This is what your Love looks like at this very moment. Love itself as an emotion looks like a crystalline green disc that fits perfectly in the palm of your hand. Your Love is just as it is because you don't believe that you can allow yourself to Love and be Loved. You believe that with everything that you feel in yourself and of others, it isn't fair to fall in Love. You've grown your Love into a protector of itself. It scares people off. It pushes people back, and it hurts them if they get too close. And it's fast. When I opened up the alterheart when we got here, it was dying. Do you see the burnt part? That was all of its head. Its heartbeat was so shallow I had to use dierscope to detect it. There was no color to any of it except on the very tips of its tendrils. I didn't want to worry you, but I was afraid that I couldn't save your Love.

And then it called out to me in that moment. I held it, and then released it and it found its way into my hands that held Hope. They lay pushed up against each other as your night went one. Love gained color and movement, and its heartbeat swirled into motion all through its body. It's only been getting clearer and clearer. It sent me its SOS, and I heard it. It was like nothing I had ever seen or felt in my life to witness it slowly coming back to life. And now, I believe I know the answer. Which is why I came to get you tonite from the Room of Lost Things."

Kai thought, 'So, what's the answer?'

Hendrix didn't say anything, he just placed Love in Kai's right hand, and there it settled down slowly, very slowly. It drew its tendrils in, the burned skin peeled back and disappeared. Its shape settled right into the palm of Kai's hand. It sat there perfectly. Kai smiled. He felt it. Then Hendrix got up and placed the blue Hope that still wore its mirror and smoke in Kai's left hand and slowly, little by little; Hope began to clear as well. Until all that was left in Kai's hands were two bright crystal clear discs.

Kai turned to Hendrix and thought, 'Does it work like this for everyone?'

"No, I think having you here, experiencing things, split from me has helped to Uncover your feelings faster. But I do think that it may be helpful for others to realize that the emotions can help one another sometimes."

Hendrix took the two crystalline discs from Kai and placed them in the cupped palms on the wall of his space, then took a long look down the counter at Kai's other emotions that needed to be Uncovered. He was looking with a deep reverence. He continued, "Kai, no one here takes their job lightly. It's an honor to do this work and, in a way, it's life or death work for each of us. I'm your shadow self. I live inside you in the other world. I feel everything alongside you, actually, I feel everything whether you choose to allow yourself to feel it or not. I'm your raw emotions. I'm the hate, the jealousy, the sadness, the frustration. I'm the side of you that longs to haul off and hit the idiot standing next to you when he says something about you under his breath. But I'm also the drive, the longing and the spitfire passion that overtakes you and makes moves and lays down women in your bed. I'm the sadness and depression that weights the couch cushions for days at a time. I don't think about how I feel, I just feel and I react. I send impulses and thoughts and daydreams through your body, and you do what you will with them. Sometimes you follow my instincts and sometimes you don't. Do you understand?"

Kai shook his head, he picked up his guitar and let his fingers crawl along its neck, just a few notes poking out from behind his minds wandering. He was trying to put it all together for himself. He thought to himself, "Kind of like the Id and the Ego. I bring my mind into situations to help temper my emotions, and you're pure emotions and working off that."

Hendrix who was listening for Kai's thoughts said, "Exactly! And I'm a very important part of you. When we're together in the other world, there are two things at play inside you. There's me. I'm there, and I feel things just as you feel them, but I don't define them, judge them or hold them back. My job is to let you know what I feel and what I'd like to do about it. Think of me as this world. Whatever you see in these glass containers of your feelings is okay. I don't judge any of it. We know that judgement isn't a concrete thing, it's of the mind and boxes us in. I've been in you and I know you've felt the itch to kill, you've been turned on by things you feel shouldn't be turned on by, you've wanted to do things you know are wrong. All of that is okay and I Love you anyway. You haven't done these things because you have a healthy relationship with me and allow my impulses to flow through a stream of check and balances.

The other thing at play inside of you is the state of your emotions. I only feel the emotions and relate my experience of them to you. It's what you do with your emotions that dictate the state of them. Too often in our world people deny emotions, sit on them, push them down, twist and turn them into other emotions. That's when they start to look like what they look like here in this world. That's when the emotions start to build defenses, outer layers, doppelgänger emotions, sometimes fortresses and man caves. This all happens when your emotions begin to qualify themselves and believe the judgement that you put on them. And this is where they can get very powerful, and a person can get unbalanced. Here, in this world, the emotions that need Uncovering are from childhood. And childhood is a time where we don't actually take responsibility for our feelings. Often as children, as you well know, we're given information from adults that isn't correct about feelings, but we absorb it and take it in regardless, because we trust the adults around us. There's really no way for us to know any better. Our feelings get all sorts of mixed up. But that's why this world is here. It's the chance to experience our own emotions and feelings on our own, to own them, to be responsible for them and to get to know them! It's really very exciting. I can imagine what it will be like to explore the world with you when our emotions are Uncovered!"

Kai was listening, he had heard this before, but it was hitting home in a different way now. Because Kai was so empathic, he had felt the impulses of others. He had felt the struggle to detach from the impulses as well as the struggle to hold onto impulses that should be let go . It was all beginning to make sense to him. It was something that Hendrix had said about judgement that opened everything up to him. He was caught in a thought. It was that his world had taught him to judge almost every emotion, even if he reacted on it or not. He was thinking how unfair it all was, thoughts and feelings didn't always equate to actions.

"I understand what you're thinking Kai, and it is unfair that in your world we're taught to judge emotions that aren't acted on. And to be honest, it causes a lot of problems, emotions that aren't validated in some way can start to grow wild and big and powerful and people can become unbalanced. The shadow selves lose control of the beast within and terrible things happen in the name of insanity, rage, mental illness, and addiction. No one knows how to override this kind of unbalance. For the most part, people tend to take things like medication to try and put the emotion to sleep, but there are problems when you do this too. Because just like your Love and Hope healed one another, emotions are connected. You affect more than just one emotion when you do such a thing."

In an attempt to lighten the mood a little Hendrix said, "Imagine life without me, your shadow self, your guide. Without me, you wouldn't be able to decipher what you truly wanted or needed. You wouldn't get to the core desires. Your mind works in a very spidery way, but shadow selves, we are direct, and you know when we converse with you. I give you gut reactions and every so often I override your system to make a move. If you know what I mean." Hendrix chuckled. "Remind me to take you back to the hidden room later where all the really dark work is done, it might enhance your music after seeing it."

Kai's interest was peaked. He looked at the time and saw he had about an hour before he was going to find Grace again. He decided to take the time to write her a song. Hendrix was back at his work, kneeling down and saying hello to all the emotions that still needed to be Uncovered. Kai picked up the guitar, closed his eyes with all the new information he had learned about the worlds and about himself. Who knew his shadow self was so enthusiastic. He mused about Love and the fact that he had begun its journey. He had written songs about Love before, but never a song that was written from his own experience of it. He listened for his own heartbeat and the way it beat a little higher in his chest this time, and he found the rhythm that was waiting patiently for him to pick up with his fingers. He let the scent of Grace's body linger on him as he played.

Part Five:

Discovery

Chapter 27

When they arrived at Sen's the smell of incense pulled her inside and Sen greeted Grace and Anika at the entrance. She ushered Grace in quickly and sat her down on a carpeted plush chair thick with a plaid design. Grace imagined in her world the chair would be full of yellows, browns, and oranges, stuck in the Sixties with Sen. Grace swore this chair wasn't in this place when she was here last, but, then again, nothing seemed that concrete in this world. Sen motioned to Anika that it was okay to leave.

Anika said to Grace, "I have some work to do, for now, I'll see you later?"

Grace replied, "Sure. See you later." She still couldn't quite wrap her head around talking to herself and seeing herself do all of these everyday things like standing in front of her and talking casually. It was so strange to see herself from the back walking out of the door

As the quiet began to seep in and Anika left, Sen began, "No need to thank me now, there's more important stuff to talk about. I've always been a sucker for Love, and I want to hear all the juicy parts, but for now, I need to teach you something and give you a little of my own history! I don't tell just anyone about me, but I think it'll help you to understand the bigger picture here. And I'm kind of excited to finally share it with someone! To most here, I am a mystery. So make yourself comfortable." Sen had a wide smile across her face. She continued, "Then, I need your help."

"My help?"

"Yep. You'll see. "With this Sen sat down in her own carpeted chair and as she did Grace had to think back to a few minutes ago to figure if the chair was here when she walked in. She thought to herself how quickly things shift and change in this world.

Sen began with a tone of excitement in her voice and a buzzing in her body, "I sent you to meet our Founder, I needed you to understand what this place was about, it was important for you to meet him. For what reason you ask? Ah! Well, let me tell you! You are here, and Kai is here, and there are more of you here than ever before, at this very moment. So many more! It's unheard of! You are gathering on the shores here. More of you come here each day. Now, your kind, you all are different from the others who come here to do their work. For one thing, you're quite a bit older than the others when you get here. I don't know if you've noticed, but most shadow selves travel here when they are between fifteen and sixteen, and you're eighteen, as is Kai. Your kind come here later than others, mostly between seventeen and nineteen, as far as I can tell. I don't know for sure, but my guess is that because of who you are, your ability to hold more in your hearts combined with an overactive empathy for others and a high tolerance for change, you are all somewhat groomed from your childhood to be more resilient in the area of feelings. So it takes you longer to reach your moment. There's more that builds up inside of you, and I imagine that this adds to the dramatic nature of the events that lead to your journey here. Often your choices are quite unnerving and would be final if it weren't for the splitting. You can thank the founder for that one, otherwise, a lot of you might find yourselves living here permanently. It's not that living here is bad, but it has its limitations.

Your kind come here with both sides of yourselves, which I bet can be a little strange, to say the least, but you all seem to handle it pretty well. You go with whatever is in front of you like a chameleon; it's a trait that you all possess."

At this Grace felt a tug of something, like she understood exactly what Sen was saying without needing further information.

"I've learned, from conversations with others of your kind in the past, that your kind are called here so that you can do your work when you Merge again in the other world. Your alterhearts are very tangled up because of the amount of time it takes you to get here and the ways that empathy plays throughout your young lives. The added benefit of having you here with your shadow self is that you often Uncover emotions very fast working together. You can learn more about who you are and why you're here later when you can talk with Anika. In fact, you may not need to even work with Anika, because since you have been here you have Uncovered feelings for yourself by simply by living here and being moment to moment within this world. You, Grace, have already begun untangling your own heart."

"How many of us are here? Do you know?" Grace asked.

"There are many of you here, and to give you an idea as to how strange this truly is, since this world has existed, there have only ever been one of your kind here at a time. Never has there been more than one of you at a time. I'm not sure what this means or what consequence this is having back in your world, or if there will be a consequence if you ever find each other in your world after being here. I think we've all assumed you came one at a time for a greater reason. It points to something big happening, wouldn't you say?"

"Only ever one of us at a time and right now there are many at once." Grace was staring off trying to come up with a reason for why there might be so many of her kind her, not comprehending what her kind was and what she was here to do. Everything had seemed so cryptic since she'd been here. Just the fact that there seemed to be a gathering of people, with whom she had some ancestry felt right, somewhere inside. It didn't scare her or worry her or make her tense.

Grace added, "We are where we need to be." She didn't know where the words came from but they hung in the air for a moment before drifting along with the thick scent of incense.

Sen took in the words then began again, "Me, I get to travel back and forth, whenever I'd like, between the worlds. I play in both of them. I travel back and forth; You never know where you'll see me. I'm not like you and Kai, and I'm not like those that live here permanently, I don't do one person's work. I create. And it's through my creations that I travel. Actually I found this world by accident!"

With this Sen began her own story, becoming visibly younger as she did so. Her gestures became more childlike and her excitement pulsed through the air. Grace could see that Sen had longed to tell her story. Grace had known this feeling, she had held in so many stories after what happened to her when she was six, that she's surprised she didn't blow up from all the truth she swallowed down.

Sen continued on. "This world is so magical. It really is! I want you to appreciate it for it's magical possibility. If you understand this, you can tap into it just as I can. If I tell you how I got here, I think you can understand just how easy it is to tap into the magic. And this is what your people need. The Magic. And you will be the one to bring it to them, to help them understand."

Chapter 28

Sen began, "I came here one day, a while back, by accident. In the other world, I'm an artist. That's my job. It's pretty amazing! Now, my art is hanging all over the city I live in, from small coffee shops in my neighborhood to galleries downtown. I didn't start out as an artist. And I could never have imagined that I would be as successful as I've been! I started out not knowing what I was supposed to do or be. I was a wanderer who listened to music, took classes on everything from meditation to massage to quantum physics. I practiced yoga, and I danced all night in dark rooms with wooden floors, sweat and djembes. I always talked to people I met and recorded their histories in my memory. I loved anything to do with spirit and energy. I read a lot of books and wrote in journals. I always had a creative life, and I've always been a searcher. But some time after I turned thirty, everything I had done and learned had hit maximum within me, and my guess is that it all started to mix and match itself up. I had the most incredible urge to give what was happening inside of me a reflection outside of me. The only thing that made sense to me as a way to do this was something I did when I was a child in school. I went out to a magazine shop and bought a bunch of magazines, on everything from food to home to sports and news. I brought them all home and when I walked into my house, I spread all the magazines out on my kitchen table. I remember the day; it was dark and grey and rainy outside. I've always thought there's something magical about rainy days.

Once I began rummaging through the magazines, I pulled out pictures and words that spoke to me and started cutting paper, ripping paper. My kitchen table became a refuge for pieces large and small, I threw away nothing, figuring I could use all of it if I needed. I chose a cardboard box to paste everything onto. I cut out a flat shape from the box and began to layer these pictures and scraps onto it. It was a moveable picture that shifted with my thoughts until I decided to start pasting it down. My hands were guiding this picture. I had let my mind wander its way into a sleeping state while I worked. But my hands never stopped. It had felt like something bigger than me, or even a bigger part of myself was speaking through my hands as I worked. And when I awoke, I looked down, unaware of the amount of time that had passed. In front of me, in my own hands was a collage that screamed integration, putting all of me back together. And it was a picture of the shore of this world. It was black and white, and the rain outside had stopped, but the grey was still present everywhere. I could see the shore like it was moving and when I looked up from the collage in my hands, I saw that my toes were dug down into the very same black and white sand. I held where I stood for a very long time, long enough to see my first black and white moonrise. I was just breathing, holding my collage and staring at my feet wondering what had happened. As far as I could guess, I had astrally projected somewhere. That was my educated guess, and I had figured that all of the work I had done on myself, my energy, my mind had allowed me to take advantage of a rift between worlds."

Grace was listening mesmerized by all that Sen was saying. She couldn't believe that making a collage could bring her here; there had to be more to it.

Sen continued, "As you can imagine, I was pretty lost here, all by myself, not sure what happened, with only a collaged-on piece of cardboard in my hands. I wandered around when I eventually got the courage up to move from where I stood. I called for help, but no one was nearby to hear me. As I called for help, I noticed that sounds of wildlife answered me back. I found the path that led to The Hall and I followed it. You have to understand that when I got here, I had no idea how and no clue how I could go back to my kitchen table. I was stuck, and I didn't have my other self to guide me. I knew nothing of this place. But I forced myself to walk on the path through my fear so I could find my way home. As I got closer to The Hall, I noticed that on the edges of the path small animals had gathered on my way with me. And even a small red fox was staring gently in my direction with kindness in his eyes. It was then that I knew I was safe."

Grace interrupted, "I know that fox. Anika led me to it last night. I slept curled up next to it; I had such beautiful dreams."

"Yes! There are all kinds of animals here. On my first trip here, I only saw the woodland creatures. If you call out to them, they'll come and say hello, you should try it sometime."

Sen continued with her story, "Well! My presence in The Hall created quite a tizzy! Everyone stopped, there was a murmur like I've never heard and I was rushed to the Room of Lost Things without a second thought. It was here that I was given a glimpse into what happened while I was collaging , it was more like I was given a shot of understanding. I didn't witness anything or see any pictures in the room, I simply walked in, the door closed behind me, and I was hit by something, without warning. And I just knew how I got here and how to get back. I had an instant knowledge of this place, what they do here and how it came to be. I was also given a glimpse into my magic and how it works. I finally understood how all of the pieces of my life fit together to get me to this place. I imagine it was a similar experience to what the shadow selves get when they land here. I suppose it was the information I lost on my way to this world that I got back."

"What I now understood was that when I created my collage and quieted my mind, I basically allowed my own shadow self to speak through my hands. In its own way it was a split, I gave her a voice all her own. But I was too old to be Uncovered, nor did I need to be Uncovered. I simply found a loophole in the design of the world that allowed me to visit when I gave my shadow self her own voice in my creations. But it also took a keen focus on what I was doing and a sacrifice to her will. I would allow her to move my hands. It's something that I had practiced many times, getting lost in rhythm, settling my mind into meditative states. I hadn't realized it, but I was actually preparing myself for this world! I now knew, that in order to find my way back into my own world, I just had to take what my shadow self was telling me and Merge it with the rest of me. When I left the Room of Lost Things, I knew just where to go, and my feet led me to this space. When I first arrived here, it had everything I needed, and it was a beautiful and perfect rendition of my personality It was as if this world was welcoming me in. It felt like home. The space didn't look much different from what it looks like today. I guess I haven't changed that much." Sen laughed a big belly laugh at this, it was so genuine that Grace found herself laughing as well.

"Isn't it amazing how sometimes we do things to prepare for other things ... all the time having no idea why we're drawn to these things? But we do them and learn them anyway! I know that's not a very poetic way of saying it ... but it's really amazing! It requires a trust, which most people don't have."

Sen took a moment to walk over to the counter and asked Grace if she would like some tea before she continued with her story. Grace, having remembered how good she felt the first time she had the tea, said yes. So Sen quietly went about collaging a white teacup with bits and pieces of white paper, linen, fabric and such from the counter, then she picked a word out of her word jar and pasted it right in the center. This time, Grace could see the word clearly. It was Trust. Just as she saw the word Trust pasted in the center of the teacup, the collage began to grow into an actual white porcelain teacup with steam rising from the warm liquid inside.

Grace asked, "Why do you choose a word to paste in the center of the teacup you collage, what does it do?"

Sen replied," It gives you what you need. I placed the word trust in your teacup, because I'm about to show you how to use magic for yourself and in order for it to work, you need to trust. You need to give over a part of yourself to the process, and in doing so, you need to trust. It flavors the tea, but it also infuses it with whatever word chosen. Here." Sen handed the teacup to Grace. She accepted it and took a small sip from the side of the teacup. It tasted different from the tea she had last time. It was a stronger flavor, one that melted in her mouth; it was almost like a caramel. As Grace swirled it around her mouth to taste it, she felt herself open up to what Sen wanted to tell her. Even if she had been wary as to what Sen might say, do or show her, she wasn't capable of anything but putting trust into her. She was still herself; she was just more open to the ideas put forth in front of her and willing to try anything as long as Sen was the one who offered it.

Sen then continued her story as she created her own cup of tea with the word Truth pasted in the center, It was strange, because her tea was clear. It looked just like warm water in a teacup. Grace thought maybe that was what truth was. Pure, plain and simple. No matter what it sounded like ... it just Was.

"In order to find my way back to my world, I had to Merge my selves back together again with a sense of integration, which is what the collage continued to scream out at me. I sat down in this very space and put all of my knowledge about energy, states of mind, rhythms and sound together. I pulled on everything that I had learned from classes, teachers, gurus and I allowed the collage to speak to me. I had no need to create a new collage to find my way back; I just needed to learn from the one that I came here with. I sat in quiet, relaxed my mind, allowed all of the walls inside to drop and for all of me to co-mingle. It was fascinating. I let go and called out to my shadow self, it was fascinating to have it all swimming alive and together inside of me. I watched the symphony of it all with my mind's eye and as I did, time stopped again. I was lost suspended in it. When I opened my eyes, I was back at my kitchen table holding my cardboard collage. But when I got back here, I had all the memory of what happened. And I had new insights into my own life. I was meant to create; I was meant to piece together broken parts, to use everything I had learned up until that point. I knew I needed to weave the creative and the spiritual, and that in between the two was where I was meant to dwell. So after my first journey to this world, I began to create collages of all sizes and shapes. My work fused the conscious with the subconscious. And the more I created the more I was commissioned to create. My work found itself all over

NYC. I decided to move into a small little apartment in the village where no one would bother me, and I could continue my studies and my art."

Grace interrupted, "Wait, you found a new world, one of magic and mystery, you came here on your own by accident, through a collage of all things, you found your way home and you didn't have an urge to come back and discover more?"

"It is strange, isn't it? My urge to come back hadn't appeared until I was thirty-five. I guess I was infused with enough purpose for quite a while that I didn't have the need to refuel it." Sen paused for a moment and then continued, "It was when I was thirty-five that I got the idea for a new collage series. It was to be a series about emotions and what they look like if they had a body all their own. Not what they look like with someone wearing them on or dressed in a human body, but rather if they themselves had their own unique bodies. I started with my own. I delved deep into my own heart. I hadn't called on my shadow self for quite a while, but I inherently knew how to do it and knew it needed to be done in order to begin this series. I sat down at my same kitchen table, on a rainy NYC day, and I set my intention. To see my heart and to greet my own sadness. At first, I had all these ideas as to what it would look like, I chose all the taboo colors, the blues, and greys and it was like my hands rejected the papers. It wasn't until I set my hands down on the table, breathed into my own heart and began listening for her voice, looking for her help, calling on my own shadow self. And again it happened!

Time stopped, and I found myself in The Hall, I looked down at the collage in my hands and the canvas was bright lime green, with a heavy dark green haze all around its glowing center. There were growing vines all along the outside of the canvas, and it was almost growing buds as I watched. This time I knew where I was and what I was looking at. I went to my space, and this time no one stopped what they were doing or hurried me to the Room of Lost Things. I just made my way to my space and worked on understanding my collage.

After that visit, I came back more and more often, doing my work. I love this world, but I also love my own world, I respect both. Since I've been coming here, I've watched things change each time I arrive. I've taken up the art of prediction and I'm trying to understand why this world is changing, and how I might be of help to it. That's why you see my cards, my tea leaves and candles and crystals and wind chimes. There is a magic here that can be tapped into easily here, and I do it willingly, in hopes of helping this world survive. Without it, the future of our world is more than grim. A world without a balance of adults who can feel clearly and have a purpose, a world without adults that can hear their hearts call, is not one I would want to live in. And if you think about it, the problem only doubles. As one generation births another into their ideals, the problem compounds. Do you understand the layer of the problems this world is facing and the urgency to change course as soon as possible?"

"I think so, from what the Founder said, there are two problems. One problem is that less and less shadow selves are making it here to be Uncovered."

"Yes! This is due to a manipulation, manufacturing, and spreading of fears. These fears then create a questioning of the very ability to parent one's own child. And when these fears get big enough the larger institutes sweep in with their protocols to alleviate them. The problem is how they alleviate these fears; they do it by wiping away emotions from our children's lives, through pills, and therapies. So, the children of this generation are not making it here to be Uncovered, because their emotions are missing, fading or dying inside of them. There is nothing to Uncover.

"The founder said the other problem is that more and more people are making it here permanently without the splitting, which means they've died at heir own hand?"

"Yes, These are the children who have been used and abused and unheard and discarded at the hands of an industry that experiments with their lives. Sometimes they make choices not from their own heart, but as a side effect of the very protocols put in place by the institutes that say they are here to protect them. I know that what you are learning is a lot, and it goes in the face of all you believe about our world. But think about it. How many people do you know in your life right now, who are on some kind of medication to temper their negative emotions? How many people do you know that take a pill instead of looking into the depth of their heart for answers? How many people do you know who have illness creeping inside of them, who can no longer handle loss or anger, how many people do you know that have disconnected to their hearts. It's started already."

Sen nodded gravely, her smile all but gone. "There are forces at work that suppress feelings, that alter the brains of our youth. There are organizations that prey on the fears of parents, and they cater to a living devoid of ups and downs. At the same time these forces are using drugs and therapies to wash clear remembrances of feeling from our youth. The side effect of some these methods has led to more suicides than ever. The counterattacks have to start now, or I'm afraid it is a generational problem that gets harder to fix each time we miss a shadow self. I believe that is why your kind are gathering on the shores. I believe that you have the answers to igniting the counter attacks. But to be sure, we need to work together. What we learn together you can bring back to your people that have gathered here. Are you willing to join me? To quest for the answer with me?" Sen paused waiting for an answer from Grace

Grace said, "Of course! But I don't know what you want from me; I don't have magic."

"Yes, you do! That's what I'm telling you! You are a story-teller; your magic is as ancient as we are! You are a truth sayer. You lineage goes back to the very beginning, and add to it the ancestry that you come from, being that you are of your own kind. You are magic in and of yourself. I'll help guide you, and we'll work together on a collage, you'll know what to do when it's time. No more talking!" with this Sen waved her hand over the table in the center of the room and invited Grace to sit in a chair at the table next to herself. Grace joined Sen and looked over the table. It was full of scraps, clippings, fabrics, edges, ribbons. In the center was a large canvas blank and calling out to be filled. There was a vat of paste with 2 paint brushes in it.

Grace, looking over the table of supplies felt unsure of exactly what to do next, but she trusted Sen, and whatever she needed her to do, she would. Sen grabbed Grace's hand and held it while she said, "Listen, do not think. You'll breathe with me. We're going to quiet our minds as best as we can and then set an intention and lean into the sacrifice of who we are."

Chapter 29

While still holding Grace's hand, Sen began to breathe in a deep and easy way, her eyes closed and her lips slightly parted. Grace followed, she didn't like to close her eyes when she didn't know what was going on, but she trusted Sen, the tea had worked.

"In order to set an intention," Sen began, "you hold it like a crystal sphere in your third eye. Have you ever wondered about the marking that Anika, and now you, have over your third eye and what it means? It is an ever-flowing spiral. One that flows both outward and inward. It opens us up to the travel between the conscious and the subconscious. It resonates the vibration of surrender and the journey. Like a path, the leaf takes from the tree to the ground below. It represents connection with what is inside to that which is outside. The spiral is a symbol of our evolution as humans, as a planet, as a world, as time itself. When I look at Anika, I understand that you, Grace, are a conduit between worlds, between evolutions of beings. You have the power to expand and contract in whatever direction you put your attention on. I'm telling you this, because it will help you to visualize a moving spiral in your third eye. It will focus you quickly and easily. So, as you breathe and allow your mind to settle like a pond after a rock has disturbed its surface, you can allow the image of the spiral to be projected in your mind's eye. Just watch it spin without attachment."

Grace did as she was told, and found it quite easy to settle her mind. The spiral energy in her third eye started moving without even a thought; it was like as soon as she opened the door and sent the invitation out, it all began. Grace, without realizing it, had a huge smile on her face as this was all happening. It felt good to her, knowing that she was part of something bigger than herself, knowing that she was helping.

When both Sen and Grace were in a calm, relaxed and meditative state and with full awareness, Sen began again, "It's time to set our intention together. We are asking for an answer. One to the question of the role we play in the larger healing. You can allow the thought of the barren Hall, the empty shores here and the gathering of people who live here permanently, then allow it to pass as you ask about your role in the healing. In your third eye, focus on a small ball of white light and ask for the answer inside of yourself. I'll be asking my shadow self; you just need to hold the intention inside of you. Our magic can work in tandem and show us the answer, we just need to trust it, and surrender to its movement. "They both sat, eyes closed, intentions being set and when they finished, they opened their eyes at the same time. Grace had felt the moment that her intention solidified inside of her and she just knew it was time to get to work.

"Are you ready to give of yourself? To surrender to your magic?" Sen asked

Grace, feeling very confident, calm and strong, said "Yes."

"Okay, put your hands on the table and simply allow them to move across it. Allow your fingers and hands to collect and shuffle and arrange whatever they want to touch. We are being as present with the moment as we can. Your hands will do the work, if you have a question or thought come up to the surface of your mind, simply say it out loud to release it and then move back to your hands across the table. Don't try to dictate an idea, picture or anything of the sort, if you do, we may end up somewhere we do not want to be! We're letting the magic work through us, we're calling on the deepest part of who we are and asking it to lead us to the answer, so just allow your hands to guide you. To do the work. Surrender to the movement."

They both got to work. At first, Grace was tentative and questioning the process, her mind shifting in and out of trying to hold onto the control of her hands and fingers. But she spoke through it, releasing her mind's skepticism out into the air and trying to keep her thoughts still as she grew the trust between Sen and herself. She continued moving and releasing, moving and releasing until finally, her hands began to move of their own purpose, Grace's mind following along. The tabletop became an altar of spirit and magic as their hands moved at a furious pace over its surface. It was like a dance of intention, never once did their hands bump one another or grab for the same piece, even though they sat almost shoulder to shoulder next to one another. They worked in complete unison and silence. The collage was slowly coming together. Grace had been collecting bits and pieces to arrange on the edge of the canvas where her hands seemed to want to work, as Sen worked directly in the middle of the canvas. Before long the collage began to take shape. All of what Grace created was holding in what Sen had created. And before they both knew it, time was slowing down, their hands began to move at a slow-motion pace, and Sen reached out to grab onto Grace's arm before it happened.

Chapter 30

I

When time caught up with itself again, Sen and Grace were back in their world. They knew this, because of the color peeking out from between things. Though it almost seemed as if their world was a black and white world, as from where they stood, the walls were white; the desks were white, the computers were white, even the uniforms and shoes everyone wore were white. Grace couldn't quite tell where they were; there were desks like it was school but there were also men and women walking around with clipboards and wearing white lab coats. There were kids her age and younger everywhere, sitting at the desks, looking out the windows, working on computers and handheld devices of all sorts, hanging out in the hallways. It was almost like the combination of a school and a doctors office or a wing of a hospital. There was something that Grace couldn't quite place. She knew it was her world, but it wasn't her time. It was in the way people styled their hair and the little nuances of what they wore. It certainly wasn't from any of the interactions between people that she witnessed, because she realized no one was interacting with one another. Grace thought to herself that this must be the future, a picture of what the future brings. She thought back to the intention she set with Sen, what was it? What is her role in the healing? She had visualized The Hall, barren of shadow selves doing their work, the empty shores of the world she just came from; she had visualized scores of people living there permanently and then she had asked very clearly, "What is my role in the healing?"

Where she and Sen stood in this future world, it certainly did not look like a healed place. It was in need of healing. Grace and Sen were standing in a shadow in the corner of the building, they were as of yet undetected, getting their bearings on the situation. From where they stood, they could see the layout of the floor in front of them. Everyone went about their work in their own way, but no one smiled, or talked to one another. It was quiet except for a white noise that permeated the walls of this place.

At first, Grace couldn't place what was missing, but then she realized that it was the sound of conversation. It was chatter, the gossip, the discussions, the talking, the sound of communication; it was missing. The adults in the room only spoke in the hushed tones of matter-of-fact with one another. It was obvious to Grace that there was no personal attachment in any of the things they said to one another. It was all business. What was missing was the carefree tone of a conversation between two people being themselves, in a present moment. It was a sound that Grace knew very well but hadn't actually thought of as a sound in her everyday life; it was just so ingrained in everything she did, everywhere she went. People talked and laughed and conversed; it was always in the background. And now, in this place, she missed the sound, the one she didn't even really know existed as a soundtrack in her life. There was sound here, but Grace could only describe it as a hollow kind of sound, and it made her nervous; it brought all of her anxiety up from her belly into her throat. She tried to push it back down, but she was no longer in the Shadow World, and the air was no longer was thick with magic that could settle her anxiety. She looked around again at the place in front of her. It wasn't outwardly scary in the sense that no one seemed scared or afraid or angry. No one seemed sad, unhappy, no one seemed bored even, they all just went about their business, so why was Grace so uneasy, other than the hollow sounds of the place?

Sen whispered to her, "Stay close to me, you're more powerful than I even realized" at this, she looked down at the canvas. "I imagine we'll be shifting quite a lot, I've never created a collage quite like this one and I'm not sure how this trip will play out, stay close." With this, she motioned for Grace to look down at the canvas alongside her, as she pointed out the landscape of the collage which looked more like a graphic novel on the outside border of it.

Grace looked down. She had collaged the entire outside border. She ran her fingers along the work she had created on the border. It was boxes and circles and thought bubbles collaged out of tiny pieces of paper and fabric. It ran along the entire border of the canvas. Grace had really never seen anything quite like it. All she had remembered from being at the table at Sen's was the energetic pull to work on the margins, to create the border, nothing else. She didn't remember putting the images together or drawing the lines and divisions and boxes that defined what she looked at now. She had a moment of wonder as she looked at it. How could she not know what she was creating? The only answer she could come up with was that it all came from her subconscious, that she was able to let go of her mind. In the center of the canvas, Sen had created a collage of this very space. It was whitewashed across all surfaces, though there was color on the people. And there were many people. There were many many young people. They were sitting down watching TV, standing up, leaning against walls, playing games on devices. They were sitting in chairs looking out windows, sitting at tables drumming their fingers. There was an overall feeling of blah everywhere. No excitement, no anger, no sadness, no happiness, no anything. It was exactly the scene in front of Grace and Sen right now.

They both stood there looking out at the world in front of them. There seemed to be work getting done; there was a lot of attention paid to things in everyone's hands. There were people reading, writing, drawing. Grace whispered to Sen,"Where do you think we are? Is this some kind of future?"

Sen answered back, "I would imagine it is. It's not like it seems all that bad, but if I had to think of an image to help explain how it feels to be here, I would say that it feels like there's a wide crack in the floor and part of what makes us human is slowly draining out through that very crack. My curiosity is going with it. It's like a vacuum."

"Yeah. I can see that." Grace responded. "Should we explore this place a little? How do we get out of here?"

"We have to learn what we've come here to learn, and then I imagine the canvas will take us through to the next place we need to see. Once we've seen it all, we need to integrate it into who we are so that we can find our way back."

"Well, I think that we need to find what we need to see here if the scene won't shift until we find it, staying in the shadows isn't going to do us any good, we should get out and start looking for it."

"Don't go far, you need to be close to me when we shift again, I don't know what will happen if we're separated when it shifts, one of us could get lost here."

"Oh," Grace replied, understanding now the gravity of what they did. Realizing she actually in that very moment existed in the future, or rather a future. They weren't just hopping from place to place in some subconscious cloud traveling in the mind of one of them; they were literally five senses in the future.

"If you step out from the shadows, remember, they can see you. You look young Grace; you could easily be mistaken for one of the children here, so be careful, we don't know enough about what this place is and what is going on here."

"I'll be careful, as careful as I can be, I guess." Grace answered, and then she quickly stepped out from the shadow that was hiding her, thinking that if she didn't do something now, she would never move and in never moving she'd never get back to the shadow world and in turn get back to her own world.

As she stepped out into the open of this strange and quiet place with the song of white noise everywhere, she realized she was going to have a problem with how she was dressed. She was still dressed in the swatch of material she dreamed up in the shadow world. As she looked down at the material, she realized for the first time that it was every hue of the rainbow. She hadn't seen the fabric in a world of color before. It was beautiful. Regardless, no one here was dressed like her. All of the young people here were dressed alike, almost as if they were in a school uniform, except the uniformity was in the shape of their clothes not the color or patterns of the fabric. She would be singled out almost immediately. She wondered if the magic she used to find the material in the first place would work here in this world. So she closed her eyes, putting her full attention on what she was wearing and imagined something more like school uniform, basic, boring and something that didn't call all sorts of attention to her. When she opened her eyes, she was still standing there in the open draped in one large piece of material that gathered perfectly around every curve of her body. She knew it was inappropriate for this kind of place but before she could think another word of it a woman in long dark pantsuit that zipped up to her neck came pushing her back into the wall behind her, which happened to be an open door. It was a door to a bathroom on the floor. She seemed nice enough, kind enough.

She said to Grace "I didn't mean to push into you like that, but you cannot go around this floor wearing what you're wearing. Can I help you change your clothes? If you walk around like that you could set off the middle road and take down the quiet time everyone is enjoying. Not to mention that it could be quite dangerous to you depending on what gets recalled and triggered."

"Oh, I don't have a change of clothes, I just got here."

"Oh, okay, if you stay here, I can see if I can find you a change of clothes in the nurse's station, there has to be something. I'm sure we can find you something." She said this with a small smile, and a tone of caring.

"I can stay here. Whatever you need me to do." Grace replied. The woman left to find her a change of clothes, but as soon as her way was clear, Grace made her way out of the bathroom. She needed to figure out what it was she needed to learn so she could get out of here, it was creeping her out. Middle road? Triggering? Recalling? What did it all mean? And where was Sen with the canvas, maybe if she could look a little more closely at the collage they created she could learn from the canvas as well. Grace looked around for Sen, but she was nowhere in sight.

Grace decided she needed to pay closer attention to the details that surrounded her, like when she was on the hunt for the stories she strung together as a child. She needed to investigate, to listen for the spaces between and to sense the truths that were around her. She started by taking in the entire scene in front of her. She saw all the kids, not one of them was interacting with another, and there didn't seem to be a need to interact between them. No one was trying to get anyone else's attention; it was all very lackluster. Grace shook her head at the scene in front of her. Then she looked at the adults walking around. They had more movement than the kids, but it was very pleasant, no one gave a backward glance behind anyone else's back, it was all just happening. After looking at the people, Grace decided to watch how they all moved from space to space to see if there was a pattern she was missing. She pulled back the vision in her eyes, so she was no longer focussing on smaller details but rather taking in the overall picture in front of her. She noticed a lot of movement coming from a room on the left. The adults were all coming and going out of there, maybe a teachers lounge or a nurses station? She still hadn't decided if this was a school or a doctors village. She did notice in her vision that every so often there would be a moment where all of the kids would have some kind of movement in their body, though it was minor. They would all cross their leg or rub their nose, it was like a uniform moment of movement, but the movements would all be different. Grace wasn't sure what was triggering it. Trigger, Grace shook her head again, she had these words stuck in there, and she would hear them repeated throughout her journey here. Grace narrowed her vision again and looked around at what people were eating and drinking. There was a lot of water and snack bags; there was no snack machine, so she supposed they either had the food here or it was brought from home. Some kids had backpacks with them and headphones on. And there it was again, the not-so-spontaneous movement of all the kids at the same time. What was this? When it happened it was like an orchestrated beat in time, like they were all on the same inner clock.

Grace figured if she could delve a little deeper she could maybe figure out what was going on, so she attempted to look into space between, to read the scripts that wrote themselves out there. First, she set her intentions on a boy with his feet up on a table, his eyes were closed, his backpack was on his lap, and he had headphones on. She focused her energy and intention on the space all around him ... First, she opened up her vision to colors to see if his aura was bright or dim. She squinted her eyes a little, but as hard as she tried, she was unable to see anything. She began to allow her mind to release its grip on her, because panic had crept in without her even realizing it. Grace was getting desperate to leave this place. She was afraid the woman would be back soon and see she wasn't in the bathroom and maybe she would try to come find her, and a scene would be made. Knowing that there was a pressure building up inside of her to finish this process, she purposefully released the pressure valve and just let her eyes settle. With this, she let a sound slip out of her lips and she called to the space between. As she was watching, she could see just the faintest of faint glimmers sparkle and then fade. She could see a shadow start to push free from the dimensions they are kept in and come to converse with Grace, but as quick as it placed a hand in the in-between to push free, *poof* it disintegrated into thin air. It was like someone trying to blow a bubble with a bubble wand but not getting enough air to actually release it into space. Grace never had this happen to her before. She was so confused. She tried again, but nothing. She even sang a little song she sang when she was a child, in a hushed voice to tease it out, but maybe she had been too loud, because before Grace knew it, she was being led by three men, down a hallway into an intake room.

Everyone was being polite enough, no one was pushing her or yelling at her, but they all had a firm hand on her and directed her through the hallways and rooms. She was brought to a brightly lit room, with one lone light bulb hanging from a wire in the ceiling. It was bright because there was a large window overlooking the city below and it was a sunny day outside. Grace, looked out the window and the world looked different out there. There were no advertisements outside. No ads on top of taxicabs, no signs on sides of buses. All the cars were driving at the same speed it seemed like. There was no honking, no yelling, no cars cutting off other cars. It seemed like a well-oiled machine. Grace thought to herself, This is what it'll be like when we finally get self-driving cars. No hassle." That's what Grace thought. Only the words came out of her mouth as she thought them.

One of the men who led her into this room spoke, "No hassle."

Then another of the men spoke, this one with more authority than the last, "Well, I'm glad you don't want to hassle with us. But young lady, Ms. Delfonte called you into security as soon as she saw that you had gone missing from the bathroom. She was worried that you might get hurt or disturb the environment here at the Institute. You cannot wear clothes like that here. It can cause problems. All kinds of problems. If you are going to attend this Institute, you need to abide by our rules while you're here in our care. Dress doesn't always lead to problems, but it can cause a glitch in the work we do, it can trigger recollections and set our path backwards and sometimes backwards can be hard to reverse, once negative emotions get a hold of you, all kinds of complications occur."

Everything had happened so quickly from trying to tease out the space between to being here in this, interrogation room? Intake room? She didn't know what to call it. Singular lightbulb, chair, desk, clipboard. The people who had led her here were about to leave the room, but first they placed her directly in the chair. Before she knew it, she was alone in the room. The sound of a lock clicking into place as the men left, decided her level of panic as she was left alone in this place. Grace didn't have her head fully back in the game. Her fingers began weaving in and out of one another, her leg jumping in feral anticipation of something bad. She wasn't sure why she couldn't converse with the space between. Was is it because she wasn't in her world anymore? Had she lost her ability? She called out quietly to Sen, "Sen! Are you here? Where are you? What's happening? Where are we?"

But no one answered her.

After a short while, a man walked into the room.

"Well. You are quite a mystery, quite a mystery indeed." He was shuffling through some papers. Then he took a seat on the opposite side of the table from Grace. He was a taller man, but he looked like he had kind eyes. "No one seems to know who you are or how you got into the institute. No one knows how you got around our security, or into our environment here at the Institute. You must be very eager to join us if you've taken the time to make it into our environment unharmed. If you're looking for entrance here, I can make that happen, but first, we'll need to get you up to date with our protocols immediately." At this, a woman entered the room and began slipping sleeves of pressure detectors on her arm, her leg and around her head. Her wrists felt weighted down by something but when she looked down they were free to move. They just didn't have the impulse or the strength to move. Grace thought it had to have something to do with the pressure sleeve that was on her arm. It all happened so fast, that Grace hadn't the time to push away from it.

The man with the kind eyes continued. "By looking at how you're dressed, I'm going to assume that you haven't seen our dress code here at the Institute." The man's voice was calm and centering, it wasn't too loud, it didn't fluctuate tone or pitch very much, it was steady, and it exuded warmth.

He pulled out a sheet of paper and placed it on the desk in front of Grace; it was a girls dress code for The Institute of Higher Learning for grades 10-12.

He continued, "If you would like to attend our institute then you cannot simply show up in our building ready to go, there are some things that happen first. You need to be evaluated for triggers and recalls. We need to find your middle road. We have to make sure that you're capable of doing the work, that your parents approve of your choice to come here, and are willing to take all the precautions to keep your home environment-friendly and that you really want to be here. We're a free institute, and we are happy to take in anyone who would like to experience higher learning in grades 10-12. However, you need to be a good fit with us just as we have to be a good fit with you. There's a little bit of testing that is done on any candidates, but it doesn't take long, and we can probably have you on our attendance sheets by the end of the day. Do you understand everything that I'm telling you?"

"Yes," Grace nodded as well as giving an answer in the affirmative figuring maybe this would be what she needed to learn to get out of here. Her blood pressure was skyrocketing with anxiety, and she didn't want to set off any alarms on the pressure sleeves they put on her.

"We strive to keep this Institute as distraction-free as possible. We work very hard to make sure that our students are comfortable and at ease in their day, they don't experience anxiety, sadness or anger. We don't want to trigger any of the deeply suppressed emotions in anyone, especially for students who in trial mode here at the Institute. The tests will discover how you handle stressful situations and we'll get you updated with the right cocktail so that your day is easy and fluid. It's all very non-invasive, it's a process we all go through her at The Institute, teachers, students, janitors, parents, etc. If we are striving to give you the best possible experience, we need to make sure everyone is on board and no one is recalling the feelings that we work so hard to keep at bay. Actually some of the parents and teachers here are on higher cocktails than the kids, just so we can keep calm around them and give them the best possible chance at a successful outcome. But before we start your actual testing, let's talk about dress code."

As the man was talking, Grace took notice, not of his words so much as how he was talking to her. His voice still remained steady and calm, and kindness permeated every syllable. She actually felt quite relaxed in his presence; his voice had a kind of lullaby quality without the lilt. His voice was helping her through the anxiety that was trying to rise higher every moment that she was without Sen and without the canvas. It was like his voice was reminding her to Trust. At the same time that his voice was playing on the strings of trust, his words were commanding her to sit up and listen. Grace was trying to read between all the lines and make sense of it all so she could integrate it and be gone from this place. Did she understand him correctly? They strive to create an environment where nobody feels anxious or scared or sad or angry, and in doing so they also work with the environments at home. I mean it sounded crazy and pleasant all at the same time to her, a life without anxiety without her mind taking over her bodily functions. But then she brought her mind back to this place, and how no one smiled, no one talked to each other. She wondered what would be the side effect of taking away all of one's bad feelings.

The man began again, "Okay, to begin with, you cannot walk through our halls wearing what you are wearing. Our dress code for girls is simple, undergarments must be worn at all times, and must not be shown through outer layers of clothes, legs must be covered from the calf up, and no chest can show below the collar bone. Clothes must not be form-fitting against the shape of your body. How you obey these rules is up to you, use your creativity and style. The dress code is put into place to keep our environment safe for everyone." As the man was talking and looking at Grace, she noticed that his voice was wavering just the very slightest of bits from the steady tone he had spoken in when he first entered the room. She looked up and caught his eyes with her bright green eyes. As they caught eyes, Grace felt something like a spark flare or a flicker inside it was definitely something being turned on. She had a quick thought that she might have done something bad. She quickly looked away from the man. She had a sudden impulse to run, but her arms and legs were useless in the chair she was in. Her mind reasoned that even if she could run, they would just find her again and bring her back to this room and things could get worse. Right now they were being kind and understanding. She turned off her questions and sat on her impulses and continued to listen to the man, "While it is a lovely color and looks very comfortable against your skin, it could cause a glitch and we try to keep things on even keel around here, there are enough hormones coursing through everyone as it is and an outfit like yours could set a whole new viral hell storm of negativity loose among our population. It could make a child crazy for something he doesn't know he needs. It could arouse a need that hasn't been met in a very long time." At this Grace looked up suspiciously and saw the man's eyes clearly travel down her body from her eyes to her shoulders to her chest to her waist to her legs and back up again.

Looking at the man now, Grace could see something had changed. He was breathing a little heavier, he was beginning to sweat, his movements weren't fluid, and he was beginning to get up out of his chair. Grace swore that she saw his lip tremble and he tried to bite it back as he got closer to her, he was breathing the air around her into him, taking pieces of her into him then pushing them out just as fast. There was a literal, physical struggle this man was having not two feet away from her. She could see it. He was right in front of her, between her chair and the desk he was just sitting at. He was leaning against the desk, struggling with himself. She could see the struggle. She witnessed the man visibly wipe the beads of sweat gathering on his brow, the space between cried out for her. And here she was stuck, unable to move. Her body's motive for movement had all but gotten lost. The space between Grace and this man grabbed at her neck and spat in her face. She jumped back in her chair, and the man continued to lean against the desk and talk at her. "We're going to have to get you changed into something less distracting before we go to the testing room, we don't want to trigger anyone now do we."

The space between started to howl at her in tongues, and she remembered how to hear it, it howled, "I want to fuck you, You fucking whore of a girl. Take it off, Take it off."

Just as the man was about to lose whatever battle was raging inside of him, he lunged toward her to begin his glitch of a rampage. At that very moment, the possibility of the answer to her question what happens when you take away all the bad emotions came to her. Then she was whisked away. Things began to move. The world began to spin. The floor fell out, the walls flew out in a dance of freedom from the box they were being kept in and before she knew it, the expanse settled in and she was next to Sen again. The canvas was between her hands, and they were staring at one another.

"Did you see any of that?" Grace asked her

"I didn't need to see any of it, I heard it. Something wasn't right, something was unnatural. We need to go back to put all the pieces together. But first, it looks like we need to find our answer to this world. Stay close."

II

In this new place, Sen and Grace found themselves again in the shadows and witness to a new scene in front of them. This time it was a dark and dusky kind of basement vibe that greeted them.

There was the smell of pot everywhere. There were vinyl records strewn across the rug that lay in the center of the space. There were candles and posters and the low lights of a group of people who didn't want to be found. It felt to Grace like a den of best friends where no secrets left the room, and everyone was safe to be a freak for as long as they needed. The judgement here didn't exist. It may have felt that way since she had been inhaling all the second-hand smoke that drifted her way, but nonetheless, it was safe here. It wasn't whitewashed; it wasn't quiet. There was music playing that rambled on in the beautiful tide of a jam band. And there was actual conversation. She took a deep breath, full of gratitude. Oh! There was a conversation! She heard laughter and serious tones and a mix of tone and pitch that was so comforting to her right now. There was a melody and rhythm to the words and thoughts and voiced opinions. Grace immediately picked up on the honesty of the place; she became hungry to hear more. Sen interrupted her reading of the place.

"My kind of tribe," Sen said with a quiet smile. Making reference to all the textures and materials that brought cushioning to the stark reality of a concrete basement floor. Grace smiled quietly at this too, taking in all the thickness around her, and realizing her life was void of this kind of thickness, there was no padding or safety to her childhood, she stripped it all down to get to her own answers. But sometimes you need some cushioning in order to build the courage up to hear your truth, she understood that in this very moment.

Sen put her finger to her lips as she motioned for the two of them to listen in on what was being said.

Grace looked over toward the group of people sitting on a few velvet chairs and on the rug. They had to be seventeen maybe eighteen years old, Grace's age. They were all relatively good looking and had an air of the creative surrounding them. There were instruments among them though none were currently being played. They were all passing a joint around and talking. There was a genuine feeling in the air, the exact thing the Institute was missing. Grace noticed that one of them, a younger girl of the group had very bright blue eyes similar to those of Kai, and she sat with a sketchbook just drawing as she listened and joined in the conversation as she had something to add.

Grace listened in as one of the kids was saying,"I don't know how much longer we're going to be able to get it."

A boy with long blonde hair answered "We'll be able to get it as long as people have any question as to whether what they're doing to all of us is right."

Another girl in the group said, "Yeah! They need to settle their own minds, but they won't take the same shit they give us, they take the all natural stuff, this shit right here!" as she said this she held up the joint that was passed to her.

The first boy spoke again. "But if they find out kids are getting a hold of it, I think they'll stop the production. What would we do then?"

A girl, it seemed the oldest in the group answered "We'd survive like we did before we found it."

The conversation continued

"That sucked dude."

"It sucked but we made it here didn't we? We're almost aged out ... just a few more years before the only one who has a say over ourselves is us."

At this Grace noticed that all of the kids had scars on their hands and their arms. She pointed this out to Sen, and they continued to listen in.

"Calm down; you're ruining my high."

"Now you sound like everyone else outside. I like it rowdy give me some passion any day, anything other than the bullshit everywhere."

"Alright, alright ... I get it."

"I mean really man, I can't take any more of this middle road bullshit. It makes me want to scream. It makes me want to set off a huge trigger to wake everyone up out of it. I should be naked in the streets fucking my way to the truth, waking up everyone with an orgasm. Giving away my Love on the streets like Jimmy Hendrix, waking people up to the Love all over the fucking place!"

"You know that's not how it works. Maybe one day, when we have the numbers."

"It's gotta start somewhere."

"It is. You know we have to wait until everything's in place. We can't do it by ourselves. We have to be patient."

Then the girl with the bright blue eyes looked up from her sketchbook said something. She said it quietly and to her group, but as she said it she looked directly at the shadows that hid Grace and Sen.

"We're not alone. We're not the only ones. You'll see what they're out there doing."

And with that the scene changed again.

III

When all the worlds atoms settled back into their place, Grace and Sen were smashed up against each other in a dirty bathroom stall. There was a conversation going on outside the stall, and they both knew they couldn't move, not even an inch. They needed to breathe as quietly as possible, which was a little hard at the moment because Grace had always had a very strong reaction to pot, even if it was through second-hand smoke. That is, she would laugh uncontrollably at the slightest hint of it and just now, as they landed in the bathroom stall, with Sen pushed up against her in a tiny stall and a canvas between them, the scene was just too much for Grace to handle. It all seemed so ridiculous. It blew up inside her like a huge bubble gum bubble, and it wanted to pop. Everything that had happened in what seemed like a day or two, it was unreal, was it a fucking dream? And now, here. She was trying to contain the sweet pink splatter of ridiculousness from spitting out from between her lips, trying to hold in uncontrollable laughter, and she was ultimately failing at it.

Sen covered Grace's nose and her mouth letting out just the smallest stream of air, and just at the minute she couldn't hold it back anymore, Grace let out a rippling cry of laughter just as a bonafide scream pierced the space and ricocheted off every ceramic tile in the room. The scream bounced into echoes of itself as it rung out in the small bathroom. The scream was primal and enough to pull Grace out of the contact high she'd been sporting since first entering the basement pow wow.

Both Grace and Sen peered out from between the metal frame door of the bathroom stall and saw three young boys; they were thirteen years old at most. They were leaning over a bathroom sink, and one of the boys was holding his hand his head thrown back and his chin jutted forward as he screamed in pain. The other two boys were staying cool and waiting for the first boy to calm down stealing guilty glances at one another as the screaming continued. When the screaming finally stopped, the first boy brought his hand back down to the sink. Grace heard one of the other boys ask, "Can you handle it? Are you ready? Three more times, You can do it."

"No, give me a minute. Just a minute."

All three boys relaxed their stance in a grateful sigh relief and hung their heads as they waited for the first boy to get ready again. They were looking everywhere but at the first boy, obviously feeling shame about what they were doing, but not enough shame to stop. Grace noticed blood dripping onto the tile floor from the boy's hand and turned her head away.

"It's worth it. It's the only way to keep it going."

"I know."

"My brother says that it gets easier the more you do it, and it doesn't take as much pain to bring it back each time."

"That's what my sister says, She says we can use her stuff if we need to, she says it doesn't hurt as much once you get it back, and if we use her stuff, then it becomes easier."

"We should do that. Why aren't we using her stuff now?"

"We can't yet, not until we've all gotten it back, until we recalled it all, then we can use it to stay, awake."

"Okay, I'm ready, let's get it over with, before I pass out."

All three boys leaned back over the sink and then

"Here I go, 1, 2 ..."

Screaming pitched itself forward into the room again. Grace and Sen couldn't see what was happening and what was causing the screaming, but they did see that one boy was holding the first boys hand down into the sink and the other boy was doing something to him. The first boy was not only screaming but his body was convulsing while he stood there making it hard for the boy to hold his hand down in the sink. He was fighting the urge of the first boy to pull his arm away. The first boys head was turned away from the sink, and the one boy yelled, "Look at it happen, watch it! It makes it last longer, gives you more to work with! Don't turn away!"

The boy turned his head toward his hand, and the screaming continued. It lasted for another twenty-five minutes at least as Grace and Sen stood still and quiet in the bathroom stall sweating on top of one another unsure of exactly what was happening.

There was a point in the boy's screaming, where his screams turned into an almost exalted sob. And this sob gave way to maniacal laughter that rounded itself down into a joyful sigh of relief. The boy was folded over practically into the sink in tones of satisfaction with the presence of a long lost friend returned. His voice rang out along the porcelain and ceramic of the bathroom.

Grace and Sen both looked at each other in confusion.

When it all stopped, and the boy was finally quiet, the boys left the bathroom and made a promise to meet there again tonite so the other boy could have it done to him, whatever, 'it' was.

Grace and Sen practically fell out of the stall the minute the boys left, from sheer inability to stand in the same place for any longer. They looked down at the floor and saw a trail of blood from the sink to the door of the bathroom. They walked over to the sink and looked in. What they found were five full fingernails laying on the side of the sink. Each fingernail had been ripped off of the boy's finger in its entirety, in one piece. Grace almost puked. She heaved a bunch of times and then was able to gain control of herself. Sen's eyes began to well up and pour over, but she was careful to keep her tears away from the canvas in her hands. There was no way she would be stranded in a world where thirteen-year-old boys felt they had to do something like this to themselves to survive.

The tile floors fell from beneath their feet, the walls flew up, and the tornado of their seeing took off again.

IV

This time both Grace and Sen had closed their eyes when the scene changed and when they opened them again, they did so tentatively, afraid of the next scene that might be in front of them. When they did open their eyes, they were in a forest, not that different from the forest of the shadow world, but they both knew that they were in their world from the color that shone through the space around them. There was dirt beneath their feet, and they were up close against a tree. They were quiet for a moment, just glad to be away from the bathroom, but also listening to hear what was going on around them. There was no noise, except for the nighttime banter between wildlife.

They looked at each other wondering why they were here. Sen said, "Just wait. It'll present itself to us. Remember stay close."

Grace responded, "I will."

They stayed in their exact places for about ten minutes waiting when all of a sudden they heard fast footsteps coming straight toward them. They could hear the rustling of dried leaves crunching under the feet that seemed intent on running right into Grace and Sen. In a panic, Grace and Sen stepped around the tree behind them to the other side, the footsteps still coming toward them. Then as quickly as they came toward them, they were moving past them and away from them. The quiet settled back down to the forest floor. Not two minutes later there were another set of footsteps running in their direction. Sen motioned to Grace for them both to squat down. It was dark outside, obviously night in this place, so they wouldn't be as easy to spot, but Sen figured if they weren't at eye level, they would have a better chance of remaining unseen, or taken for a nighttime creature. So they both squatted down on the side of the tree the canvas held tightly in Sen's hands.

More footsteps began to run toward them. Someone spoke, "Hey, am I going the right way?"

"Yeah, just follow the sounds of the footsteps."

"Thanks!"

Grace looked at Sen and mouthed the words, 'Meeting in the forest?' Sen shrugged her shoulders unsure of what they would be witness to this time.

More footsteps.

Coming and going.

Coming and going.

Coming and going.

Then more voices, "Hey man! Good to see you!"

"Glad you could make it!"

"It's just over here."

"Don't worry, it's safe, no one else knows about it."

"Right up there you're going to go to the left and then follow the voices."

"So glad you could come!"

"We're doing it."

There were so many footsteps and voices now that carried over from the other place, that Grace had figured this was, some sort of secret gathering. It didn't sound like something that she needed to be afraid of. All the voices she heard were of kids her age and younger. They all seemed happy to be here and to bring others in. It sounded like some of them had been here before and knew what was going on while others seemed to be coming for the first time and had a nervous tone to their voice when they spoke. Then a piece of paper floated down and landed at her feet. It was a flyer; someone must have dropped it. It read "Third Official Meeting of The Children of Heart. Join us to find out how you can feel things again. It's not easy, but it's worth it. Follow the hearts into the forest."

Grace showed the flyer to Sen, and in that moment they made a decision to follow the footsteps to see what it was about. They waited until all was quiet and then walked together in silence in the direction of the gathering. They snaked around a few more trees, and then the forest opened up into a wide circle of generous space filled with young people of all backgrounds, races, shapes, sizes, genders. In the crowd of young people, some were having conversations. Others remained still, waiting and yet others were working the crowd. There was a momentum that was building itself up among the people attending this gathering. Grace and Sen stayed in the background of it all, but they squatted down and watched and listened on the edges of whatever revolution was rising here.

A fair number of the young people seemed to be here for the first time. These first-timers Grace could pick out the first timers from others by their lack of excitement and the fact they weren't worked up about the gathering like the others that were present in the circle. They more meandered from one space to another without much of a thought about it. They seemed to be friendless until Grace would see one of the older more confident looking kids in the group come by and pull him or her into the world that was surrounding them.

Grace was wondering how people knew to come here, how the flyers got around, how they found the people they needed to find when she noticed a girl start to gain attention among the throngs of young people. She stood up, to see who this girl was. As soon as the girl entered the circle, the attention turned to her in waves of acknowledgement. She was not tall. So much so that she needed to stand on a tree stump in order to be seen and heard across the circle. As she stood on the tree stump of a forest life that was cut down too soon, Grace noticed that she was very young. This took Grace a second to register. Grace had assumed someone who would be at the forefront of this revolution would be older, maybe her age if not older than that. This girl looked to be maybe fifteen at the most. She had her hair pulled back into a high ponytail. She was wearing clothes that Grace might wear in her own time. There was nothing futuristic about her. In fact, if anything she reminded Grace of herself when she was just a child. It was how she held her head on her shoulders, and the way her fingers danced with one another while she held her hands together waiting for everyone's attention. There was something like a recognition that presented itself between Grace and this girl It was something familiar, something Grace knew. Then the girl started to speak.

"Welcome!"

Everyone cheered at this.

"I'm so glad everyone could make it tonite. This is our third official meeting! As most of you know already, we've been meeting for some time as a smaller division of our work, but we've decided it's time to bring everyone together. We can do more together than we can separately."

Again, everyone cheered at this.

"For those of you that are new to our meetings, I'm especially thankful that you've decided to join us or at least give us a chance. I know it's amazingly hard to rise up from the fog that's penetrated who we are from the time we can speak if you've made it this far, to this place, here with us... you have the strength to make it into the clearing!"

The crowd roared with this last statement.

"Come! Come into the center of our circle; you can feel all the Love right here!"

Grace noticed that with every roar of the crowd, the people who were new to the meeting, who were walking around somewhat separate from everyone else, who were making their way into the center of the circle, they began to make eye contact. Their lips were beginning to shape themselves into the edges of a smile. It was like the unity of the young people here had an effect on the individuals that came here to be a part of this something.

The girl went on, "Let me quickly tell you about how we started. It was Jonathon and myself, who, years ago woke up by accident. We were home in a daze of nothingness induced by protocols that were supposed to be answers to a fear that wasn't ours. It was a nothingness that we didn't have the chance to reject, a nothingness that stole the childhood out from under us. Our daily life consisted of studying and working and getting good grades, but we had nothing to show for our childhoods, we had no games, no friends, no risks taken, no laughter that ran us over into delirium. Sure, we were free of anger and sadness and jealousy, but we didn't feel any happiness, any joy and most of all we didn't understand what Love was and how it felt. There was a fog that was cast over our lives, and the Love couldn't make its way through. And believe me, the Love is worth going through everything else, you just don't know it yet because it hasn't broken you free."

And with the word Love repeated three times, on the third time, a cheer broke out among the crowd that raised thunder in sky. Grace and Sen looked up to see a cloud break open and shed some moonlight into the center of the circle. It all seemed so destined. Everything in that moment seemed to join together into what can only be called one-ness.

The girl continued, "Love couldn't find its way through that fog. I had Jonathon with me, but we both had no idea what we were missing. We lived in the same house slept in the same room, and I didn't even know who he was. We didn't know our own parents, but we didn't bother to care, we didn't even think about what had happened to them. The questions had been erased from our memory. We were walking around our lives instead of living in them. We were accepting whatever was presented to us by those around us without even a question as to why.

"It wasn't until we were in our bedroom and I was laying down in the bottom of our bunk bed that we were blessed with an awful accident. Jonathon was jumping up onto his bed, and a piece of the railing broke off that he was using as leverage to get up. It was a metal rod, and I don't know if it was fate slicing through the fog once and for all or a beautiful and painful accident that it happened, but Jonathon fell down to the floor holding the broken off metal. As he fell, the metal rod came down on top of my leg, slicing it open to the bone. In the moment that it happened, everything flashed before my eyes. Everything that I had been missing came back at the boiling point of pain. At first, I writhed and screamed, the heat of it burning into me. I released the screams from my body and then what happened was amazing. My heart burst awake all at once. My screams became cries became sighs of Sadness became Pleasure became Laughter became Joy became Love. A warmth settled around my heart like the arms of someone I love. Once it all came back, the questions began. I quickly looked to repeat what I had experienced for my brother, but without the pain, and it didn't work. I tried everything, but that made me no better than the people who have created the fog they call the Middle Road. Through my questions and my experiments, I learned that it's all connected. Pain is the big glitch itself. Pain can be the trigger for the recall. Pain is the doorway back to our hearts. So I forced myself to inflict it on my brother until his heart burst open in the same way as mine. Together we've paved the path back for others, and it is here that we'll take it to the next level. We will change things. We will remind people of all we can be. We'll remember for them what's important and we'll hold their hand as they take the steps to awaken their hearts.

My brother and I were taken away from our parents by the very people that tell us they're trying to protect families and keep them together. We were taken away because my parents questioned the manufactured fear, they spoke out against it, they penetrated the fog before it had its hold on us all. They exposed the protocols for what they really are, human manipulation for power and wealth. They were forced into hiding, their voices too loud against a fading backdrop of revolution. They were charged with crimes of revolt against the heartless regime. No longer could they speak for us. My brother and I were left in the fog, but for some reason, we found the way out on our own."

As Grace was listening she noticed the bright green eyes this young girl looked out from behind.

A smaller group cheered this time.

Everyone broke their listening silence to cheer the girl on further.

"I don't blame any one person for what happened to my brother and me. I don't blame any one person for what has happened to any of us. I don't blame my parents, the doctors, the teachers, the officials. I don't blame any one of them. There's a larger picture at play, and I don't think that the individuals that are painting it have any idea who they're working for or what they're doing. Everyone is reacting to the fear. They're reacting out of misunderstanding and ignorance. They've been so steeped in fear for us and who we'll become, that we've taken away our choice and our free will to live our own lives.

When I received my pain back and my anger back and my sadness back, my happiness back, my joy back ... It all came to me. I also received my capacity for forgiveness back and my depth of empathy back, and you will too. You'll understand the panic that has driven them to alter our emotional fibers and connectivity to others. Our hearts have been turned off, but we will turn them on. We will take back our hearts."

A lone cry out from the back of the circle, "We will man! You'll understand everything they felt, you'll feel it too,"

The girl continued, "You'll also feel the Love. I felt Love for the first time. And while I felt the anger at my loss, the rage, the grief, I also felt the Love multiply within me and search for places to plant the seeds of change for you all. "

"For those of you that are new tonite, these words may be foreign to you but I promise you that if you follow our instructions on how to awaken your hearts again, you'll understand, it will come back."

At this, people in the gathered crowd who were new, began to be pulled into the fold of others with gentle and steady touch and assurances.

"Once you have opened yourself back up, you can keep it open with a daily maintenance. We're working on ways to do this without the pain, and we're finding out that just relating to others stories of pain and heartache, Love and loss, these can keep you awake. Touch of any kind can keep it alive, connection to others and honesty can help you through. We've brought with us pamphlets for the guide to waking up and suggest that you find at least two other people to connect with outside with whom you can begin your awakening. You'll support one another through it. Nobody should do it alone. Once you find your group, please tell someone who is already in maintenance to hold you to task, until you've been awakened it's very easy to fall back into the daily fog."

She continued, "And as promised, my mother is here tonight to inspire us in the ways of revolution and the ways of our hearts. We found her after we woke from the fog and she found us, and now she is our voice, our calling, our answer. She's here to tell us a story to tap into our magic and to give us the courage to survive. Welcome mom, Welcome Grace!"

A wide and pounding applause welcomed a woman about thirty-four years old onto the tree stump. It looked just like Grace only sixteen years older. She had the same voice, the same mannerisms and the same bright green eyes, only her body was bruised and marked, scarred and tired.

Grace, from the Shadow World, fell back into Sen, the weight of her body too much. Sen dropped the canvas and Grace flew into it. It was like falling through a black hole. Grace's stomach lurched as she was spun one way and then another. When she came to, she was back in Sen's space. All she could think about was her daughter, leading a revolution. The heartbreak, the poetic and disturbing way young people pushed themselves to feel again, awakening pain of all feelings. And the prospect of having left two children to fend for themselves, in such a world. What would have made her do such a thing.

Part Six:

Love

Chapter 31

Grace, wasn't sure how she got back to Sen's, it was different from how she traveled to any of the other spaces. It was more violent, more forced. Grace looked around needing to find Sen and needing to process what they had seen, but Sen wasn't there. Had she been left at the gathering? Why had Grace come back without her? She looked around for the canvas and saw that it too was missing. Grace wasn't sure what to do.

She looked at the table in front of her where she had created the collage with Sen and right in front of her was a word from Sen's word jar. The word was Trust. It was a cutout from her tea. She remembered what Sen had said about the magic here and needing to trust it. She let the word sink in and thought about how Sen had been traveling through collages for a long time and was probably all right and would make it back safely. She knew Sen would eventually call to her when she was needed. In the meantime, she looked at the clock and realized that she was sent back here just in time to meet Kai again. But she wasn't sure how she felt about it. Should she tell Kai about all she had seen and learned? She wasn't sure she really understood any of it. She couldn't talk with Kai; he had no voice. What would they do?

But she longed to see him again. She longed to touch him again. Had Sen purposely sent her back to meet with him?

Trust.

Grace stood up from the table and walked out of Sen's space down toward the Room of Lost Things.

Chapter 32

As the hour passed in melodies and chords tied to the Love taking hold inside Kai, The Love glowed more true to its perfect crystal essence. When it was time to find Grace, Kai threw his guitar over his shoulder and walked out toward the Room of Lost Things. He stood in front of the door unsure if Grace would be in there or if she would have stood him up, or maybe he was early. He had no prior need to be in this room and yet now, here he was, for the second time, eager to place himself inside the door once again. The pattern on the outside of the door wasn't one of storm clouds or fear. It was a beautiful portrayal of the lines on a flower's petal. There were veins that extended out from the center of the door in all directions. Kai put his hand out to push the door open. When it opened, he saw Grace standing there. Her back was to him.

He walked up to her. He placed his hand on her shoulder and kissed her neck. Her shoulders rose up to meet his lips as if they knew exactly what he was going to do. She closed her eyes and allowed her breath to fall from her chest to her stomach. She reached up and behind her and grabbed his head turning the side of her face into his. They stood there like that for quite a while just breathing and greeting each other. It was like centuries between them that had been crossed, and they needed to gather the stillness when the movement stopped in order to stay on their feet. Some might say it was an epic Love. Others might question how it could happen so quickly. I'm not sure exactly what kind of Love it was. Destined? Tragically Beautiful? Home?

Chapter 33

As they stood there breathing one another in, standing in the middle of the Room of Lost Things, the lights rose . If either Grace or Kai had looked up at that moment they would have seen a golden America; their breath would have been taken away from the sheer vastness in front of them. Each inch of space out beyond them held the possibility of frontiers to be explored. It was rich with beauty and unmarked lands. But Grace and Kai were both standing there, eyes closed, together, letting themselves sink into one another intentionally. Allowing their weight to shift into the center between them. They were building the trust that lived there. The breezes that swept past them only brought them closer as Grace turned into Kai's chest and Kai held her safe against him. She could feel the movement of his heart, it was right there in the center of his chest, beating strong and steady. She placed her hand right over it, her fingertips tracing around the movements it made. As she did this, she noticed her own heart catching up to his, Her own heart racing to meet his. Her own heart finding his beat inside of her and as it caught the exact rhythm in time to his, she locked in. She felt his strength and his longing for her course through her veins. She felt the pull of her blood to meet his. Everything, became warmer, and right in the center of her belly, a fire was beginning to smolder and snake up her own spine. She latched onto Kai grabbing his arms hard and pulling her face toward his. Her mouth closed in on his. He tasted of raspberries and salted tears and memories of a childhood steeped in adventures. Her tongue was making up for every minute they were away from each other. Her hands were trying desperately to hold on to him and keep him from ever leaving her again.

Kai pulled himself away from Grace, He looked at her, the Love that had sprung up inside of him growing roots with each moment they spent together. He wanted to see her body in front of him. He knelt down in front of Grace and grabbed the fabric that gathered at her thigh, unknotting it with both of his hands. As the fabric hung loose, it slipped from Grace's body to the ground. The room shifted to accommodate the situation, and Grace found that she was leaning against a smooth tree, her weight supported by its trunk. Kai was kneeling in front her. He leaned in and rested his mouth on her belly. It was warm and slightly salty, rising and falling with the gravity of her hunger for him. He wanted to race down her body, he wanted to meet her desires, he wanted to be inside of her, he wanted to consume her in that moment, but he didn't. He simply rested his mouth on her belly and slowly wrapped his arms around her waist, waiting for her agreement to what was to come next.

Grace's skin prickled at his touch, like it was carving a path out of her flesh for him to find the fire brewing inside. Grace was becoming impatient for him; she felt her own body stand a little straighter in an effort to let him know what she wanted. She placed her hands on the top of his shoulders pushing down as her hips lifted to meet him. Kai needed nothing more. His lips shed their gentle demeanor and pushed into her skin; His hands firmly spread her legs which were all too eager to receive him. His tongue and his teeth finding the space between her legs where she melted into him, where the fire inside her poured itself into his mouth, between his lips. As he pushed his tongue into her, he felt himself push up against his pants pleading in persistence to be let out. Grace was up against the tree, head back against its trunk, eyes closed, breathing in short but deep spasms of breath when Kai came up to meet her eyes. Without a word, he spoke to her, he told her. "Grace, take off my clothes, I'm going to make Love to you."

Grace opened her eyes having heard the words he said. But did he actually say them? She looked at him. His mouth closed as he looked at her. But she didn't have time to think about it; her hands were already pulling his shirt off, and unbuttoning his pants, her hands, spurred on by the urgency of her body's need to swallow him up inside of her were grabbing for him.

The room shifted again and this time, Kai, naked in a small dark space with just a strand of light dancing on the ceiling, laid Grace down on a four-poster bed, and she took him into her.

It was a period to their sentence. It was what they would both refer to as Home. It was right. It was Love recognized for the first time by both of them. They rode it out until the Love gathering all it could and placed itself at the foot of their bed waiting to be picked up again. And it was picked up again and again until Kai had left a piece of himself inside Grace, for her to nurture and Love back.

They were silent laying next to one another when Grace said,"I heard you. I heard you talk to me; I heard your voice, I heard you say my name."

Kai smiled. He knew she had heard him. His hand came around to her belly and his fingertips gently ran in circles around her skin.

She continued, "I don't know how or why I heard you, I can only think it's because we're connected somehow."

Kai used his fingertips to trace the word Love into her skin.

Grace felt the letters L O V E burn into her like a warm wax from a candle cooling quickly.

At this, Kai sat up and at the foot of the bed was his guitar leaning against the bedpost. He picked it up and looking at Grace; he began to play the song he had written earlier.

His hair fell over half his face as he leaned into his instrument, his hands finding the words his voice couldn't. The melody poured from him like Grace had poured into Kai. It wasn't sweet; it wasn't light, it wasn't gentle. It was heavy and full of the weight he had carried around all his life. It was purposeful in its journey across strings and lit up pieces of his life as he played. It was haunting, and it spoke of shadows and death. It spoke of ashes that spread across his life in deep-rooted friendships lost. It spoke in sharp edges of his fear of Love and how it might slice him open, bright blood washing from his wrists. And then it spoke of Here. It wasn't sweet. It wasn't light. It wasn't gentle. It was intentionally beautiful in the weight of each note as it rang out in the space between them. It was rippling through water echoing something recognizable. It was the perfect pressure of her lips on his. It was a salty melody of two strangers meeting and falling in Love in an impossible place with impossible tasks ahead of them. It was a question.

When Kai was finished, he laid his guitar back down, and he looked at Grace. She was crying. She was trying to gather herself back up but wasn't able to. Kai brought himself over to her and put her head into his chest. It was right there, at that moment, that she cried... knowing what the future could possibly hold.

Chapter 34

When Grace was finished, she looked up, and there was a pact made between them, a promise, an understanding. Both she and Kai put their attention on their clothes, and before they knew it, they were dressed again, and the room looked more like a boardroom than a bedroom. There was a large circular wooden table that matched the wooden walls of the Room. There were pads of paper and a handful of pens lying on the table, and chairs surrounded it. More than just the two chairs that Grace and Kai needed, which got them both wondering who they were waiting for. It was now bright in the room and Grace and Kai looked at one another taking in all the little nuances of each other's faces. The way Grace's hair had a natural wave to it that accentuated her cheekbones and the way Kai's eyes smiled at her when he was concentrating on her.

Grace and Kai sat down next to each other at the table, and Grace began slowly, "I've been through so much in the last couple of days. I don't even know where to start, but I have a feeling that you need to know what I've learned because I think we both have a part to play in it. I don't know how I feel about what I've seen, but I know that I don't go through it alone."

Kai nodded and continued to listen as Grace explained all about her journey with Sen. She told him about the Magic and the collage, the Institute, the boys in the bathroom, the forest, the girl. She told him about her daughter, the gathering in the forest and seeing herself come out from behind a tree to the raucous cries of revolution. As she spoke of her own daughter, something woke up in Kai; It was a presence of destiny that was, as of yet unnamed by him. For now, he just felt the pull of something foreign. She told him everything, and he just sat there and listened trying to make sense of it all. As Grace went through her day moment by moment, she too, was piecing together the information and trying to sort it out into nuggets of truth that could speak to her and reveal the story that needed to be told here, but it was so much information all at once, that Grace had become overwhelmed by it all.

Kai had been thinking to himself what the connection was between all the other people who were here in this world that were like Grace and Kai. His mind kept going back to something Grace had said that Sen told her. She had told her that there was only ever one of their kind here at a time in the past, but now they were gathering on the shores for something. Kai had seen a few others like himself, though none of them called to him except Grace, and he didn't often see them walking around, he wasn't sure where they were or what they did all day long, he only knew what he did with his work with Hendrix. But he knew there were others, he could sense them. He noticed that they walked a little different, they held purpose in their strides, and they seemed to be putting themselves to a test. He had seen them all going in and out of the Room of Lost Things. Though he hadn't had an urge to go to the room until he met Grace. He had seen a few of his kind go in and come out. He had seen the confident way they walked in and the defeated way they walked out. He had seen them stand in front of the door challenging themselves to go in again. There was something about this room that called to them. Were they all here looking for something, or someone? Did they know what they were seeking in the room? What exactly did they all have in common with one another?"

As he was thinking all of this, without a second thought about it, Grace responded. "You've seen others like us?"

Kai was taken back as Grace responded to his thoughts. Grace looked up at him to see his mouth slightly open, and his eyes narrowed looking at her. He stopped thinking entirely and just took her in. His heartbeat quickened at the possibility that she heard his thoughts, not just in the heat of moments but how Hendrix was able to hear his thoughts. That their connection penetrated past the boundaries of the physical.

Grace looked at him and smiled, "What? I heard you; I think I can hear you now. At least I think that's you, I hear the words in the back of my mind, it's not in the front, and it's not words strewn together, it's more like whole thoughts that come to me at once, and they're attached to a feeling. Like I can sense you're searching for answers and the urgency that your mind is racing with. I don't know. Is this because we're connected now? Can anyone who is part of our tribe, one of our kind, do this or is it because something else is happening between us? All I've wanted since I saw you was to hear you say my name and here you are, saying it in my head."

All Kai could think was, "I Love you."

And he didn't want to think it but it somehow took hold or his mind, and it swirled there for Grace's taking.

She grabbed for it, and she said out loud for the both of them, "I Love you,"

"You know, I can give you a voice here. I know that Hendrix can do it too, but I can give your story a voice. You just need to tell me it."

Kai thought, "I will, but first we need to figure out what is going on and how we fit into everything. We need to put together a timeline and see how the rest of our tribe fits into the world that you saw with Sen."

At that they turned their attention back to figuring it all out.

Kai thought, "Where is Sen now? Maybe she can help us put it all together?"

"She never came back here with me, and neither did the canvas we created, I think she actually sent me back so that I could meet with you in the Room of Lost Things. I think she thinks that we were meant to be here together. She brought us together when she created the collage of the Founder, and even then she winked at me and said I could thank her later. I'm assuming it's because she brought you into the space with me."

The two of them sat there in silence, until Grace broke it. She said, "We need to find others like us, maybe they know about who we are. Maybe if we bring ourselves together, we'll find the answers we're looking for. The only hint Sen has given me is that she's said I am more powerful than I realize and that I'm a storyteller."

Kai thought, "You're powerful, and you're a storyteller. Tell me about your gift, let's put the pieces together ourselves." With that he picked up his guitar and began to play while Grace told her story to Kai.

Grace said, "Okay." And she reluctantly started, making sure not to skip any details. She began the telling of the story of her gifts. "Ever since I was a baby I had a fascination with stories. They calmed me and settled me. I loved fairy tales and short stories, I loved the adventures and the love stories. My parents would read me stories from all over the world. They read to me at the level that I understood them, and I was far ahead of my age. They started with nursery rhymes and fairy tales and progressed to the Grimm's tales and Shakespeare and the Greek myths. By the time I was five, I was reading the stories by myself, though my parents always read to me at bedtime. That's when I would get the most lost in the twisting tales, sure to never fall asleep until the very end. I guess all the stories I listened to when I was young influenced me because my parents used to say that as soon as I began to speak, I began to make up stories of my own. They were simple at first, reflections of the stories that I had been told. But as I got older, the stories that I unfolded and performed for everyone took on a different weight. I was still young, but by five and six I was consuming lore that teenagers would read. And the themes that captured me were ones of Love and War, Power, and Darkness, the stories that weren't afraid to tell the truth behind human behavior. These influenced the words I chose to speak.

I told stories. I would watch everything around me. I watched for details and I would look into people's faces and I would just know the truth of a situation. I would have intimate knowledge of all the angles that made up the present moment for someone. I would sense the past and the future of it too. Then I would look around for parallels of those threads of truth in my childhood and weave it into a story. Sometimes my stories would be about a bird or a cloud I saw in the sky, sometimes it would be about an imaginary character that came to me while I was looking at the ground and saw a crack that looked like it could be someone's home. I would take the truth that I found and give it a home inside a story that wasn't exactly its own. In that way, the person whose truth it was, knew what I was saying, but others listening didn't. When I was younger, my family were the subjects of most of my stories, and as I got older and read more and more complex stories of others, my stories became more global and my parents didn't have answers for the truths that I spun. They could no longer be constant witnesses to the truths I told. I believe my mother fought off depression and my father had anxiety. I don't know. But they stopped listening to my stories. Then there was one story, in particular, I needed them to hear. But they were shut off. I had told too many stories I guess. I hadn't remembered the story I told that brought about my silence, but when I came here, the Room of Lost Things gave it back to me. And I realized that I held the truth inside of me all along. I had just altered the reality of it and spun it into a boring rehearsal of an everyday. One that I would overlook if I ever happened upon it..."

With this, Kai remembered how he first saw Grace, walking up to the room, the storm that formed on the door and then how she entered. He remembered seeing her walk out later that day and how as she walked past him and he had felt her. He had lived inside her, even if just for the few moments she walked by him. He remembered the collusion of feelings. The confusion of it all, the mass of it trying to break free at once and how all of the feelings wanted to find their own path to acceptance. And still, she had walked out with confidence and strength.

"You were there when I walked out of the room for the first time?"

Kai nodded yes. He thought, "I didn't see the memory, I just felt all of the emotions inside of you, I could feel them coursing through me, I can only imagine what would have caused that kind of reaction inside of you."

"But how? How could you feel what I was going through back then? We hadn't yet met."

Kai thought,"That's part of my story and how I came to be here. Just like you're a storyteller, I'm an empath. And we had met. We had looked into each other's eyes."

There definitely was something about their eyes. They both had very bright eyes, filled with color. And when they looked at someone with intent, and with longing, they unlocked something. They cleared a fog.

Grace continued, "Well, the memory was forgotten for so long, I didn't even know I had forgotten it, and yet, it directed my life. It became a character in my own story, only I didn't know it. I tried to tell the story of what happened to me to my family at the time, but they blamed my imagination, and I was told to stop telling lies. I guess the child in me just gave up. I sort of knew then what it felt like to be unheard, like a book on a shelf that's never read. It was easier for me to sit on the shelf and never be picked up rather than open myself up to be read and have someone slam me shut. So I stopped. When I stopped telling my stories, other things started to happen. I actually thought I was going crazy for a really long time until I just gave into it, and that's when I just didn't care anymore."

Kai thought, "What started happening when you stopped telling stories?"

Grace continued, "Well, I started to close my eyes to the truth of others. But it was like the truths still wanted to be seen." Grace stopped for a second, afraid to tell Kai, afraid he would think she was crazy, but he was looking at her with Love in his eyes and with honest intrigue that she forced herself to say it out loud, for the first time in her life.

"The truth still wanted to be told. When I stopped being open to seeing it in others, it started to make itself heard in other ways. I began to be able to taste it and smell and hear it and see it. It started to take shapes in the space between."

At this Kai looked like he wasn't understanding, so Grace continued, trying to explain it better to him.

"See, for me, the space between people and the energy and the world around them is moldable, it's tangible and thick. When a truth wants to be told, well, it kind of uses what I've always called the space between, to find shape and to speak to me. It usually speaks in tongues, but for some reason, I understand exactly what it's saying. Sometimes it takes the shape of a person or a child. Sometimes it takes the shape of a creature or a thing. It usually calls out to me and sometimes it speaks directly to me or sometimes it just repeats the words it needs others to hear so that I can say them. Only throughout my life, I've ignored them. I've heard it, and I've witnessed it. It's been impossible not to. But that's all I've done. I haven't strung anything together; I haven't given most of it a second thought, it just is. It's someone's truth, and they've chosen to ignore it, to crush it, to hide it. And I certainly haven't told any stories."

Kai was listening intently to everything Grace was saying and she saw this. She felt the need to qualify what she said. As she heard her own words, it seemed so selfish. It seemed so mean and wrong, and she wasn't either, she knew this.

She quickly added, "I was stuck on tracks that led me to darker places than even that, I was on the hunt to remember a memory that I hadn't even realized I'd forgotten. I was trying to make sense of a physical reminder of what happened to me and that was slowly choking my sense of right and wrong, and I was trying to find that same feeling outside of me. So instead of telling other people's stories, I was trying to re-live my own vacant and horrible memory and make sense of it so that I could free myself of its grasp. It's all so fucked up. I just got sucked in further, and I was so lost. I don't know what happened; I just found myself stuck bleeding from the wounds of a relationship, unable to tell the truth from the space between and the lies that kept me there. And something about being controlled felt good, I made him feel good and I don't know why, but damn it if there was a part of me that was okay with how I was treated." As she was saying all of this her voice was heightening, and she was losing control of her calm, the anxiety was rising in her. Her fingers began holding onto one another in a panic of pulling, rubbing, scratching each other in her lap. Her cheeks were flushing red and she was having a hard time breathing normally. She was saying this out loud for the first time. She was admitting the abuse that had clung to her past, and her own hand in it. It all had such an effect on her to actually say it. And then to be saying it to someone for whom she was falling in Love.

At the same time as she was saying all of this to Kai, he began to open his heart to her and her experience and all at once he let her in. He broke open for her. Whatever she was saying she needed to say, but she couldn't hold all of it. At once, Kai understood. Grace was a storyteller; she gave away her stories, she wasn't meant to hold them inside. All of her own stories finally wanted to come out at once, but her mouth couldn't move fast enough, and her mind couldn't let go quickly enough. She was beginning to drown under the anxiety of it all rising to above sea level. So, Kai allowed himself to be her vessel. He broke open, and she came rushing in like waters through a broken dam.

There was a flash inside Kai, a recognition of what she was saying in the words that she wasn't using. It was like he was struck in the side of the face by a hardened fist. The pain in all areas of his body that took the rage of others. He started bleeding from his nose, His heart palpitating, his lungs trying to catch some air to breathe as it began collapsing under forced pressure. The tight grip of invisible fingers threw him back from his chair and held him to the ground. His eyes shut tight, his mouth writhing open and shut, his hands manically trying to free his neck.

Grace started screaming, "What's going on! What's happening? Help!"

But when she looked up again, Kai was on his chair, his guitar in his hands, he was playing furiously. He hit the strings with intention, their song roaring out in heated arguments, in "Fuck you's" dripping with the honey of apologies and broken promises.

He played, the oxygen draining from his lungs and the sweet descent of the air finding its way back in. He struck the chords of longing for more and the sound of the word No. As he hit each string and they rang out backwards calling to her childhood in the unison of six notes, she heard the response in each of those six strings, of how good it actually felt at first, how she wanted to help him, how she told him to stop, how she may have wanted more but how she was scared, how he pounded her voice quiet and how blood pooled between her legs. Kai played on through it all. He strummed the monotony of mistakes and his persistent plucking of a discordant melody reached into her and pulled out the very last of it; he had found his way to the drip dropping of wet tears on bathroom floors and the shame that brought her here to this world. Kai was dripping sweat from his forehead, his hands and his back, he was a machine playing it out, not getting caught up in his feelings for Grace, but letting those feelings drive him forward through to the end. He played, at once broken and healed. The song was loud, it was righteous, it was determined, it was full of pain, and it curled up into a ball at Grace's feet when it was done. When Kai was done. When it was over, he laid his guitar down and then his own head in Grace's lap. They both sat there. Free.

He didn't even know he was capable of his own Love. Let alone that he could Love someone this much.

Chapter 35

When Kai came to, his head was still in Grace's lap, and she was stroking his hair. He was tired and he remembered everything. He stayed still for a moment and gave his brain a chance to connect the feelings with the thoughts; then he looked up at Grace. Tears had dried on her cheeks and her eyes were open, red and swollen from the release, but there was a smile on her face. She said, "I Love you." Then she added, "Do you know that you're an amazing musician. How did you do that? You took everything I was feeling, not even knowing the details and you turned it into sounds that played through me and took all of the shit out with it."

Kai was too tired to think; he was working just to keep his eyes and his mind open.

He sat up and all he thought was this, "So, you're a story-teller." And he smiled with huge grin widening his tired face.

Grace laughed. "I guess I am. But I'm a little rusty at it. It's been a long while since I actually told anyone a story of any substance."

Kai thought, "I think it's time you start telling stories again."

Grace said to Kai, "Actually, I think it's time I tell your story.

We have to find out the places where we intersect. There has to be common ground in our stories and I know that I can find it and make sense of it. It'll speak to me, I think. I know you're tired and quite honestly I'm not even sure how you did what you just did or what you even did. But we need to keep going. Would it be okay if I tried to do something? You inspired me. You don't have to do a thing, just close your eyes and rest; I want to see if I can open a window into your life so I can see where our lives collide."

Kai squeezed her hand, and he closed his eyes and fell gently back to sleep.

Grace got to work. She didn't need any art materials or a guitar. She didn't need candles or incense or cards or tea leaves. She was in a world of magic, and she was a storyteller. Kai was right. She just needed to set the story in motion and then follow its lead; she just hoped it would lead her to Kai's past so that she could piece this entire journey together.

She started with speaking out loud. She hoped this would work. She was going on a random idea that came to her when Kai reminded her of what she was, A Storyteller. She focused all her intention and attention on the words as she spoke them. She could feel the heat rising from her belly to her third eye and it began to swirl with the search for truth. She began.

"Once upon a time there was a girl. Her name was Grace. She became lost in a world full of struggle and survival. The struggle to fit in, the struggle to please, the struggle to be heard, the struggle to understand and the struggle to give voice to a darkness that got buried in between her thighs. It burned there like two handprints pinning her to the place where it all began, only she had become estranged from the memory and it cast itself into the crevices of who she was. It was lying in wait for a time when she would find it again. It was waiting for her to grow into the scars that it left. As a little girl she ran away from the monster, and she didn't scream when she ran because she heard that little girls who tell on the grown-ups get their voices taken away. She figured it was better to take her own voice anyway, that way she could keep it in her pocket in case she ever needed it. She got along just fine without it for twelve years. Each year the memory of it all burrowed deeper inside the scar tissue. Of course she would put her voice back in once in a while just to keep the boredom at bay, but for the most part, she let her body do the work her voice ought to be doing. Her body worked hard for her too. It had a lot of catching up to do if it was going to turn around and face the monster she left behind eventually. She had to grow into the scars, harden her skin; she had to plaster all the holes where she was falling part under the loss of it all. She had to drown herself in hatred so she could come up for air and remember. And that's just what she did. And when she came up for the bright gulp of beautiful air, she found herself on the shores of another world. She was staring at herself. She was watching her sanity split in two until right before her eyes, and she gave herself over to it all. It was in this world that she had finally done enough work to turn back and face everything. And she did. She did it with the help of a boy. A boy whose name was Kai. Kai had beautiful bright blue eyes and a heart that could jumpstart just about anything his eyes could touch. It all started when ... "

At this last sentence, the world before grace began to change. She had hit the part of the story that needed to tell itself if it was to be heard. And it wanted to be heard. She heard its excitement in the creaks and the splits that made way for her. Grace stayed as silent as humanly possible as Kai's world unfolded before her. It was like a time-lapse movie rewinding itself for a private viewing and when it got to the beginning, the story started.

Grace looked around. She was in a kitchen, it was all wood and yellows and browns, and Formica counter tops and cabinets. The lights were on, and there was something cooking in a big pot on the stove. It smelled wonderful. There was a lot of noise in the background, loud voices and the movement of feet on a hardwood floor. Here in the kitchen though, there was silence, except for a tiny "shhhh" that came from beneath the kitchen table. It was a little boy hiding. A little boy with bright blue eyes and shoulder length hair. He held his knees up against his chest and hid his head in between them. Grace just sat back and watched as she heard him talking to himself. He was saying things that made no sense for a little boy to be saying.

In the room next to the kitchen Grace could overhear an argument. It was between a man and a woman, there were raised voices and sharp words being hurled. Grace could feel the tension of it being sucked into Kai's little body under the table. And yet, Little Kai said nothing. He lifted his head for a second and Grace could see in his eyes a growing hatred and a pregnant sadness crying out for a friend. It was in his eyes. She saw it all in his eyes, the bright blue reflection of the argument in the next room. She immediately understood. The word empath rolled around in her mind trying to find its way to the center. At the exact moment of her understanding, the space between she and Kai gasped for breath, taking the opportunity to be heard. It was a looming solid form in the image of Kai as he is in the present. He had a voice, and he said, "It's all too much. Make it stop. I'm the reason they hate each other."

As fast as the scene unfolded, another one laid itself out before her. This time Kai was a little older outside playing ball with two older boys. Grace assumed they were brothers from the similarity of their features. One of the older boys was throwing the ball to Kai and Kai was mid-air catching it. He tossed it back to the other boy with a smile on his face and as the boy dove to catch the ball he landed in a bush. The fall into the bush was brutal and painful. Grace turned to look at Kai as she heard the other boy yelling for help and screaming in pain. Kai was doubled over, one hand holding his ribs the other raised in a fist pounding on his own temple over and over again.

As the scene changed to the kitchen; Kai was sitting down with his mother, she was talking to him about his grades, she seemed concerned about his performance in school. She was saying, "If you don't bring up your grades, what will be left for you in this world. Look at your brothers, look at how well they've done, because they made good grades and went to college. I hear you aren't even in class half the time, how am I supposed to answer to the school, when I have no clue where you are either? What is going on?" She said this with not so much passion as with routine.

Kai didn't respond at first but then he opened his mouth and the space between dragged his head to turn toward Grace in slow motion, and it said through his open mouth, "I can't be in school, there's too much there. I will die."

The scene changed to a classroom in the local school. Kai was missing, he wasn't there, but Grace was sitting in his seat. She was part of this memory. The teacher called on Kai and looked straight at her. She didn't understand at first, but then realized as everyone laughed and pointed in her direction, that she had become his stand-in. As the attention in the class turned back from her, she sat in her body in the seat. She just sat with her body in the seat at the desk in front of her. She was paying attention to everything that she was feeling and it still crept up on her. It crept up on her so slowly that at first it was just a twinge and tingle and questionable thought that passed across her head, And then it was just a feeling of her body being uncomfortable, a silent reminder between her legs of last night, then a passing remembrance of something sad. Before she knew it, she was being pulled in twenty-three directions at once by twenty-three different people having twenty-three unique experiences in their body and she was picking up on at least one of them in every person in that classroom. Her heart was pounding with anxiety for the boy two seats in front of her to look back. There was an ache in her bones craving the next possible high, jumping her knees in uncontrollable anticipation. There was the tears streaming down her face from the heartbreak of a first Love. The anger pressing up against her chest at nothing in particular. The shame clamped along her backbone of being someone on the outside that she isn't on the inside. The feelings and emotions kept piling up until Grace stood up from her seat and ran out, almost crashing into the wall on her way from the delirium of hunger starving itself in one girl sitting in the front row.

"Holy shit!"

It was all Grace could say as the scene changed yet again. She was under the bleachers outside, where Kai was quietly breathing, hiding.

She was watching television sitting on a couch next to Kai. He was staring at the news. There was story about the women of Iraq and the laws that bind them to their men. Grace knew what to do in order to understand. Though she was so afraid to actually do it, she did it anyway. She grabbed his hand, and with that, her gut dropped from her body, replaced by what can only be called absolute fear. She went numb and limp but just before the pain of persecution called her name, everything shifted inside of her. The righteous pride of a man's fury stampeded its way through all the pieces of her pleading for mercy. Its round belly full of fire scorched her and Grace passed out from all of it. She woke up on the floor of Kai's bedroom and looked down to see the river of blood flowing from her forearms, the quick strokes of scar tissue that had been called on again. And then the sound of a young Kai playing the guitar over her, coaxing her back into her own whole and healed body. The space between them forming syllables of language. It sang to her, "You need to find something to quiet the beast. You need to find a way to give it all its own voice. Once people hear it, they can change it."

And with that Grace was back where she had begun. Kai was sleeping in the chair next to her. His eyes closed his breath deep and relaxed. Grace looked at him with utter reverence for who he was and what he had done. How could he possibly have ever held all that inside of him? How could he ever know what he, himself was feeling? How could she not have seen this in the depth of his eyes when she first looked into them? Or did she see it?

Looking at Kai, having lived his story, if only for a few minutes, had brought her clarity. It had lit up the intersection where their lives crossed. She understood. They were both truth-sayers, they were both conduits of the heart. They both were in service to others, only she had the words, and he had the sounds. She was made up of pieces of him from the very beginning. Without sounds, words would not exist, and so he was the beginning, and she was the end. She watched it all fall silently down around her with tired eyes as it played out in the space between.

Grace didn't wake Kai up. She let him sleep; he had given her the gift of freedom from her past. She pulled her chair up next to his and laid her own head in his lap. As she did this, she noticed that the markings that Hendrix had on his forearms of the river rushing were manifesting on Kai's forearms as she watched, only it was just a gentle movement under his skin, not as pronounced as the markings on Hendrix. It was like a small reminder of who he is, and what it took for him to get here. She closed her eyes and together they slept.

Part Seven:

Change

Chapter 36

It was a few hours later when both Kai and Grace were woken up to the murmuring sound of others. But it was a gentle touch of Sen's hand on Grace's back that brought her to the present. Both she and Kai sat up. They were surrounded by about twenty people including Sen. "Thank goodness!" Grace thought as she saw Sen back in this world, safe. She wanted to go to Sen right then and there and tell her about her travels, because she had learned something new and she had put something together that Sen needed to hear. But right now wasn't the time.

Sen asked everyone to take a seat at the table which seemed to grow to the size it needed to fit everyone perfectly around its circumference. Grace looked around the circle and noticed that everyone seated at the table had bright eyes like hers and Kai's. She noticed that everyone seemed alert and awake. Though it didn't seem as though anyone knew each other. Everyone was about the age of eighteen, and they all looked very average except for their eyes. There was nothing special about anyone except that they all had some kind of marking that looked like it was pulsing under their skin. It was akin to the spiral swirling on Grace's third eye and the river rushing on Kai's forearm. One woman had little star-like freckles all across the bridge of her nose that were twinkling like light playing across a mirror. Another man had horizontal parallel raised scars all along his fingers that raced from side to side while Grace watched. Another man, whose chosen outfit was more than a little dramatic, had neatly sewn stitches right at the spine of his mid-back that looked like they were struggling to hold something inside.

Both Grace and Kai sat as part of this larger unique group of people for whom they immediately felt a small affinity toward, if only because the marks they had on themselves had begun to pulse and move in rhythm with everyone else in the room.

Sen, lifting her arms and bringing them down hard on the table in front of her, began.

"I've learned a lot. I've called you here so that we can make change happen. Grace and I have been traveling to realms of your world in order to make sense of all the changes going on here, in this world, right now. We thought there might be a reason why there were so many of you gathering at the same time here, and we were right. As you all know, there have only ever been one of your kind at a time here in this world. This is significant. The reason for its significance is the power that rests in each of you." At this Sen raised her arm and almost as if she had a crystal ball in her hand she brought her arm overhead and back down to her side in a sweeping motion the shape of a rainbow above her. As her hand came to her side, a flurry of cards rained down on the table all resting neatly in two spreads of ten cards each. The two spreads were separated but connected by the space between that Grace could see was holding on tightly. Each card had a different depiction on it. These were tarot cards, but they weren't the typical swords, cups, pentacles, and rods of a tarot deck. These cards were the Major Arcana, telling a tale of epic proportions using the ancient archetypes called forth in all mythology and religions and handed down stories. Grace was drawn to the spreads immediately. She didn't know what any of it meant, but for some reason, as the cards were laid out on the table in front of her, she could read their story. And her temperature began to rise with a new level of understanding.

Sen began again, "There are twenty of you in total here around the table. On the table's surface, there are twenty-one cards. There are ten men and ten women in this room, and the cards have separated into two distinct yet smaller spreads of ten cards within the larger spread. They are all connected by this card." Sen pointed to the card labelled The Wheel of Fortune. It had a picture of a large Ferris wheel with bodies in all sorts of contortions hanging from it.

"These cards represent your path. The Major Arcana take the reader on a journey through a lifetime, or in this case through a revolution. It starts here with the fool." Sen pointed to a card with a picture of a man stepping off a cliff, a dog at his heels and wings at his back. He was carrying a guitar. Below him lay the rough waters of an ocean calling for his demise. Sen continued, "It then travels through the path to the very last card here." Sen pointed to the card labeled Judgement, where a woman with bright green eyes and a swirling spiral on her third eye overlooked a community of people, Her arms were open as was her mouth as she looked as if she were about to speak. Looking at this card Grace couldn't believe the resemblance she had to the woman in the card. She looked from the card to Sen and then back to the card. Sen just held her finger up, as if she was telling Grace to hang on , she was getting to it.

Sen began again, "Each of these cards represents one of you here at this table. It begins with Kai, and it ends with Grace. There is one card from the Major Arcana missing, and I can only assume it's because he or she hasn't been born yet." With this Sen looked at Grace, And between the two of them there was an understanding of the role that her future daughter would play.

Sen continued, "The last person is represented by the World. This card is the end of one journey and the beginning of another. It can represent unity and peace, but it can also represent the failure and restriction of a world that hasn't stepped up to the challenges that it faces."

"Listen to me now; you are more than merely these cards. These cards are only here to show you the path, the destiny that you, as a people, need to work toward. I threw these cards years ago and have awaited your arrival. I have continued to throw them out in the same patterns the same spreads with the same outcomes over and over again through the years. Then you started to arrive on the shores, and I counted you one by one. You started to arrive last week. And now there are twenty of you, and each of you has an element of the card you represent. There is a revolution that needs to happen in your world, and you need to understand it here and gather your resources in order to set it into motion. Grace and I have seen a future that holds a void of the heart. Its adults act out of fear for their children. Afraid to let them feel anything. They give them drugs to tame the flames of anger, anxiety, frustration, instead of giving them ways to express it and understand it. They teach them how to train their brains to not feel through rote repetition that numbs their minds and slowly etches scar tissue around their hearts. They do this because they, themselves, are uncomfortable with the vocabulary of the heart. The adults of this future are the children right now.

What Grace and I witnessed is just one generation away. They are the children who, right now, are being labeled with disease in order to catalog the creative, the emotional, the quirky. They are being identified and dosed and quieted. They are being judged and marginalized because of their ability to dress themselves on the outside with what they feel on the inside. It's a trait they all have and it is a gift. The children living right now are an answer to the peace everyone has been calling for. They are the children who know Love. Only the powers of the world right now don't see it this way. They see these children as threats to their hold on humanity, and so protocols have been put in place, by schools, governments and the medical field to monitor and maintain a level of fear that keeps people running to them, trusting them and ultimately putting the lives of their own children in their hands. These children don't have a choice, and for most of them, they have been numbed and placed on medications, and they're being watched, so they stay that way. The parents will lose their choice as this movement goes forward, children will be taken away from those that don't follow the protocols. As these children get older, they will become the adults, they will have lost the Love and have forgotten its calling. They will do the same to their children and ultimately we'll all live in a world where thirteen-year-old kids rip off their own fingernails one by one just to feel something that they know should be there, but isn't. They will try to kickstart a fire in their hearts by raising the pain they feel to the highest of levels.

For the families who have refused to buy into all of it, and there are a few, they have hidden in the mass of the mainstream, pretending to buy it all but secretly they teach their children how to survive, all the while tending to their children's creative quests. These families will join the revolt in years to come; they are your allies. They will risk their lives for their children and they know the heart in all its intimacy."

With this Sen took a sip of water that appeared in front of her. One of the others at the table asked, "But why are we here, why couldn't we meet in the other world and what do we have to do with all of this?"

Sen replied, "That's a good question, you're here because it's safe for you here. You're meeting here because this is a world made up of emotions, the whole purpose of this wold is to Uncover the essence of all the emotions that got tangled up in childhood. You are here to learn the ways of Uncovering. To watch closely as the shadow selves go about their work. It's true that the magic doesn't exist in the same way in your world, but the process of releasing emotions is very similar. You need to translate the process into the work that's done in your world. While you're here, you need to get to know the essence of each emotion intimately, watch the process that Uncovers them, understand the language of each emotion and what it needs to be freed and bring this information back to your world. From there, you will disseminate the information in your own unique way.

You all come from different corners of your world, and together you'll knit the message across oceans and skies. Here you must learn how to speak the same language with the same accents so that it connects in your world. You are here to learn together and to help one another to understand.

When your time here is up each of you will go back to your homes in your own world and start your work. You'll each use your own unique gifts to start the change, to awaken both the adults and children of the world before it becomes too late and revolution certain."

"I must warn you though." And at this Sen looked from Grace to Kai and back to Grace and mouthed the word, 'I'm so sorry' and then began addressing the whole of the room "The last thing I learned when I was in the other world gathering information, is that any of you who are in this room, if you are to meet up again in your world, you need to stay away from one another. You cannot risk an unbalance. I know that there are only twenty of you and it should be easy to avoid one another, especially as you'll have no remembrance of this world. You'll only have the instructions you need to do your work. But should you run into one another in your world and should a spark fly, should a fire ignite a memory or a touch open the door to where you once were, the plates on which you reside on the earth in your world will shift and resonate calling for this world. That shift will bring our two worlds together. This world and that world would collide, giving birth to chaos. So please when you design your personal instructions for going back to your world, please make sure you design a mechanism for detection of others of your kind and a way to dampen any sparks that might fly."

Sen gave a sad smile toward Grace, a tear starting to well in her right eye. Grace was stunned with the information she was just given, unable to process anything further.

"Any questions? If not, I have a few shadow selves that are going to take you all on a tour of our hidden spaces. This is where the darkest of dark emotions are Uncovered. It's important for you all to see this process. It can be disturbing to see, but please remember, you're in a world where there is no judgement on what we feel, and anything is done to Uncover emotions. These are the emotions that started out small and trivial and then grew into powerful entities from lack of acceptance or refusal to admit; sometimes it grows from pure curiosity as to why it can't be tapped into in your world."

A girl with gemstones growing from her earlobes like a trailing ivy raised her hand and Sen said, "Yes Summer?"

"I understand that we won't remember this world once we go back, but when you speak of designing our instructions. What does that mean?"

"You will know when it's time to go back to your world. When the impulse to leave starts to happen, you'll gather all the information that you learned, and you place it deep in your subconscious. You'll know exactly how to do it when the time comes. When you do this, you'll be able to place markers on the important things to remember; you'll choose what these are and which information will be most useful to you according to the job you have in your world. And from there you'll be sent back."

Sen continued, "Each of you is unique. You are all connected. You weren't born this way. You weren't born connected. You weren't born special. You were born like very other child in your world with a gift that you chose to enhance. What connects you is how you have, as children, harnessed the natural gifts that were given to you. In that process, most of you lost your families, they gave up on you, they moved on without you, but you became part of a larger family of your own kind. As you embraced your very gifts, your hearts called out to others of the same. Your hearts have literally beat for one another. They have literally inched forward in your body to call out to each other. You all are amazing and ordinary at the same time. Your superpowers are self-made. And you have born your own family. Because of this, you will always have a call out to one another; this is where you must design a mechanism of detection, a way to forget your time here." Everyone looked across the table at one another, witness to each other. They all listened intently to each word Sen said.

"Each of you has a unique self-made superpower. Kai, you're an empath with the ability to play the essence of other's feelings into the space so they can experience them with senses other than those that reside inside of themselves. Summer, you can hear the whisperings of desire and internal conflict, and you can whisper it back into people. Drayden, you can heal with your hands, you can recall memories with just a touch. Forrester, you can see the angels and the ancestry back through time. You can recall faith in people. Margaret, you can see in angles and degrees and cornerstones and chart out bigger pictures for those to witness. Grace you are a story-teller, you can affect millions at a time with your words. You all have your gifts. Find a way to communicate in the other world without tipping off the memory of here."

"Grace, do you have anything to add?"

But she was dumbfounded. She was shocked; she was frozen in a grief that hadn't made its way to her heart quite yet. She thought of her daughter, she thought of Kai, and of a lifetime without him.

Grace forced herself to speak, giving the information that she learned to everyone at the table. "I learned that the answer is in giving people back their voice. However we each do that, our job is to help people remember. We can speak for their hearts, remind them what's really important. We all are conduits of the heart, capable of tapping into the feelings of others and translating it back to them in ways that they can hear it and understand it. We will all do it in our own way with our own gifts. I've learned that we need to use our gifts for others actively or else it drowns us. The more we tap into others the more we can translate, the more change we effect. I've learned how important our shadow selves are and how integral our pain and all of our emotions are to our well being, not just the emotions that feel good. I've learned that it's not easy to be human and that it's okay, that we're okay and we always will be okay if we're honest with ourselves." With this Grace began to cry, loud sobs that deep breaths that got caught in the air around her. The rest of the people in the room got out of their chairs; Kai included and surrounded Grace in a kinship and solidarity that lifted her up. This solidarity, placed her at the head of a revolution to come. As it did, the room transformed and the table was no longer a circle. It was a rectangle with two chairs at the head. One, a red velvet throne made from the trees of the ancient forest, held up Grace and another held up Kai. Everyone found themselves sitting in a chair around the aged wooden table. Kai took Grace's hand as her place among this new family was staked. Her weight growing down into the red velvet of a timeless story waiting to be told. Grace allowed herself a minute there, an impossible minute filled with hope and wonder and magic and Love before it all faded with what lay ahead of them. She gathered all the power she could from the throne beneath her and then she stood. One by one, everyone stood up with her, a new sense of purpose, no more words needing to be said between them.

Sen spoke one last time, "It's important for you all to understand the different ways that emotions speak through people and the ways that feelings try to get our attention. It's also important for you to pick up on how they retreat and react so that you can see this in your world and help before they get submerged. You all have had time to live in this world and learn from it. Now, you need to integrate what you've learned. You will all use your powers on levels that reach far beyond the individual. It'll take shape as you return to your world with the knowledge and urgency you imprint before you leave here. Follow the shadow selves into the hidden spaces and allow yourselves to let go of judgement. It won't help you here or in your world as you move forward. You need to cleanse yourself of good and bad, right and wrong, black and white. You need to find the grey in between. Use this as a chance to let go of any judgement that you hold once and for all. Good luck on your journey."

With that, they all left. Sen stayed behind and solemnly looked at the cards on front of her on the table. Grace had stayed behind as well. She didn't have the motive to leave just yet. She approached Sen.

"So, I won't see Kai anymore once I go back to my world?"

Sen replied, "No."

"I can read the story of your cards. It's plain as day to me. Kai is the beginning, and I am the end, and our daughter will be the new beginning. I can see the division of genders, the call back to the womb. This journey is anything but simple. It's crossed by karma and cycles that have circled around one another for decades now. It's built up, and it needs to get worse before it gets better."

"Yes, but you can put a stop to it now. Your kind can influence destiny. You can make the change. Just remember what you learned here, how we made magic. How you let go of your mind. This will help you to be a conduit. I have to go, and you need to see the hidden space. You will do it. You will be the leader we all need."

With that, Sen disappeared. Almost like she was never really there. Grace ran off to catch up with the rest of her kin.

Chapter 37

As Grace had walked out of the room to find the Hidden spaces, she was floored by what Sen had said about seeing Kai in their world. Sen, of all people, had pushed her toward Kai. She had made it happen. She had brought them together. And now she was telling Grace she could no longer be with him. That she had to forget him.

She found everyone in a large room next to the Room of Lost Things. She had never seen it before, though its door was directly next to that of the Room of Lost Things. The room was sectioned off by large glass walls. The shadow self who was guiding them started to speak.

"This is where we work on the large and powerful emotions that can bring people down with them. They are kept away from the others so that they don't infect the other emotions. They're that powerful. They've been given this power by those they live inside of. They often grow wild and out of control and are extremely hard to Uncover. It takes measures beyond what we are capable of in The Hall. Often we give into the needs and allow them to play out so they can unwind back to their essence, But this doesn't always work. Try to allow yourself to see these, not as perverted, wrong or bad, but as emotions that have been hurt and are in need. They're just feelings that have gotten out of balance and have taken everything to its farthest edge. This is your chance to witness an emotion Uncover itself to its truest potential. I'm bringing you to one of the hardest emotions we've had to Uncover this last week. But we believe that we know what to do with it finally. We've just been waiting for you to come so that you can witness the magic."

The shadow self led them to one space, surrounded by glass.

He continued, "This emotion was originally Love. Somehow it became twisted up with hurt, rage, and jealousy. As it got twisted up, the essence of Love was choked out."

Everyone looked in the glass space. There was a tangle of three colors, green, yellow and blue. All the colors swirled and meshed together in a form that was not unlike a child crouched over his own knees. There was a rumbling sound echoing from the space. And the boy seemed to be shaking uncontrollably. All Grace could think of was an earthquake. It sounded like the rumble of an earthquake to her. While they were watching the shape of the boy, his shake became more violent until, BOOM, he blew up into an explosion of green, yellow and blue ashes that landed in pieces all over the floor.

"This emotion does this at least once an hour; we're trying to time it so that no one's in there when he blows up. The ashes that come out of him are toxic and have caused three shadow selves to take time off to heal. This emotion, in particular, has been growing stronger and stronger inside of this boy. In fact, the moment that led him here was one that would take out many other people with him. Thank goodness we caught him before it happened."

Everyone watched this emotion, trying to tame their judgement. It wasn't hard. The emotion had taken such a shape that it was like watching a little boy wither under the weight of the world.

Grace wondered to herself why people in her world couldn't see it. Kai came up behind her, and he thought the same thing. He silently took her hand, and they listened, understanding how emotions are the fibers of their world. Emotions and feelings drive everything.

"So, I think we're ready to try the next phase of Uncovering for him, especially since it'll be a while before it blows up again. We're trying to tease out the anger to release it so that the Love can come back. So we're using a method that some of you will not agree with, and that'll be hard to watch, but we need to Uncover this emotion, and quickly."

The shadow self pushed a few buttons and said something into a microphone on the outside of the space. In no time, the lights within the space went dim, and the walls lit up with images and videos. Every image and video was a gruesome depiction of death and dying. Nothing was pretty or poetic or mechanical about it. Every depiction had fierce emotion tied to it. As the images played the sounds of death and dying boomed in the space.

Everything from war to shootings to illness and back again. The green yellow and blue ashes gathered in the center of the room. At first, the mixture of the colors created a lime green, but then the shade darkened to a brown and then a red. The shape that the emotion took was a grown man, seven feet tall at least. There was a sense that he was hyperventilating in the space from the heaving of his chest.

Grace yelled "Stop it!"

The shadow self hit a few more buttons, and suddenly every image and video and depiction ran backwards. Every death had life. Every dying person had youth. Every sick person had health and a family that Loved him. The emotion sank down as the videos played right back to the very beginning. The emotion sank down into a red brown puddle on the floor. The shadow self said, "It's my time. I'm about to go in and Uncover the Love that was lost."

The shadow self opened the glass door and walked in, unafraid. He knelt down, picked up the puddle, which had the consistency of slime. He sat in a chair in the corner and he held it, he rocked it. As he held it, the color shifted from red to brown to blue to yellow back to green. After a while, the puddle became a solid beautiful green crystal disc."

Everyone watching this was amazed at the transformation and to see what became of the boy that originally held the space. When the shadow self was done, he came out of the room with the green disc. He said, "It's taken some time for us to realize what this emotion needed. It needed to be reminded that every end scene has a beginning. When that was recognized, it needed to be held. Don't we all though?"

With that everyone left the hidden spaces. They all left with a renewed understanding of emotions and how they become weighted, tangled, lost, wild. They all left with more questions than they came with, but judgement wasn't part of the equation. And that was the purpose. Everyone found their way back to their own shadow self and dove into their own emotions to learn more.

Chapter 38

Goodbye. Goodbye, it's one word, sometimes it's two depending on who's writing it. Sometimes it's hyphenated. Good-bye. It's complicated; it's hard. Sometimes it's final, sometimes not. It's different for everyone.

Change. The word is simple, succinct, understandable. No question as to how it's spelled. But change is just as hard, if not harder than goodbye. Most often they work together, in tandem. A goodbye will bring about change.

The time had come for both. Grace and Kai drifted along the aisle, hand in hand, back out the double doors that lead to the path into the forest. And the other's drifted back to their spaces. Grace and Kai spent a long time in silence, not even thinking, just staying present with one another.

Their goodbye would be the hardest.

As Love had finally sparked for them both, as Love had finally rooted in both of them, they needed to move on. They needed to give in to the forgetting.

Grace thought, "I don't have to program a way to forget you if we meet in our world."

Kai answered in thought, "You wouldn't risk that, and neither would I."

They held each other. They kissed. They breathed as one.

They stayed there until at once, they both felt an urge to walk toward the willow tree in the center of the forest. They got up and walked there together. The space between them pregnant with a future's hope, but heavy with loss that weighted every footstep on their path.

Chapter 39

When they arrived at the willow tree, they found eighteen of their kin, all called there as well. But no one could decide who had called them all there.

It wasn't until Kai has read Grace's heart that he realized she had called them all. She was tired of goodbye and wanted to move on from it. Kai had felt the exhaustion, the limp presence of purpose that was hanging on to its last thread. He realized that if she didn't do this now, a goodbye would never happen.

Grace had the impulse to speak, and so she started, placing herself at the forefront of the revolution. She spoke "We all have to do our parts in our world. We can't find each other, but somehow we need to work with one another to create the change that needs to happen, and it certainly needs to happen from everything that I've seen. Sen's urgency is right on target. In our world, they're going to make enemies of our emotions, and today we've seen that emotions are our lifeblood as humans. We can eat healthily we can exercise we can ace our tests, but what do we have if we don't feel anything about it all. There are factions of people who will rise up, who will call to us and their neighbors, we need to tap into them, we need to travel the margins and make them heard somehow. I suggest everyone get a really good handle on what your gift is and to know for certain how to tap into its magic here in this world. My gift is storytelling and I've learned how to tap into the magic of it, I can tell a story to show the truth, I can also tell a story from someone's past by speaking it out loud. I don't know how this will play out in our world, but from what Sen says, we don't need to know that right now."

Grace went on, "I imagine that how we tap into our own magic is the same. I've learned that it's about quieting our mind and trusting our body. If we can all find ways to do this everyday back in our world, it will create the synchronicity we need to start the changes. We'll work together, though we may not know it in our world. Remember to program a detection mechanism for recognition among us into your instructions. I wish we had more time here, but I can feel it waning even I stand here. Go back to your space, and take in everything you can before we must leave. I'll see you all on the other side, and though you may not know it, you will all hold a place of gratitude in my heart."

Instinctively Grace put her hand on her heart, Everyone else in the willow tree did as well. As they all did this something sparked. Something lit up, and they were all thrown backward. In a moment of unity, they were given the truths of each other. Grace and Kai now understood all the stories in the space. In that moment as the truths sprung free, Grace and Kai and everyone else there, knew instinctively that it was time.

Everyone dispersed to their spaces to gather their instructions

Grace found Anika and together they filled her alterheart with crystalline discs of bright hues and new beginnings. Anika said, "Your emotions were easy to Uncover, I assume it's because of Kai, He did something to you, he cleared you practically by himself."

Grace lowered her head. Anika could tell she needed silence. Grace had an urge to find Kai in her instructions, but she knew that it could be catastrophic for not only her but others in her world. Kai was right; she wouldn't risk it.

She closed her eyes visualizing everything she needed to remember. She placed it all in the swirling energy of her third eye. Everything else, she discarded among random thoughts. She opened her eyes and in front of her was Kai's face, like it refused to leave her. It looked like it was made up of the particles and molecules of the beginnings of Love. His eyes reflecting the beauty Kai had found inside of her. She reached out to touch him. She held him in her sight and then she blew him away like the seeds of a dandelion. That was it. That was the last thing she saw before it happened.

Chapter 40

It was just like Sen had said it would be. All of a sudden, she just knew it was here. It felt like time was catching up to itself so she could be hurled back into her own world. Grace knew that there was no stopping it. She had just a few moments before all of the knowledge of this place would leave her, the Love, the Magic, the Pain, the Boy.

Her heart, even though it had been Uncovered and glistened with the essence of pure emotion, began to break. A small and life-altering crack began along the perimeter. It made a quiet rolling gesture along the surface of her heart and then as time found its trail of breadcrumbs back home, the crack made for the center. It struck with the force of lightning. All it left in its wake was a single Love letter. A song he sang to her playing over and over again filling the void where her memory once was.

When she opened her eyes, she was alone in her bathroom again. The knife she held so long ago, was lying lifeless in the sink and all she could do was hum a strangely familiar tune, though she wasn't sure where she had heard it before. Time had stood still for her.

She stood up with a renewed sense of purpose. It was light, and it called to her from somewhere distant. Somewhere she couldn't quite place. She had the idea for a story. A story, she hadn't wanted to tell one of those in a long time. But the urge to tell this story, in particular, pushed her on and she immediately got to work investigating, questioning and weaving the truths that surrounded her.

Chapter 41

Grace put her story down on paper, to make sure she had all the details just right. It hadn't taken her very long to finish it. The words just kind of flowed out from her fingers as she typed. It was like she was channeling something bigger than she was. When she had finally gotten everything down, she carried it everywhere with her. She always kept it in large black canvas messenger bag that she had tied a rainbow silk scarf to. The rainbow scarf had somehow felt right; it was a silken cotton that soothed her whenever she began to doubt herself.

It was one day in the local bookstore, with the black messenger bag strapped across her, that she had met the woman who would produce her story into a feature film. Margaret had bumped into her at the bookstore and made mention of the rainbow scarf on her bag, and how she had one just like it at home. They began to talk, and before she knew it, Grace was handing over her story to Margaret to read.

They were currently in the process of finishing the production of the film. Margaret had talked Grace into doing the narration of the film, and now she wanted her to hear her voice over the soundtrack that had been commissioned for the film.

Grace gathered her bags and her coat and her hat and took the bus to the production center. When she arrived, she saw a man sitting at a sound board in the editing room. He had long brownish hair. He turned to say hello as he heard her enter and Grace caught sight of his beautiful blue eyes. He said, "Hi, my name is Kai, I'm the musician who recorded the soundtrack for your movie. It's a fantastic movie. The telling of the story is what pulls you..." And he stopped. There was an acknowledgement, a remembrance.

Grace was still, unmoving, paralyzed in space. She was stuck where her feet had planted themselves. There was something about hearing this man's voice that made her put her hand to belly. As she rested her palm on her outstretched skin, she felt he baby inside of her kick. In a moment of recognition, Grace's heart began racing toward Kai's.

Kai had felt the acknowledgement of the baby inside Grace. He picked up on her sense of home and completion. He felt her Love radiate.

It took a few moments for the moments to catch up to themselves. Everything that was happening between Grace and Kai was being filtered through a colander of the baby inside of Grace. The cobwebs of rules and instructions and change and goodbyes, it all got wiped away. They hadn't thought about the call of their daughter when they created their instructions. Grace wasn't sure she was pregnant, though she thought she might be. Kai had no idea of any of it. And so neither of them included her in their final instructions. She was here, purely here.

It was their daughter that brought them together here in this world. And so far nothing major had shifted. Chaos hadn't overrun the world.

And then, Grace's water broke.

A note from the author:

This book has held space inside of me for about thirteen years. It's my answer to some of the major issues that we face in our society today. I invite you to take a closer look at some of the themes I've written about in The Storyteller's Throne and see if they resonate for you as well. I've spent many years as an arts therapist for women and children and many of the themes in this book circle around matters of the heart and the landscape of emotions. Enjoy a discussion that's both academic, spiritual and personal. Allow your story to come out here, it's all we have in the end.

I've written out quite a few questions to think about ... pick and choose according to your journey.

Reader's Guide

1. What is the significance of the title, The Storyteller's Throne?

2. What are the central themes to this book?
   Where do these themes intersect in your own life?

3. Who are the main characters in this book?
   How do you relate to them?

4. How does Grace change from the beginning of the book to the end?

5. How does Kai change from the beginning of the book to the end?

6. How does the symbol of a spiral found on Anika's forehead play a role in this book?

7. What gifts were you given as a child?
   Did you nurture them or did you allow them to fall to the wayside?

8. How was your own childhood shaped by the fears of your parents or those who raised you?

9. What is Grace afraid of and how has it manifested in her life?
   How does Grace's anxiety manifest in her body?
   How does anxiety and worry manifest in your own body?

10. What is Kai afraid of and how has it manifested in his life?

11. What are you afraid of?
    How has it manifested in your own life?

12. How important is a compass of truth and why?

13. If the compass of Truth were an actual thing you could hold in your hand, what do you imagine it might look like?

14. Are there any stories that you needed to tell and no one listened, or believed you?
    What was the fallout, if any from that?

15. What's the difference between compassion and empathy?

16. What could Kai have done differently, if anything, to avoid drowning in other's feelings?

17. Have you ever felt that you had feelings that were not yours?

18. Why do you think Grace and Kai are so drawn to each other from the very beginning of their interactions?

19. Do you believe in fate, or do we have a hand in our own destiny?

20. Have you ever felt an epic and destined love?

21. As a teenager, did you hit any moment or event that felt like your rock bottom?
    If so, what do you think led up to it?

22. If you split and had a shadow self, what would you name him/her?
    What would you choose as your outfit in the shadow world?

23. If you were in the shadow world and your shadow self had your alterheart what emotions would be inside of it?
    How do you imagine those emotions might look?

24. Have you ever lost a memory and then found it again?

25. Do you believe in magic?

If Magic was tangible, what do you imagine it might look like?

26. Why does Grace feel a mother/daughter bond with Sen?

27. Have you ever felt like you straddled two worlds? Two ideals?

28. If sen was to make you a cup of tea, what word would she give you in your cup?
What word would you hope she gave you in your cup?

29. If you possessed the magic of childhood, what world would you create?

30. Where do you think people go who have committed suicide?

31. How do you judge others feelings, whether they have been acted on or not?

32. Have you ever felt like you were being manipulated by fear? What are the means of manipulation in our own society?

33. What emotional triggers do you have that could unlock feelings held deep inside?

34. How have you lived in your own middle road?

35. If you were a mother to a teenager in this book at this time, and you were an ally to the children of the heart, how would you parent your child?

36. Do you think there's any truth to the paradigm in the book of the world as it changes during Grace's lifetime?

37. Do you have a favorite story that changed your life or altered how you see things in your life?

38. If you could tell one persons story from beginning to end who's story would you tell?

39. What story does the world need to hear from Grace in order to change, in order to open to our hearts and not fear them?

40. When has pain been a blessing in your life?

41. Do you agree with Grace's decision to forget Kai back in her world?

42. If you knew that you had to forget the love of your life, would you play by the rules and design your instructions accordingly or would you allow for the chance to meet again regardless of the consequences?

43. If Grace were alive in the here and now, what story do you think she would be telling?

44. What do you think will happen next?

Ackowledgements

Thank you ...

-Veronica, Cole and Piper for reminding me how important a story can be and for putting up with all of my time in front of the computer ... I love you always and forever no matter what, you will always inspire me... Xoxo

-Matt, My Love, for helping me through all the sleepless nights, early mornings and moments of stuck. Thank you for being my partner in crime through it all, you rock!

-Mom & Dad for supporting this journey in so many ways through so many years, decades even! And for all the extra babysitting!

-Sandra Cartie for being a wonderful accountability partner through it all.

-IIN for providing the inspiration and structure to start writing this book and for inspiring me to take my work seriously

About the Author

Jocelyn Bates is homeschooling mama to three, an artist & poet and an arts therapist. Stories are the glue that holds her day together, whether she's reading them, hearing them, telling them or creating them. She writes in the elusive early hours of quiet that holds space in a house of seven people. Reach out and follow her, say hi, let her know what you think. You can contact her here:

jocelyn@jocelynbates.com
jocelynbates.com

Made in the USA
Columbia, SC
06 May 2018